DEATH OVER EASY

AN EMMA TRACE MYSTERY

DEATH OVER EASY

TOBY SPEED

FIVE STAR
A part of Gale, Cengage Learning

GALE
CENGAGE Learning®

Detroit • New York • San Francisco • New Haven, Conn • Waterville, Maine • Lor

GALE
CENGAGE Learning®

IBRARY OF CONGRESS CATALOGING-IN-PUBLICATION DATA

Speed, Toby.
    Death over easy : an Emma Trace mystery / Toby Speed. — First edition.
        pages cm
    ISBN 978-1-4328-2722-9 (hardcover) — ISBN 1-4328-2722-7 (hardcover)
        1. Young women—Fiction. 2. Murder—Investigation—Fiction. 3. Fear of flying—Fiction. 4. Long Island (N.Y.) —Fiction. I. Title. II. Title: Emma Trace mystery.
PS3619.P4385D43 2013
813'.6—dc23   2013014025

Edition. First Printing: September 2013
us on Facebook– https://www.facebook.com/FiveStarCengage
ur website– http://www.gale.cengage.com/fivestar/
t Five Star™ Publishing at FiveStar@cengage.com

ico

on   7 16 15 14 13

For my mom, Jean Braun, who always said I could.

ACKNOWLEDGMENTS

I could not have written this story without the encouragement and help of many people: my team at Five Star, particularly Deni Dietz, for her generosity and the gift of this opportunity, and Alice Duncan, Tiffany Schofield, Nivette Jackaway, Tracey Matthews, and Marcia LaBrenz for their skill and expertise; Tom Sisk, former police criminal investigator and former criminal defense investigator in North Carolina; Officer Mitch Savino and his dedicated staff at the Suffolk County Police Department Citizens' Academy; pilot Michael Mancuso for the ride that started it all; my flight instructor, Lou Ballester, who taught me, with grace and humor, to "fly the airplane"; the late Vinny Nasta, my aerobatics and tailwheel instructor, for his immense knowledge, caring, and confidence in me; my friends and fellow pilots at Brookhaven Airport and on the blue and red boards; the librarians at Middle Country Public Library and Port Jefferson Free Library; Phyllis, Rebecca, and Emily Reed; Karen Leibowitz; Lisa Sansonette-Martin; Clara Gillow Clark; Marileta Robinson; Sam Levitan; Leslie Schwartz; the late Mary Lou Stewart, for the hiding place; Donna and the gang at the former Blue Sky Diner; Lea Tala, MD; Mike Gasparino; Michael Davis; Jim Shannon; George Chris for his careful reading, multitudinous realms of expertise, and loving support; and my children, Vanessa, Kate, and Zoe. Special thanks go to my fellow author and friend Howard Gimple, whose patience, suggestions, and constant support kept me writing and rewriting and never giving up. I am grateful to you all.

DISCLAIMER

As much as I love Port Jefferson, in the spirit of storytelling I have taken occasional liberties with its geography, inventing streets where there are none, altering topography, and creating shortcuts where necessary. All errors and misrepresentations, intentional or not, are solely mine.

"Three may keep a secret, if two of them are dead."

—Benjamin Franklin

CHAPTER ONE

Friday

The little gray cat with the notched ear crouched on the dumpster. He'd had nothing to eat since yesterday, and every hunger pang felt like a knife in his ribs. Shivering, he pressed closer to the window filled with flickering blue light.

The Feeder hunched over a table, mixing something in a bowl. Her yellow hair bobbed as she worked, her elbow pumping in and out. But something was wrong. Usually the Feeder hummed while she worked. She was not humming today.

The little cat's eyes narrowed. Someone was with the Feeder—a tall figure in a hooded cloak. The figure lashed out in a torrent of spits and hisses. There was a harsh laugh, and a spoon clattered to the floor. Chair legs scraped as the Feeder jumped up.

His tail fat, the little cat watched the two figures circle the room. Now the Feeder's back was to the window, and now she faced it, arms outstretched, fingers curved like claws, while the cloaked figure swept by in the opposite direction.

The room went dark, and the hooded face came close to the window.

The little cat pulled back into the shadows.

Then the door burst open and the cloaked figure ran out and vanished into the night. The smell of cooking oil wafted through the open doorway. After a few moments the little cat jumped down from the dumpster and crept to the open door.

"I got an idea," said LaRue. "Find a place to stick your foot, a hole in the brick or something. I'll give you a boost."

It was pitch black behind Hoyt's Greenhouse, except for the halo my flashlight made on the wall. I trained the beam on a metal sign someone had tacked up.

PRIVATE PROPERTY
TRESPASSERS WILL BE
SKEWERED AND EATEN

I shuddered. A few blocks away, boats creaked softly in the harbor. A warm October wind blew some leaves through my path of light and sent them scattering up the wall and onto the roof. Angling my flashlight up, I knew we had a good half hour until sunrise—more than enough time to grab the Buddha and be gone. Still, I felt uneasy.

Guilt, that's all it was. My family had been friends with Mr. Hoyt forever.

On the other hand, maybe it was bad timing. Bad timing had played a big part in my breakup with Sam. More to the point, twenty years ago it had put me on the losing end of the annual birthday bet and upside down at six thousand feet. Not something I particularly wanted to repeat now, at thirty-five. Or ever.

That's the only reason I'd agreed to be here in the first place. To win the lousy bet and uphold my nineteen-year winning streak.

Men shouted in the distance, readying the ferry for departure. It was only a matter of minutes before cars started rumbling by.

LaRue chewed and cracked her ever-present stick of gum. "Earth to Emma."

"This was dumb. We shouldn't have come."

A year younger than me, my best friend was unabashedly confident. "Well, we're here. And I have to be at work in ten, so this is all we got. Hold that light still, will ya, Em? Stop bopping it all over the place."

I aimed the beam at the wall. The cracks in the bricks looked more like the commas and semicolons in the manuscripts I edit than places to wedge a foot.

"You sure it's up there?"

"Of course I'm sure."

"How high is this shelf, anyway?"

"I don't know. Ten, twelve feet. Give me that."

I handed her the flashlight. Looking over my shoulder, I saw a sliver of pink in the eastern sky and again felt a quiver of unease.

"Ta-*da*. A hole in the brick."

"LaRue."

"What?"

"If you get us arrested, I will never forgive you."

"Oh, here we go again. I'm not getting us arrested."

"I'm serious. Everyone in town knows me. I've never broken the law. I've never even gotten a speeding ticket."

"You can do it. Hey, I got it, Em. Pretend we're back in improv. You were good at that. Pretend you're Indiana Jones, and you have to get the Sankara stone from the evil high priest and save the children and stuff. Come on."

"But this isn't improv. It's real life."

I thought about the places we had already looked. We'd hit practically every Asian restaurant and yoga studio within fifteen miles. Why couldn't my present have been in one of *them*?

"LaRue."

"*What?*"

"How do you know it's not in the shed?"

15

She sighed and lowered her arm, illuminating her freckled chin and the miles of flame-red hair I'd always envied. My own thick brown mane didn't come close in the glamour department. Neither did my legs, which were a Misses size eight regular, not a four extra long, like hers.

I was stalling, and I knew it. Most Traces didn't stall. Most Traces went walloping into everything head first. Like my dad and his three brothers, who had devised the bet—they grew up to be bungee jumpers and pilots, occupations that required split-second decisions and nerves of steel. They weren't thesis editors. Most Traces wouldn't have been fazed by a little pre-dawn trespassing.

LaRue's chewing gum went pop-pop-pop like mini firecrackers. "I know it's here, 'cause I've seen it a million times. I used to work here, remember? Mr. Hoyt always keeps the Buddha on the shelf. Anyway, it fits the riddle."

She unfolded a piece of paper from her jacket pocket, and we read it silently.

> *Over the eyes that cannot see,*
> *under the ears that cannot hear,*
> *in the belly of an eastern icon*
> *lies the true Long Island sound.*

" 'Over the eyes that cannot see'—that's us. 'Under the ears,' and 'in the belly'—that's him." LaRue pointed up at the shelf. "The 'eastern icon' himself. Big Buddha."

"What if he—"

"Emma Trace, put your freakin' foot in the wall and get up there."

I remembered the time I'd found my gift in the eagles' cage at the Holtsville Ecology Center. I'd slipped the animal handler ten bucks to climb up after it.

"Not me. You know I don't do heights."

"It's only a ladder, Em, not a flippin' airplane."

"It's still up."

"Wuss. You got a tissue?"

I dug one out of my pocket. LaRue squished her gum into it and handed it back to me, with a hard look.

"Swee'pea, that was *one* plane ride a hundred years ago. You gotta get a grip on this thing. I love you to death, but one of these days I'm not going to be around to save your ass."

Turning away she wedged her cowboy boot into a gap between two bricks and pulled herself up by the drainpipe. The rhinestones in her denim jacket glittered in the dim light from the municipal lot a block away. She tilted her head down. "Hey. If I find it, do I win?"

"No."

"How do you know I won't go to your dad and uncles and tell them you were too—"

"It's *my* bet, LaRue. My lousy birthday. So just shut up and climb."

I put my hand under her skinny butt and hoisted. One of her boots found purchase on a jutting brick and the other sank into my right shoulder, pulling a few hairs from my scalp. I smothered a cry.

"Ho-*ly*, it stinks up here," LaRue said. The light swept back and forth above me. "Okay. I see the Buddha, but I can't reach it. Scootch over a bit."

I grabbed her ankle and made a little hop to my right, nearly tripping over some junk. The heel of her boot dug into my neck. I hoped I didn't pass out. If my mother saw me now, she'd shriek, "Are you crazy?" That was her favorite expression when I was growing up. "Are you crazy?"

"I'm going to balance on your head for a sec, Em. Pull off my boot. Okay, now I'll pull myself up by this gutter thing, and—aha! I got it! I got Big Buddha. Shit, this sucker's heavy."

17

"Open it," I grunted, my cheek squashed against the bricks.

"What? I can't understand you."

"Open it. Open it."

"Good idea, Em. I'm taking his head off now."

I heard the scrape of pottery. A moment later there was a loud screech of ripping metal as gutter parted company with roof, and everything, including LaRue, came crashing down on me.

CHAPTER TWO

After LaRue headed to the Sunny Side Up diner to work her shift, I went home and waited to be arrested. LaRue had landed on me and escaped without a scratch, while I, absorbing the brunt of her fall, ached all over. I was lying on the couch with my cat, Bergamot, on my chest when my cell phone rang.

"Brace yourself," said LaRue. "I have bad news."

Bad timing. I knew it. Growing up in a family of gamblers, daredevils, and practical jokers, I've learned a lot about timing and its first cousin, dumb luck, concepts I was introduced to while still in the womb.

Take my name, for instance. If I'd been born a mere six minutes earlier, I would have been called Bernadette, which means brave as a bear, instead of Emma, healer of the universe. I'd have been named by Uncle Pike and not Dad, who put all his money on two-seventeen a.m. Uncles Sherm and Ned, betting on a pre-midnight arrival, weren't even close. But if Dad aced the time pool, he lost his shirt in the gender pool. In fact, all of them did except for Aunt April, who, after calmly raking in her winnings, spent the next Saturday at Elizabeth Arden.

"We're being arrested for trespassing," I said.

"Worse. Jennifer Hazzard's dead."

"What?" I sat up and knocked Bergamot to the floor.

"She drowned in pancake batter."

"Hazzard's *dead*?" Jennifer Hazzard was Sunny Side's slutty short-order cook. She lived in a rented house in Port Jefferson

Station with a lot of smelly dogs, and among her many star qualities was a talent for stealing other women's boyfriends. I knew that from personal experience. "What do you mean, she drowned?"

"She was doing the dead man's float when I got there, Em. She was sitting up with her face in the batter."

I stood up and stepped over my bloody, ripped jeans. Aside from the shock, an evil little piece of me was disappointed. Over the months I'd developed an elaborate fantasy of revenge that included rope, train tracks, and a sharp writing instrument. It was very complex. It could have won an Oscar.

"When did it happen?"

"I don't know. Jenn gets in at four-thirty to take deliveries. Rita opens at six, and I'm there right after Rita. So it happened in there somewhere. Maybe when we were futzing around with the Buddha."

"Oh, man."

I heard coffee being poured. "Wait'll you meet the detective. Mr. X-Ray Eyes himself. He held me like forty minutes, Rita even longer, since she found the body. He asked me a million questions. 'What time do you usually get to work? Do you have keys to the premises? Do you know anyone who had a problem with her?' Yada yada yada."

"Where are you now, home?"

"Yeah. When I left they were talking to the customers. All the regulars showed up except you."

"Great." I examined my face in the mirror. Miraculously, I had only one small cut on my cheek. My eyes looked hollow. That was nothing new; they'd looked like that for the past three months. "I can't believe she's dead."

"Tell me about it. I can't even feel the rug. I feel like I'm on Mars."

An engine purred outside, and I went to the window and

pinched the blinds. Two floors below, a cop car was cruising slowly through my parking lot. It stopped behind my green Honda Civic and sat there, engine idling.

"You there?" LaRue asked.

"Yeah. There's a cop car outside."

"What's he doing?"

"Sitting there, looking at my car."

"Probably Zahn. X-Ray Eyes."

"It's not a detective. It's patrol."

"Now, listen, Em. When he knocks on your door, don't tell him about Hoyt's. Tell him you were home in bed. That's what I said."

"What? You lied to the police?"

"I didn't lie, I just left out that part. You think I was going to say we were across the street while Jennifer was getting snuffed?"

"I'm not lying to him, LaRue. We had nothing to do with this."

"Exactly. We didn't hear anything, we didn't see anything, and it's not going to make any difference. What cop is going to believe us, anyway?"

As I watched, the car door opened and a big, beefy police officer got out. He went up to my car and looked in through the passenger window. He had to be six-foot-six at least. He whipped out a pad and wrote something down.

"Now he's looking inside my car."

"Okay, so he's looking. So, what's in there?"

"I don't know. My dry cleaning." The cop tilted his head up toward my window, and I stepped back quickly.

"What does he look like?"

"Big dude, black hair."

"That's not Zahn."

"I already told you that." I looked out again. The cop was squatting down, poking at my right rear tire with his pencil

21

point. It looked like he was scooping something into a plastic bag. "Maybe it was an accident, LaRue. Maybe a pot fell on her head."

"Nah. The back door was open. And if it was an accident, why is the neighborhood crawling with cops? What's he doing now?"

The officer returned the pad and pen and plastic bag to his jacket pocket, got back in his car, and made a U-turn. "He's driving away." I let go of the blinds. "So, what's your theory?"

"I think one of the customers got tired of burnt biscuits, and he turned her into toast."

"Very funny."

"Well, why not? She was a pain in the ass, Em. She knew everybody's business. Her neighbors were always complaining about the dogs. And she was a man-stealer. There's a bunch of reasons right there."

"Still, murder? Rita liked her."

"Rita likes anyone who likes dogs."

My ex's face floated up before me. "Sam used to leave Ruby with her when we went away for the weekend."

"I know. That's what started that whole thing. The louse." LaRue's cockatoo, Petey, began screeching in the background. "No, she was definitely iced. And you know what *that* means."

"What?"

"The cops'll be looking at everyone she was pissing off. I think you better get that note back before they find it."

I felt faint. I had forgotten about the note. Three months earlier, when Sam had hemmed and hawed and slithered out of our three-year relationship like a greased pig at a county fair, I'd written a poison pen letter to my replacement, Hazzard. Then, instead of burning it, I'd mailed it. After that we were enemies, even after she'd dumped him for her next victim. A few days ago I'd been eating breakfast in my usual booth at

Sunny Side when I felt someone's gaze on me. I looked up and saw Hazzard giving me the evil eye through the pass-through.

"Doesn't your mom have a cousin or something who's a cop? Someone on the inside?" LaRue asked.

"You mean Mad Melvin? The one who moved to Vermont?"

"Oh. Well, how about your dad? Petey, shush!"

"I'm not involving him. He's working on a screenplay and hasn't been up from the basement in months."

"Since when does your dad write screenplays?"

"Since the band he managed broke up."

"I thought he was into restoring cars."

"He was. Life moves on."

She slurped coffee. "When does your mom get back from Seattle?"

"Next month. How about your cousin Jimmy? Isn't he a cop?"

"Yeah, in Delaware."

"Oh." I went back to thinking about the note.

She hesitated. "Maybe you should drop the bet, Em."

"Are you kidding? My entire reputation as a Trace hinges on it. I only have five days left."

"Talk to Ned, tell him there's extenuating circumstances."

"Ha. Not a chance."

"Goddess alive, you're stubborn."

We were silent for a few moments. Bergamot began doing figure eights around my ankles, my cue to serve him breakfast.

"Blueberry," LaRue said finally.

"What blueberry?"

"That's what Jennifer was making when she croaked. Blueberry pancake batter."

I wanted to throw up.

CHAPTER THREE

The local news channel had a brief story about it right after the weather. Cause of death had not been determined, and the victim's identity was being withheld pending notification of next of kin. Police were looking for anyone with information.

Frowning, I turned off the TV. A year ago I'd thought I'd be married to Sam by now and living in his beachfront house in Miller Place. I'd pictured us spending lazy Sundays on the deck together doing *The New York Times* crossword puzzle. It had all gone to hell because of Hazzard.

Now she was out of the picture. I should have been happy, or at least less miserable. But her death didn't bring Sam back, and it would put me in a precarious position with the police when they discovered how high on her shit list I was.

And the cop in the parking lot? I watch enough forensics shows to know it's a bad sign when they look at your tires.

I showered quickly, threw on a sweatshirt and jeans, and French-braided my hair into submission. Time was a-wasting. As they say in the freelance editing business, another hour, another five cents. Plus I could count on Inez, the office manager at Able Editing, to give me the dirt. I rubber banded a job, stapled an invoice to the job jacket, and trotted downstairs.

My apartment is in the "herbihood" of Port Jeff—a grid of streets named Parsley, Sage, Rosemary, and Thyme, up the hill from Main Street. Parsley Gardens is not strictly an apartment building, but a three-story shingled house that was home to a

24

nineteenth-century shipbuilder and his family. There are five units, two on each of the first two floors and the "penthouse," which is mine. It's only a one-bedroom, but what it lacks in floor space it makes up for in views. The porthole window by the stairs overlooks the harbor and the twin stacks of the power plant, the bedroom looks out on woods, the kitchen faces Parsley Street, and from my living room on a leafless day like today I can see all the way down to Main Street and right into the bread baskets at Anthony's Pizza Pasta.

The rest of my neighborhood is made up of historic wood-frame houses, many close to two hundred years old. Driving past them now I noted all the pumpkins on the porches. I hadn't bought my pumpkin yet.

I stopped at the corner of Main Street and rolled down my windows. The air smelled like pine needles, pipe tobacco, and marinara sauce. One long and three short whistle blasts announced the departure of the ferry to Bridgeport. I turned left, then right on Barnum, named for the P.T. Barnum of circus fame, and pulled into the parking lot of a small, sad office building near Rocket Ship Park.

Able Editing is the last office in the back, behind the offices of an accountant who never seems to be there. A locked box with a slot on top for CDs sits outside the door to accept work delivered after hours. I pushed open the frosted glass door and walked in.

One of the perks of being a freelancer is that I can work at home. Every time I step into Able, I am very glad of this. The room is paneled in fake knotty pine à la 1950s suburbia. To the right of the door, four sunken plaid chairs face each other over a kidney-shaped coffee table. A dusty fake ficus mopes in the corner. To the left is a water cooler and another ficus, this one covered in Christmas lights from last year.

A vomit-colored counter dissects the room from left to right, separating the reception area from the work space. Behind the counter sits a massive oak desk apparently gnawed by beavers. Mismatched file cabinets line the walls. Every surface, including the floor, is piled high with file folders and reference books. A large sign on the back wall reads: IS THERE LIFE AFTER DEATH? TRESPASS HERE AND FIND OUT.

Inez Lipchitz was on the phone when I got there—or *in* it. She was wrapped in yards of curly cord that sprang from the wall and wound around lamps and chair legs, book stacks and coat racks, before making two or three journeys around her waist. One of the last corded phones on the planet. She walked back and forth as she talked, tapping with her pumps. When she saw me, her eyes got round.

I leaned on the counter and studied a small sign that said NEXT MOOD SWING—6 MINUTES.

"Oh my *God,* you poor *baby.*" Inez hung up and unwound herself. "Let me get you a cup of coffee." Inez comes from the neighboring planet of Brooklyn, and she pronounces it "caw-fee."

"No, thanks, Inez."

She swept out from behind the counter and hugged me tight. Inez is orbiting fifty, with a horsey face and a hairdo right out of a 1940s musical. Today she was wearing a black and white diagonally striped dress with a red rose on the shoulder. The scent of Calèche followed her. "The phone's been ringing off the wall all morning. I got real worried when you didn't show up, hon. Did you go down there?"

"To the Sunny Side? Not yet."

"*Oy vey,* it's terrible. There were eight police cars—no, excuse me, nine—a van, and cops swarming around like termites in heat. You want a bagel?" Inez waved a hand at nothing in particular, shaking her head. "It's a disgrace what this world is coming to. You're not safe in your own home. Walk outside, some lunatic can blow you away with a Glock if they don't like the look on your face. Just read the papers! What kind of animal conks someone on the head like that? He should be shot. You sure you don't want a bagel, hon? I got an 'everything.' " She stepped back, looking at me. "What happened to your face?"

"I fell out of bed. What do you mean, conk someone on the head?"

"You got to put peroxide on that. I'm talking about that young girl, of course. The cook. Poor kid, she was just trying to make ends meet. As far as who turned out her lights—if I knew *that,* I'd be in business, wouldn't I? I've lived here five years, hon. You know why I moved? 'Cause Flatbush was going to the dogs. I got tired of looking over my shoulder at every *meshugener* on the street who's packing heat." Inez bent down before a brass table lamp and arranged her hair in the reflection. "I had a nice little place. I had my *abacería* and my kosher deli and my tomatoes in the back. But I moved *here* to get away from the criminal element."

"As far as I know, the police haven't said how she was killed."

"Pfooff! She was hammered."

"How do you know that?"

"Egon told me." Inez leaned forward conspiratorially. "Listen, hon, you can't breathe a word to anyone. You promise? Or I'm in deep shit. It's an in-ves-ti-*ga*-tion."

"My lips are zipped, Inez."

She took a deep breath. "I get out of the shower this morning and the news is all over the radio. Right away I'm like oh my God. So I get dressed, and I'm walking down the street minding my own business. I get to Sunny Side and the place is taped off. Everyone's craning their necks and a couple of cops are standing around with long faces. I don't have nothing to do with them, I'm just taking a walk. I'm allowed to take a walk, right? Maybe I want to buy some baby's breath. It's in my rights.

So I cross the street and go into the flower shop and Egon—you know Egon Hoyt, the owner? Of course, you do, hon—he's looking out the window and he says to me, 'What do you think of this mess?' And I says, 'Well, *I* sure wouldn't want to end up with *my* sinuses full of pancake batter, *that's* for sure.' And he says, 'She didn't have nothing up her sinuses, she got decked.' "

"How did he know?"

"From when he opened the shop. The cops were right across the street. The detective and somebody else were going to their car, and Egon heard one of them say something about 'quite a blow.' I don't know, what does that mean to you? Quite a blow."

"Maybe he heard wrong. The cops wouldn't say something like that in front of people."

"Well, I don't think they saw Egon. He was standing under the awning, and he's, you know, skinny as a toothpick."

"Did the police talk to you?"

Inez told me they hadn't, but they'd spoken to Egon and the rest of the flower shop staff earlier. Egon had asked them to come around and look at the damage to his roof. "He said he was missing some pots that used to be on a shelf back there."

My heart beat a little faster. "What did the police say? Was it connected to the murder?"

Inez turned to me and adjusted her earring. "I don't know, hon. Why?"

"What did Egon think?"

"He just said some pots were missing, and part of the gut-tah."

I shrugged. "It was probably cats."

Inez put her hands on her hips and gave me the kind of look people use at garage sales when they're trying to tell if something is a steal or a piece of junk. "Hon, you look awful. Why don't you sit down and take a load off?"

"I'm fine, Inez."

"No, I insist." With a strong grip, she steered me over to one of the plaid chairs. "You sit right here. Cuppa joe on the way."

When she came back, she sat opposite me, leaned forward, and clasped her hands around her knees. "You got to take it easy, hon. You had a big shock. We all had a big shock."

"It hasn't really sunk in yet," I admitted.

"Well, of *course* not. Whether she was your best friend or God's worst enemy has nothing to do with it. She's dead. You got to give yourself a chance." Inez picked up the coffee cup and handed it to me. "At times like this, you got to look inside yourself. You got to look deep inside and say to yourself, 'Why am I alive and she's dead? What did I do to deserve to be alive and what did she do to wind up dead?' "

We looked at each other.

"You must have seen her all the time," Inez prompted. "At the dinah."

"Every day."

"Wasn't she from Jersey? Rita told me she was going for her equivalency. *Pobrecita,* trying to make something of herself, and look what it comes to. I don't know why that good-for-nothing boyfriend of hers didn't do something."

My heart gave a lurch.

"Not your guy," Inez said. "This new one I never met. He was no good. She told me he never picked her up on a date, only wanted to meet her places. You know what they call guys that do that? Married." Inez came over and sat on the arm of my chair. She smelled faintly of tuna fish. "I got to ask you something, hon. Don't take it personal. Did you ever find out what she did to make your guy break up with you?"

"No offense, Inez, but I really don't feel like talking about it."

"I read in the paper that when a guy dumps a gal all of a sudden, it has nothing to do with her. He's allergic to marriage. I saved you a copy."

I thought about the two phone calls I'd made to Sam after we broke up. Calls he'd never returned.

Inez stood up and smoothed the front of her dress. "You going to the Helping Hands?"

She was referring to our local community service group, of which I'm a charter member. Mentally, I hit myself on the side of the head. How could I forget? They always spring into action at a time like this.

"What's the plan?"

"Rita's. Five o'clock. On account of what she's been through, finding the body. Don't leave yet. I got another job."

Inez went to the counter and brought back a CD. It was wrapped in lavender paper and smelled bitterly of stale tobacco. Taped to the lavender paper was a piece of thin foil on which was scrawled in black, *Proof and return. Do NOT rewrite. Natasha Ferrette.* I lifted up the foil and looked at the other side. It was the wrapper from a package of Gitanes French cigarettes.

"Who's Natasha Ferrette?"

"One of those cockamamie English profs at the university. Get it back by Tuesday or she'll blow a fuse."

At the door I turned around. "What you were saying before—about being alive or dead? You know why I'm alive, Inez? Because I'm lucky, that's why. Why are some people hit by lightning? Because they're unlucky. They pick the wrong tree to stand under, like Hazzard did." I opened the flap of my bag and dropped in the CD. "All I did was pick the right tree."

Her mouth was open and the phone ringing as I left.

On the drive home I pondered Inez's idea about Hazzard's new boyfriend being married. It bore looking into. When I swung into my parking lot, I stopped short. A maroon Ford Taurus was parked in my spot. A tall man in a well-tailored dark suit leaned casually against the building with his hands in his pockets, looking at the sky. I knew immediately that he was a cop, and I knew he was waiting for me.

CHAPTER FOUR

I pulled in next to the Taurus and got out.

"Emma Trace?" He stepped forward.

"Yes?"

"Detective Pete Zahn, Suffolk County Homicide." He showed me his ID. Zahn had a hard jaw and hair that was either blond or prematurely gray. His most noticeable feature was a pair of immense, pale blue eyes. "I'm investigating a death in the neighborhood. Do you have a few minutes?"

"Jennifer Hazzard, right? Sure, come on in."

Zahn followed me up the steps. I felt him staring at my back as I unlocked the door. He followed me into the living room. Bergamot was nowhere in sight, but Grandma Bea's rocking chair was moving gently.

"Please, sit down," the detective said, pointing to the rocking chair. Hard, with wooden dowels up the back, it was my least favorite seat. I sat, shifting my weight forward. Zahn walked around the coffee table and sat opposite me on the sofa. He watched me as he uncapped his pen, the expression on his face similar to Bergamot's when he smells cantaloupe.

I said, "Homicide. I guess that answers that question."

"What question?"

"That it was no accident."

His response was to keep looking at me. X-Ray Eyes was spot-on. "Right now I'm just talking to folks who are regular customers of the diner where she worked. Your name came up.

Would you spell it, please?" We went through a bunch of preliminaries, which he recorded in a small notebook. "How often do you eat breakfast at the Sunny Side Up, Ms. Trace?"

"Every day, pretty much."

"From when to when?"

"Six to seven."

"Why the Sunny Side Up?"

I looked at him, puzzled.

"And not somewhere else."

"Well, it's close by. And my friend LaRue is a waitress."

Zahn flipped through his notebook. "That would be, let's see—" His eyes were back. "LaRue Fusticola?"

"Yes."

"Did you go there today?" The blue eyes didn't blink.

I shifted in my seat. "No."

"Why not?"

"It was closed. For—this."

"How did you know that?"

My hands were sweaty. I fought the urge to wipe them on my pants. "LaRue called me and told me what happened."

"When?"

"Around eight."

"What were you doing when she called?"

"Nothing. Lying on the couch."

He gazed at me steadily before going on. "And what did she tell you?"

"Just that Jennifer was found face down in a bowl of pancake batter."

Zahn stood up, walked to the front window, and looked down at the parking lot. He turned and faced me. "Why didn't you go at six like you usually do?"

"I was sleeping." I looked back at him just as steadily. "I was out late last night."

"Where did you go?"

"The movies." It was the first thing that popped into my head.

"By yourself?"

"With LaRue."

"What movie?"

"Um, that new one with Robert Downey Jr." I gave him the title of a movie I'd seen the week before.

"Ah, that's a good one," Zahn said. "When did it start and end?"

"Started at eight, ended at ten."

"Theater?"

"Island 16."

"Buy any popcorn?"

"No."

"And after that?"

"I came straight home. *We* came straight home, I mean. What I mean is, LaRue dropped me off at about ten-thirty and went back to her place."

I knew I'd made a mistake when he raised his eyebrows.

"I watched TV until late. Didn't turn out the light till after one."

Zahn scribbled in his notebook. He must have had another pair of eyes in the top of his head, because I felt them on me even while he was writing.

"How did you spend the morning?"

"At what time?"

"At any time."

Why don't you ask the big ape you sent over here to check on me? "After LaRue called, I took a shower and got dressed. Then I went out to deliver a job. I'm a freelance editor."

I gave him Able's name and address. Then he asked how I knew Jennifer Hazzard and whether we were friends.

"No. Acquaintances."

He mulled that over. "Did you know her at all outside of the diner?"

"You mean, socially?"

The steady gaze again. "You tell me."

I looked away. "I saw her around town occasionally. Not recently, though. My ex-boyfriend used to board his dog with her sometimes."

"Did you go with him to bring the dog there?"

"Yes," I said tightly. "I stayed in the car."

That got me a look. "When was the last time he boarded the dog?"

"Three months ago."

We stopped for another little staring contest.

"I'd like his name and phone number, please," Zahn said.

I gave Zahn Sam's information. After writing it down, he stood up and walked over to the corner of my living room, where I'd set up my office. He picked up my well-worn copy of the *Chicago Manual of Style* and flipped through it. When he spoke again I had to strain to hear him.

"Now, Emma, I'd like the truth."

"What do you mean?"

"I'm doing this job a long time. It's real hard to pull the wool over my eyes. For the past three hours I've been talking to people who've lived in this town for years, some who've known you and your family for decades. Everyone tells me you knew Jennifer pretty well."

"Well, everyone is telling you wrong."

He watched me silently.

I stood up and went to the window. "Look, Detective, here's the story. I wasn't crazy about Jennifer Hazzard. She rubbed me the wrong way, as she did a lot of people. I'm sure everyone's been telling you that as well. She was a user. If she thought she could get a favor out of you, she'd go for it. But I didn't know her well. I couldn't tell you where she came from, or how she wound up in Port, or—"

"What did she try to get out of you?"

"Sometimes she asks—asked if I could make a phone call and connect her with someone who could get her a job. Who did I know at the local paper, the university. Things like that."

"Did you?"

"Once. I gave her the name of a friend who worked at *The Record*. I didn't make the call myself. Nothing came of it. She didn't have the education or the experience they were looking for."

"Why would she ask you if she hardly knew you?"

"Because that's the kind of person she was. She didn't have the social constraints other people have. She got into your space."

Zahn shut the book carefully and put it down on the work table.

"Is that the only way she got into *your* space? On the subject of jobs?"

Maybe he already knew. Maybe that's what this was about. I gained no points by not telling him. In fact, I was probably digging myself into the ground by the minute.

"No." I folded my arms. "My boyfriend left me for her. We were supposed to be married, and he left me to go out with her. Okay?"

"Now we're getting somewhere. When was that?"

"In July."

"And what kind of work does Sam do?"

"He's an English professor at Stony Brook."

Zahn capped his pen and put it in his shirt pocket. When he looked back at me, his eyes were neutral. I thought I saw something else in them, but I wasn't sure what it was.

He touched his cheek. "How'd you get that?"

"I fell out of bed."

He stood up. "By the way," he said in a faraway voice, "are you related to Ned Trace?"

"Yes," I said, surprised. "He's my uncle. Do you know him?"

Instead of answering, Zahn did a quick scan of the room and headed for the door. "Nice place. How long have you been here?"

"Two years. All my life in this town."

"What do they ask for rent?"

"I don't have to answer that," I said.

Zahn reached for the doorknob. I waited for him to tell me not to leave town. He turned back and stared at me once more with his X-ray eyes. They were like two drinking straws that penetrated my very bones and sucked out the marrow. "One more thing. Can anyone vouch for your presence here overnight?"

Go ahead, Detective, stab me in the heart. "Only my cat." I looked around. Bergamot, pain in the ass, had made himself scarce. "Good luck," I added, but was sorry as soon as I said it, for he gave me another of those cantaloupe-detecting looks on his way out.

I glanced down and saw that my hands were shaking.

After Zahn left I called LaRue. I hoped I was not too late. Zahn was obviously going to follow up on my movie alibi, and he was probably going to check my phone records, too. He certainly had asked a lot of questions. I wasn't sure why I'd lied. One lie had only led to more.

At least I'd been honest about Hazzard. Zahn had to know by now that she wasn't the most popular gal on the block.

LaRue's voicemail came on. I left a message and tried her cell, but a spunky recording answered there, too. After leaving another message I shut my phone. Almost immediately it rang. I pushed the green button without checking caller ID.

"Where are you, Rue? We have to talk right away."

There was silence on the other end, and then a muffled cackle. My confusion turned to alarm.

"Do we, now?" a deep voice said indistinctly. It sounded like someone talking through a handkerchief. "Did you enjoy your little chat with the detective, *missy*?"

I worked to keep my voice steady. "Who is this?"

"And don't bother looking for your library card," the voice continued. "The police have it."

There was a burst of laughter, and the line went dead. My heart pounding, I hit star-six-nine for call return. A recording said, "This number is not accessible for incoming calls. Please try your call again. I repeat, this numb—"

A pay phone. I slapped the phone shut and tossed it on the couch.

CHAPTER FIVE

There was a pay phone just inside the door to Anthony's Pizza, next to the beverage fridge. From that vantage point I could see all the way up Parsley Street to my building. The entrance to the parking lot was clearly visible. Conveniently, the fridge blocked my view of the area behind the counter. Someone could easily have used the phone without being seen.

I opened my cell phone to the last call received and pushed *send*. The pay phone didn't ring, and I didn't expect it to. But when I picked up the receiver, my cell phone ended its call. I went over to the counter.

"Hey, Vinny," I said to the guy flipping dough.

"Hey, if it isn't my favorite customer." Vinny gave me a broad smile as he caught the dough and slapped it down on the floured wood block. With rapid sweeps of his spoon he slathered it with tomato sauce. "Whatcha been up to, Emma? I haven't seen you lately."

"Paying the bills. I can't complain. Say, Vinny, did anyone use the pay phone about a half hour ago?"

"Nah, I wasn't looking. The high school football team just left. With the diner closed, everyone's having pizza today. Why?"

"Someone called me from here and left a message about a flat tire. They probably wanted Mort's. Our numbers are almost the same. I wanted to make sure they're all right."

Vinny shook his head. "You look outside? Maybe they're waiting for a tow."

"Yeah, no one's there. So how's your daughter like kindergarten so far?"

"Loves it. What a great kid. She's gotta be the first one on the bus, wavin' to Daddy."

"That's great."

"Here, try our new pizza."

I looked at the oddly shaped pinkish-yellow blobs on the slice he handed me.

"What's that?"

"Tuna melt."

"Tuna melt pizza? Really?"

"Yep." Vinny's smile got even wider. I always marvel at the way his features are like rubber. He can mold his face into a thousand and one expressions.

"Tuna melt's my favorite food," I said, biting in.

I pulled out of my parking spot into traffic. Before leaving home I'd removed the rubber band from the Ferrette job and spread out the lavender paper, cigarette wrapper, and CD on the kitchen table. But I couldn't concentrate and, besides, the smell was nauseating. Tackling a new job now would be a waste of time. I needed a break. I needed a plan.

Instead of continuing up Main, I circled back to the harbor and drove through town, slowing briefly as I passed the Sunny Side Up. Lengths of yellow crime scene tape had been stretched across stakes, and a big yellow "X" sealed the front door. The CLOSED sign hung crookedly behind the glass. I glanced across the street. At Hoyt's it looked like business as usual. Behind the autumnal window display customers were moving about. A police car sat quietly at the curb. I put my foot on the gas and lurched ahead.

I continued up the hill into Port Jeff Station, made a left after the train tracks, and headed east. So the police had my library card. If they'd discovered it at the crime scene, that explained Zahn's visit. Maybe they'd found it behind Hoyt's, or on the street. I always have about forty-seven loose objects in my pockets. My card could have fallen out anywhere.

Or maybe it had been deliberately stolen and planted by whoever killed Hazzard. A convenient way to direct suspicion away from him or her and onto me. But why me?

I bit back my rising panic. I was getting way ahead of myself.

Several small towns flew by, their red maples, birches, and dogwoods a blaze of color. I rolled down my window and took a deep breath. Picking today to check out the Buddha had been a mistake. It felt wrong at the time and had set in motion a chain of bad events. But sometimes one little thing is all it takes to stop a run of bad luck in its tracks.

In a few minutes I pulled into the gravel lot at Sandy's Farm Stand and got out. A busload of kindergartners was unloading, kids shrieking in delight as they jumped from the bottom step while their teachers chatted nearby. Bales of hay and painted pumpkins led the way to the pumpkin field.

Sandy's green pickup, piled high with gourds and Indian corn, and a wood-slatted open cart he used for haunted hayrides were parked side by side under a tree. Beyond them I could see people moving slowly up and down the rows of orange orbs, each looking for that perfect specimen of pumpkinicity.

A colossal pumpkin sat in a wheelbarrow in the middle of the lot, a hand-painted sign leaning against it.

15th ANNUAL GUESS THE WEIGHT
OF THE PUMPKIN CONTEST!
GUESS CORRECTLY AND WIN
TWO FREE TICKETS
TO TERROR MANSION!!!

I filled out a ballot and dropped it into the basket. Looking up, I saw Sandy striding toward me.

"Well, well," he said, grinning. "About time you made it out here, Emma."

"I need an apple pie, Sandy, and yours are the best."

"A pie, you say?" He rocked on his feet. His once red hair, now pure white, peeked out from beneath an engineer's cap. Sandy Stein has been friends with my dad ever since Dad almost blew up the high school chemistry lab, an episode that bonded them for life. A cute girl was involved, of course. The class was testing household substances to see if they were acidic or basic, and everyone was going to town with their test tubes, pipettes, and litmus paper. During lunch Dad had gotten hold of some crystallized iodine from the lab's stockroom, mixed it with ammonia back on the senior patio, and dried it in a coffee filter that Sandy stole from the teachers' lounge. He brought a little pellet of the stuff to class and put it out on the lab table where it would get the cute girl's attention. That it did. When Dad tapped the pellet with his notebook, the resulting explosion hurled a volley of pencils and pipettes across the room and blew out the lower panes of two windows.

Dad and Sandy each got two days' suspension. Luckily, no one was hurt and no charges were brought against them. They returned to school sobered by the experience and went back to the more time-tested ways of getting girls.

I walked with Sandy back to the farm stand while we chitchatted about Mom and Dad. As I paid for my pie, I noticed a wheelbarrow full of white pumpkins.

"What are those?"

"Ghost pumpkins. You like them? Take one, it's on me."

I cradled a ghost pumpkin in my arms. Everyone else was favoring orange pumpkins today, and it looked lonesome. Caressing its white skin, I had the strange feeling it had picked me, like a puppy at the pound.

CHAPTER SIX

There was no place to park in front of Rita's house, so I left the Civic in front of the library. As I walked up the front steps with my apple pie, Ronk came out, jangling her keys. Ronk is Brenda Ronkowski, LaRue's partner of seventeen years. Ronk's a mortgage underwriter for a bank. In her forties and built like a brick, she has short salt and pepper hair and sparkling brown eyes. I'd been dating LaRue's older brother in high school when Ronk blew in during my senior year and LaRue's sophomore year and swept my friend off her feet.

"Hey, there, ET." Ronk always calls me that.

"Hey, Ronk." I gave her a hug. "Where are you off to?"

"Baby shower." She made a face. "One of the women at work. Nothing like spending an evening passing around rattles and eating Oreo cookie cake. How are you doing with all this?"

"Could be better. LaRue inside?"

"Yeah. Better get your ass in there and find her. She's been trying to reach you all day."

"I've been trying to reach *her*. What's the word in there?"

Ronk shrugged. "My opinion? Jennifer had it coming. Not to sound callous, but I don't give a hoot about Jennifer. She had enemies. Take your pick. What I do care about is LaRue. Murder is real bad news for a restaurant. People don't want to eat in a place where someone was killed." Ronk spread her meaty hands, revealing a ring on every finger. "And when business goes down, profit goes out the window, and the next thing you know, they're cutting back on help and LaRue will be out on her *tuchas*. Never forget," she added, jangling her keys, "the bottom line is always money."

"Even for those who have it."

"*Especially* for those who have it."

The tiny house was packed. It looked like all the Helping Hands were there, and then some. I saw Egon Hoyt, Manny Mandel from Manny's Music Emporium, Charlie Steigbeagle from the museum, and other familiar faces. A few of the guys were trying to figure out the coffeemaker, while others twiddled with the television remote.

The pie was plucked from my hands, and I looked down to see Pearl Battley, the children's librarian. Pearl always makes me think of a white mouse. She has to be close to eighty, small and sprightly, with a silver knot of hair on top of her head. As far as I can tell, she looks exactly the same as she did when I was a kid sneaking around the book stacks and playing Harriet the Spy.

"Such a tragedy." Pearl shook her head. "And to happen in our town. I've lived here nearly seventy years. There may have been one or two incidents in all that time that shocked me as much as this." She had tears in her eyes. "I'm so glad you're here, dear," she added.

"How can I help?"

"It's Inez. She's pumping Rita. Maybe you can distract her."

Pearl grabbed my arm and steered me toward the back of the house. As we passed the parlor, I saw LaRue speaking animatedly to Theodora Silk, the head floral designer at Hoyt's. Pearl ushered me into the kitchen, where Inez was clattering cups in the sink. Rita slumped at the dinette table. At her feet sat Muffin, her apricot standard poodle, and Bruce, Jennifer's half-Shepherd-half-something mutt. All three looked shell-shocked.

"So, then what happened?" Inez asked, dumping cups into

the dish drainer.

Rita patted Muffin absently. "I called the police."

"Hi, all," I broke in.

"How're you doing, hon?" Inez asked without turning around.

"Fine, but I'd love a cup of coffee. The guys out there are so busy bandying about murder theories, I wonder if they'll ever get that coffeemaker set up."

Inez wiped her hands on her apron. "I'll take care of it, hon. They don't call me a Helping Hand for nothing." She winked as she strode past me, her curls bouncing.

I mumbled something sympathetic to Rita and went back to the parlor, where LaRue and Theo were discussing acorns.

"There should be room on the frame to hold several rows of graduated acorn caps," Theo droned, gesturing with her bony fingers. "You'll need about two hundred. If you want to see how it looks finished, I have a sample in the car. I haven't even been home to unpack yet."

"Emma, Theo just got back from a florists' convention in Rhode Island, and she's teaching me how to make an acorn wreath."

"I did a presentation this morning on nuts and seeds," Theo said pointedly.

"Cool," I said. "LaRue, we have to talk."

Theo gave me with a withering look. Her frizzy brown hair hung like curtains over her face. "We're in the middle of a conversation, if you haven't noticed."

I ignored her. "Why didn't you call me back?" I said to LaRue.

"I was visiting Nanny when you called. I didn't get your message right away."

"Would you like me to finish explaining about the hot glue?" Theo asked. "Or are we going to talk about phone calls?" She began fingering the pearl pendant around her neck.

"Chill, Theo." LaRue grabbed my arm. "I'll be right back."

The designer eyed us balefully as we left. I've known Theo all my life, and I can't recall her ever having any real friends. She was always the last girl picked for volleyball. In the cafeteria she sat hunched over in her own little world at the end of the table, eating her egg-salad-and-pickle-relish sandwich. She was the only girl I knew who carried an insulated lunch bag all through high school. Everyone else used brown paper bags that we crumpled and pitched into garbage cans.

Once we were in the bathroom with the door closed, LaRue and I began at the same time.

"Zahn stopped ov—"

"Zahn came by—"

"You first," she said.

"Among other things, he wanted to know where I was last night." I picked up a guest soap from the vanity and studied it. It was pink with a white poodle embossed on it.

"Shit, I was afraid you'd say that." LaRue sat down on the toilet. Right before it disappeared under her bottom I noticed that the seat cover was also pink with white poodles. So were the guest towels, the toilet paper cozy, and the little clock on the shelf. "He asked me the same thing."

"What did you tell him?"

"That I was home, baking banana bread. You?"

I groaned. "That I was at the movies with you."

"Shit," she said again.

"When did you talk to him?"

"Fifteen minutes ago. I tried to call you, but you didn't answer."

"I didn't hear the phone."

"Where were you, the dead zone?"

"I was out getting a pumpkin."

"A pumpkin? Are you kidding me? A *pumpkin*?"

"It was too late, anyway."

We looked at each other miserably.

"What else did Zahn want to know?" she asked.

"Basically, how I've been spending my time. And how buddy-buddy I was with Jennifer. He kept harping on that."

Her eyes grew wide. "That's a lot more than he asked me."

I started to tell her about the anonymous call, but I knew she'd start yelling. She was already getting that panicky look.

"All he wanted from me was what I saw and heard at the Sunny Side," LaRue went on.

"What exactly *did* you see and hear?"

"When I got to work, Rita wasn't at the register like she usually is. I heard someone sobbing. Real soft. It was weird because it's never that quiet in the morning. I knew it wasn't Wendy, our other waitress, because she had to drop off her car at the mechanic. So at first I thought something happened to Rita, like maybe her poodle was sick.

"Then I see the cash register drawer open, so my next thought is, we got robbed. And it's payday, so now I'm thinking I'm not going to get paid. I go back to the kitchen, and Rita is sitting on the floor, leaning against the 'In' door. I stick my head in, and—" LaRue dropped her voice to a whisper "—there's Jennifer, sitting at the work table with her feet out like Raggedy Ann. And blood everywhere, and blueberries. Lots of blueberries."

A rap at the door and we both jumped.

"Occupied," LaRue sang out.

"Hon," came Inez's muffled voice, "if it's not too much trouble, could you pass a roll of T.P. out this way? We had a little spill."

"Sure thing." LaRue reached under the vanity for a roll and passed it into the hall. When she turned back, her eyes were troubled.

"One more thing. Zahn asked me if I knew you. I don't know

how he got your name. I thought Rita told him, but she said she didn't."

"You never mentioned me?"

"Em, I don't volunteer anything to the cops. Don't ask, don't tell."

I bit my lip. "I know how he got my name."

I told her about the anonymous phone call.

"Oh, my God. Your library card?" LaRue clenched her fists. "How'd the killer get your library card?" She turned to me with a wild look. "Why the *hell* did you tell Zahn you went to the movies? Why didn't you just say you were home watching TV?"

"I didn't think of it. Come on, LaRue, he had me on the spot."

"And it probably took him five seconds to figure out it was a fish story. Why did you even tell him we were buds?"

"What are you talking about? He asked me why I like going there. Of course I told him. What was I supposed to say?"

"Your problem," LaRue said, "is that you talk too much."

We stood there, seething. I heard the TV get loud in the other room.

"Now what?" I finally said.

"You have to tell Zahn the truth, Emma. Call him up and come clean."

"Me? What about you, Miss Cool as a Cucumber? You're the one who told me to lie to him in the first place. Why don't *you* call him?"

"You're the one whose library card turned up."

"Yeah, but *he* doesn't know I know that. Calling him will make me look totally guilty!"

"Stop shouting!"

"This is great, just great." I paced to the bathtub and back. "Right now Zahn doesn't know which one of us is lying—for all he knows we both are. For all he knows we're in cahoots. And

48

of course Ronk will vouch for you."

"Of course. I told her what to say."

"Wonderful. So now *I* look like the only screw-up. Thanks a million, LaRue."

"Don't you talk to me like that, Emma." She glared at me from two inches away. "You think I don't care? I thought I was done with Zahn. He called me, for Pete's sake, while I was setting up the goddamn buffet table in Rita's goddamn parlor. I didn't have one goddamn second to think of another alibi for old X-ray Eyes. And how was I supposed to know what you told him? Am I a freaking mind reader?"

Before I could respond, her jacket pocket began to play "I'm Every Woman." She whipped out her cell phone and flipped it open.

"Yeah. I told her, yeah. She said the movies." LaRue shot me another icy glare. "I don't know, Brenda. We're working it out in the bathroom."

"No, *you*'re working it out in the bathroom. I'm leaving."

I stormed out, nearly tripping over Inez and Charlie Steigbeagle, who were mopping up spilled tea in the hall.

LaRue grabbed my arm. "Where do you think you're going?"

"Home. I'll handle this myself."

"You can't just leave. What about me?"

"You—" I glanced at Charlie and Inez, shoved LaRue back into the bathroom, and shut the door. "You're the one who told me to lie to Zahn in the first place. You're the one who told me not to come in for breakfast. So far, everything you've said has gotten me in trouble."

"You want to blame me for all that, Emma, go right ahead. But we're in the same boat now. Zahn is watching both of us." LaRue grabbed my shoulders with both hands. "We need a plan, girlfriend, or we'll sink faster than last year's American Idol. As much as you hate to admit it, this isn't just about you."

I seethed.

"Besides," she continued, "if we don't clear ourselves and get the police off our backs, the real killer might get away. You want that to happen?"

"LaRue, I am not going to go to Zahn—"

"Fine, don't. If you wait long enough, Zahn will save you the trouble and come to you."

She tapped her foot. The poodle clock ticked. And ticked.

I glared at her. "All right. I'll tell him."

The tapping stopped.

"But LaRue, if I tell Zahn the truth about last night, I'm also telling him the truth about this morning."

In a high voice she said, "Okay, fine."

"He gets the whole enchilada or he gets nothing."

"I said, fine. And if he doesn't believe us, we'll take it to the next level."

"What do you mean, the next level?"

"We'll find the killer ourselves."

"Oh, right. How do you expect us to do *that* with no resources, no experience, and the combined body strength of two jellyfish?"

"Because, Emma, you and I have something the police don't. We know Port Jeff inside and out. Between us we know probably ninety percent of the people who live here." LaRue put her hand on the doorknob. "And speak for yourself about the jellyfish. I'm taking kickboxing at the Y."

CHAPTER SEVEN

The Helping Hands had congregated in Rita's parlor before a small television. Standing before a postcard scene of seagulls, ferry, and strolling couples, a starched news reporter said, "She was a devoted daughter, cherished friend, dog-lover, part-time model, and former high school dropout from New Jersey who was trying to carve out a better life on Long Island. But now she is dead. Details next."

The room buzzed while one actor rattled off the merits of air freshener and another spoke cheerfully about erectile dysfunction. The reporter reappeared.

"Police are searching for suspects in the brutal slaying early this morning of a young woman in the picturesque Village of Port Jefferson. The Sunny Side Up, a favorite breakfast hangout, was transformed today into a crime scene when the body of Jennifer Hazzard, who worked as a cook, was found on the premises. A local business owner shared the concern felt by many residents."

The camera cut to Inez Lipchitz speaking animatedly into the mike. "Oh my God. I'm from the city, and I'm absolutely devastated. I never expected such a thing to happen in my town, and I hope and pray the police catch this evildoer right away. Meanwhile, we are all banding together here and keeping each other safe."

The camera went back to the newswoman. "Death was said to be from a blow to the head. Detectives ask anyone who has information to come forward. Now, the weather."

Everyone in the room spoke at once. "A blow to the head. Inez was right." "Did you know she was a model?" "Why don't you sit here, Rita?" Inez pranced around like a celebrity, pouring coffee.

"You're not drinking anything," a voice behind me said. "Can I get you something?"

I caught a whiff of aftershave that reminded me of summers in the Pocono Mountains and turned around. The first thing I noticed were his eyelashes. They were unusually long and framed deep brown eyes. His hair was also brown, with a smudge of gray at the temples. His muscular chest and neck seemed barely contained by the white turtleneck he wore. He was holding a glass of red wine.

"One of those would be great."

"I'm Tony Randazzo."

"Emma Trace." The warmth of his hand lingered when he released mine.

"Red or white, Emma?"

"I'll have what you're having."

Tony led the way to the buffet table. Over his shoulder I saw Inez watching us from the corner of the room. Her mouth formed an O, and she flapped her hand to mean Hot! Hot! Hot! I looked away.

"You're new here, aren't you?" I asked Tony. "I haven't seen you before."

He handed me my drink. "Since last week. Been a crazy couple of days, hasn't it?"

"A couple? What do you mean?"

"Yesterday, the fire in the bakery. Ruined a new oven. You didn't hear about that? And someone broke into the museum overnight. Then some teenagers with nothing better to do vandalized the Greenhouse. And now this. I'm beginning to think—are you okay?"

"Yes, sorry."

"You looked like you seized up for a minute there."

"It was nothing. You were saying?"

"That I think I brought a run of bad luck with me. I'm here a week, and it's been one crazy thing after another. But I don't believe in luck."

I took a sip. "I do."

Tony raised an eyebrow. "Really."

"Things happen for a reason. Good luck attracts more good luck, and bad luck attracts bad luck."

"Like momentum?"

"Kind of."

He held out what looked like a small piece of toast with chopped up tomatoes on it. I shook my head, and he popped it in his mouth. "And your life experience bears this out?"

"All the way. I've been a very lucky person. My whole family, on my father's side, is. I think it's in the genes." I took another sip of wine. "I do have my unlucky streaks now and then. How about you?"

"I've had some ups and some downs," Tony said. "A few things have come together for me lately. I'm hoping it means I'm in an upturn."

"Sorry, I didn't mean to pry."

Tony put his empty glass behind him. "I'm at the Greenhouse, working with Egon Hoyt as he transitions to retirement." He lowered his voice. "The man is almost eighty. I asked him what he wanted to do when he retired, and he said learn the East Coast Swing."

"That's Egon. So, does this mean you'll be taking over the Greenhouse when he retires?"

"Managing it, yes. We're partners."

I attempted a smile. "Was there much damage?"

"From the kids? Nothing that can't be fixed. At least they swept up after themselves." He laughed.

"They did?"

"Tidiest vandals I ever met." He folded his arms. "The police took a report. Once they have a look at the surveillance video, Egon will decide whether to press charges."

I sputtered red wine onto the paper tablecloth and watched as pink dots bloomed like little roses there. *Surveillance video?*

"Are you okay?" Tony reached for napkins.

"Fine," I wheezed. "Went down the wrong way." I cleared my throat. "When did Egon put in a security system?"

He handed me a few napkins and blotted the table with the rest. "On Monday. Why?"

"That was a smart move."

"I guess it was good luck we did it this week."

Out of the corner of my eye I saw LaRue flagging me down. "Lucky for you," I said.

CHAPTER EIGHT

The birthday bet grew out of an old Trace family axiom that, basically, nothing in the world is such a big deal that you can't put a little money on it.

The tradition goes back at least as far as my dad's grandparents' arrival at Ellis Island in 1910, when according to legend Great Grandpa Nathan Trajcevski told the agent who asked him how much money he was carrying that it didn't sit still long enough for him to count it.

I learned how to wager with the Cheerios in my high chair tray. According to Dad, by the age of three I was taking him up on bets involving ants crossing the kitchen floor. Mom ended several of these contests by vacuuming up the contenders.

My cousins and I bet on who could hold our breath the longest, which raindrop would get to the bottom of the window first, and how many holes were in a package of Swiss cheese. In December we celebrated both the Eight Nights of Football and It's Beginning to Look a Lot Like the Playoffs. If it moved, involved numbers, or had a time limit, it was good for a bet.

For fifteen years I honed my skills. I did my homework at the track on Saturday afternoons. During the spring and fall meets, when he wasn't on the phone talking horses—"Who d'ya have in the fourth? I'm going with Beach Babe and Too Much Noise in the double. No way Casino Royale's gonna win with Night Music running, he's got a good final kick"—Dad and I and whoever else was around piled into the station wagon and, to

Mom's immeasurable chagrin, drove to Belmont Racetrack in Queens, where I wrote book reports and solved math problems between races. Dad gave me ten bucks, and whatever I had left at the end of the day was my allowance.

A week before my fifteenth birthday, my uncles upped the ante. I was summoned to the living room, where Dad and his brothers were waiting for me.

"We're hiding your birthday present this year," Dad announced. "It's somewhere in town and you've got a week to find it. Sherm, Pike, and I each put fifty bucks down says you will. Ned has a hundred fifty says you won't. Good luck."

"What's the reward?" I asked, already feeling the adrenaline rush.

"Dinner out, if you find it."

"And if I don't?"

Ned sauntered up to the plate, his arms folded, a black curtain of hair covering one eye and a toothpick hanging from his lip. Ned was the youngest and wildest of the Trace boys, only three years my senior and already exhibiting a propensity for flying upside down. He was working at Radio Shack then, his first real job, and he'd saved his pay to bet against me.

I narrowed my eyes at him. Ned smiled evilly and narrowed his eyes right back. Even before he said what the booby prize was, I knew I had to win.

"Detective Zahn, please."

"Who's calling?"

"Emma Trace."

"One moment."

I bit off the corner of my Fluffernutter sandwich. Through the kitchen window I could see the blue Neon still parked on the downhill side of Parsley Street. It had been sitting there for the past three hours, ever since it had pulled out of a side street near Rita's and followed me home. Smoke curled from the driver's side window.

"Zahn."

"Detective, I'd like to correct something I told you earlier."

There was a pause, and I knew he had turned on his bullshit meter. "How 'bout that."

"I didn't go to the movies last night."

"Just a second." He muffled the phone and spoke briefly to someone nearby. I heard traffic sounds in the background. "Let's have this conversation in my office. Do you know where police headquarters is in Yaphank?"

"I think so. But I can always double check with your guy on my way out."

"Pardon me?"

"Your man in the blue Neon parked outside."

Did I imagine it, or did he say *shit*? "Find your way down here and we'll talk."

I slapped the phone shut and stood at the window, scarfing down the rest of my sandwich. A few seconds went by and a cigarette butt popped out of the driver's window. The car revved to life and drove slowly down the hill.

Thirty minutes later I faced Zahn across a desk.

I had given my name to a very pregnant desk sergeant who gave me a quick neutral look and said into the phone, "She's here." Now I sat in an office chair that was too wide for me, making me feel like a child in grown-up furniture.

A green blotter littered with sticky notes and pens sat in the middle of Zahn's desk. Three-ring binders filled the shelves behind him, along with a couple of framed photos. One depicted a younger, smiling Zahn in uniform. He held a plaque and shook hands with another man. A portrait of a dark-haired young woman and a boy of about nine filled the other frame. An NYPD police cap was hooked over the edge of that frame.

On the windowsill a spider plant drooped. The sky looked pink through the blinds.

Zahn leaned back in his swivel chair and rolled a pen between his palms. He was not smiling.

"Why don't we start from square one?"

I took a sip from the paper cone I'd filled at the cooler. "The truth is, I stayed home all evening."

"Why did you lie?"

"I didn't think you'd believe the truth."

I tossed back the remaining water and crumpled the cone in my fist. I didn't see a wastebasket. "There's more. This morning at around five LaRue Fusticola and I climbed up the wall behind Hoyt's Greenhouse looking for my birthday present."

He stopped rolling the pen. "You what?"

"Family tradition." I gave him the *Reader's Digest* version and recited the riddle. "Last year we found it in a petting zoo. If we'd gotten there any later, the goats would have eaten it."

Zahn's face looked like it was pulling in two directions. "Where have you looked so far?"

"Seven Chinese restaurants, a sushi bar, Oriental grocery, meditation center, Eastern Orthodox church, two Thai restaurants, three yoga studios, and an acupuncture clinic. Uh, and Hoyt's."

"What's the payoff if you find it?"

"Dinner out."

"And if you fail?"

I made a loop-de-loop pattern in the air with my finger.

Zahn raised an eyebrow.

"An aerobatic flight with Ned," I explained.

He tapped his pen on the edge of the desk.

"And here I thought you were going to tell me they make you write on the blackboard a hundred times, 'I will not lie to detectives.'"

I looked at my lap.

"You generally find your present?"

"All but the first one."

It was a kooky bet, that first one. It went beyond kooky to zany.

Loony. Screwy. Wacky. Pick any word you like, they all do the job.

It was a bet that nobody could win, except Ned. I don't know if Dad, Sherm, and Pike actually had faith in my deductive abilities or simply enjoyed taking on their little brother.

They handed me a few clues written on a scrap of paper torn from the Daily Racing Form.

They added a few general parameters.

And they gave me a week.

"Where do I start?" I asked dumbly.

"Always start," Dad said, "with what you know."

The clues were un-elaborate. "Hot soup," "One potato, two potato, three potato, four," and "What did Romeo say to Juliet?" After a fruitless search that took me to the supermarket, library, and high school drama department, I had no choice but to return empty-handed.

The present, a funny children's book about potatoes riding a Ferris wheel, showed up for the holidays. It had been hidden behind the concession stand at Theatre Three, where my aunt worked. But by then it was too late.

"What did you do after leaving Hoyt's?"

"Detective Zahn, I wish you wouldn't tell Mr. Hoyt about this. I'd like to square it with him myself."

"You, Emma, are in no position to request anything. Excuse me a moment." He reached for the phone and punched a couple of buttons. "Morales, is Turk back yet?"

"Yes, sir, right here," came a tinny voice from the speaker.

"Send him in, please. And would you buzz Jenkins and ask him to pick me up outside in ten minutes."

"You got it."

The door clicked open behind me. A tall, broadly built man wearing a cable knit sweater entered. He had a fringe of brown hair encircling a wide, shiny bald head, and a diagonal scar over his left eyebrow. Zahn introduced him as Detective Harris Bonomo. He took my hand briefly in a vise-like grip and retreated to the bookshelves where he watched me over Zahn's shoulder.

Zahn leaned back and touched his fingertips together.

"Emma, I'd like you to tell Detective Bonomo everything you just told me."

"About today? About the bet?" I hadn't mentioned the phone call yet and felt a twinge of dread.

"Everything."

Bonomo, hands in pockets, stood with one knee bent and his foot on the wall behind him in a casual pose while I repeated my story. He listened with pursed lips, nodding from time to time but not saying anything.

When I got to the end, I said, "There's another—"

Zahn interrupted me. "What time did you and LaRue leave Hoyt's?"

"A little before six."

"On foot, or by car?"

"On foot. LaRue was parked in Rocket Ship Park. But she was only going across the street."

Zahn rolled his pen on his blotter, his mouth set, eyes on me.

"While you were there, did you see or hear anything out of the ordinary?"

"Nothing stands out."

In a clipped voice he asked, "Did Jennifer Hazzard know about this little birthday game?"

"Not as far as I know." I twisted what was left of the paper cup.

"You never talked to her about it."

"Why would I?"

The desk sergeant I'd spoken to—Morales—walked over and handed Zahn a batch of papers. He dropped them on his desk without looking at them. "What kind of birthday present do you usually get? For example."

"All kinds of things. Museum memberships, tickets to shows, various appliances my parents think I'm lacking."

"Jewelry?"

"No."

"Cars, boats, cruise reservations?"

"No, nothing like that. Nothing valuable enough to be a big loss if found by someone else."

Zahn thought about that one. "Who else knows about this ritual?"

"A few people." The words he was using—"game" and "ritual"—rubbed me the wrong way. "Friends and family."

"Did any of them know where you were going to be this morning?"

"Just LaRue."

Zahn rose to his feet. I glanced behind him to Bonomo, who hadn't moved. The big detective's face showed no clue to his thoughts.

In measured tones, Zahn said, "Emma, are you aware of the consequences of lying to the police?"

I swallowed. "Detective Zahn, I'm sorry I—"

"Lying to the police is bad, Emma. Real bad. 'Sorry' won't wash. This is a homicide investigation. You lie to me during a homicide investigation and I can charge you with obstruction of justice and put your sorry ass behind bars." He turned and took a quick look through the blinds into the now darkness. Then he spread his palms on the desk and leaned toward me. "When I ask you a question—I don't care what it is—I want the truth. You don't give me some cock and bull story. You don't tell me which parts *you* think are important for me to know. You tell me the truth. Understand?"

"Yes."

"I'm going to give you some advice. Go home and paint a picture. Make something out of Legos. Find yourself another creative outlet, but don't concoct any more screwball stories for us. You got that?"

I felt rage rising in me. "Sure, Detective."

"And another thing." Zahn came around the desk. His X-ray stare sank into me. "Stay off private property."

I looked at Bonomo and he smiled. It was not a nice smile.

CHAPTER NINE

"See any cops?" LaRue asked.

"Hang on." Holding the phone aside, I looked up Parsley as far as I could from my kitchen window. In the dark all I could see was the occasional glint of a car fender reflected in the light of a distant street lamp. I could have been looking at a whole car full of cops and not known it. "Nope."

"Listen, Em, Brenda'll be back in an hour with the Jeep. I can take you."

"I don't want to wait, LaRue. Every minute that goes by—"

"He might already have the letter."

"And he might not. Listen, I'm going to walk." I stared at my reflection in the windowpane. Same hollow look as always. I looked away. "I'll be okay. In and out."

"All right. Call me when you get back. Be careful, Em."

"I will."

"Ten-four, good buddy."

I shut the phone and walked back to my computer. The screen still displayed the page I'd been reading. I skimmed through the information one last time to make sure I had it memorized and closed my browser.

I grabbed my fleece and trotted downstairs. There was no one in the parking lot except Mrs. Porter in 1A, who was taking out her trash. The temperature had dropped sharply, and I zipped up. Then I hesitated, looking at my Honda. If Zahn's people saw me leave the parking lot, our next meeting was going to make today's look like happy hour.

Mrs. Porter shuffled by in her pink bathrobe and curlers. "Car trouble, dear?"

I lifted my eyebrows in an if-it's-not-one-thing-it's-another expression. "It's been making a weird noise lately."

"I could tell by the look on your face. You can borrow the Olds if you'd like."

"Oh, thanks, Mrs. P. I promise, I won't be long."

"You don't have to explain, dear. I'm glad you're going to fire up her pistons. She gets so little use I should probably sell her, but I can't bear the thought. Come on in, I'll get you the key."

I followed her in and stood in the living room while she shuffled into the depths. *Jeopardy!* was blaring from the television. I'd never been inside Mrs. Porter's apartment before, but every time I went by, the TV was turned up high to the game shows. I wondered if she watched all day. I doubted she had ever lied to the police. I wondered if people in jail watched a lot of game shows.

"Here you go, dear." She handed me the key. "Watch out when you start her up. She balks."

Mrs. Porter's car was a 1973 Olds Cutlass Supreme in flame orange with a 350 rocket engine and orange pillow top velour seats. As I glided down Parsley, I glanced in my rearview mirror. No one was behind me. I felt a twinge of excitement.

Hazzard's street was lined with flat-roofed ranches, beater cars, large rusting appliances, and the occasional dim street lamp. I pulled over behind a stove, killed the engine, and gazed at the house two doors down.

The dilapidated ranch squatted in a corner lot, its backyard enclosed by a six-foot chain-link fence that went almost to the curb. Not that there was an actual curb—the property simply ended in weedy tufts that oozed mud onto the street in summer and made it a bad place to practice parallel parking.

I could see that little had changed since the last time I'd been here with Sam to drop off Ruby. Shingles were missing and a shutter hung at an odd angle. A few parched bushes hunched miserably at intervals along the cement foundation. A broken bicycle lay next to the front door like the skeleton of an animal that had died of thirst. The only thing new was the strip of yellow police tape across the front door.

Easing out of the Cutlass, my breath made little puffs in the chilly air. I pulled up my collar and treaded silently across the street.

The house windows were dark. I hurried across the front lawn and squatted behind Hazzard's Chevy pickup parked in the driveway. Before pulling on a pair of latex gloves I felt to make sure my shopper's club ID card was still in my pocket.

Keeping myself in shadow, I made a dash for the side door, ripped away yellow tape, and pulled open the storm door. Using the mini flashlight on my keychain, I illuminated the inner doorknob and wiggled it. Locked—but it was a crappy lock. I slid my shopper's club card into the crack, forced the lock tongue back against the frame, and slipped inside, being careful not to let the storm door bang against me.

When my eyes adjusted to the darkness I saw I was in a small coat room that smelled like wet dog. Boots and shoes littered the floor. I picked my way past them and into the hallway. Now which way? The kitchen was to my left. My letter was probably in a desk or file cabinet somewhere. I decided to check further and try the kitchen if needed on my way out.

To my right a den opened onto the back deck. Light from the sliding glass doors illuminated a small desk in the corner. I moved to it silently.

The desk was pre-computer age with a keyhole center drawer and six side drawers. The surface was cluttered with framed photographs. I picked one up—a professional portrait of Hazzard wearing a coy expression and little else, her platinum hair draped provocatively over a highly airbrushed shoulder. Replacing it, I saw from the dust marks on the desk that several other photos had been removed.

Putting the mini light between my teeth, I yanked open the bottom left drawer. It was filled with rubber stamps, boxes of binder clips, and other office supplies. The other drawers on that side contained more of the same. In the bottom right drawer I found a batch of letters with a rubber band around them. As I reached in, I heard a door open on the other side of the wall and light emanated from the hallway.

Holy shit, someone was in the house.

Someone besides me.

A weird moan emanated from the next room. Heart racing, I shoved the drawer back in and dove under the desk.

Heavy footsteps thunked down the hallway and stopped outside the den. A raspy male voice said, "What the fuck?"

The side door! I'd left it open. A hinge squeaked as he opened the storm door and let it slam. The hallway light blinked off.

I pulled myself into the cubbyhole as far as I could. The floor creaked as the man walked into the den and stopped in front of the desk, his legs inches from my face. He was wearing filthy, rumpled jeans over a pair of worn snakeskin cowboy boots, and he reeked of alcohol and tobacco. A hand came down, yanked a knife from his left boot, and popped the blade. It was a cheap four-inch Remington with a camo handle, the kind you can buy at Walmart. The hand and knife hung there in front of me while his other hand opened and closed drawers. I squeezed my fingers around my car keys, allowing the blade of one key to slip between my knuckles.

Then the boots backed away from the desk and stepped to the sliding door. The deck light snapped on and the door slid open.

I bent my head to get a look at him. He stood on the deck, facing right, swaying a little. Tall and gaunt, he had a reptilian face, pale gray eyes, and stringy, mustard-colored hair. A pack of cigarettes was rolled up in the sleeve of his T-shirt. The belt hung open on his jeans as though they'd been hastily pulled on. An unlit cigarette dangled from the side of his mouth.

I clambered out from under the desk. More moans came from the next room, and I realized they were coming from the TV. He was watching porn.

Leaping into the hallway I glanced back. He stood on the deck, staring at me with pale unblinking eyes. A lizard in human form. Slowly he raised the knife.

I grabbed a floor lamp and knocked it over, dashed around the corner, and pulled open the first door I came to. Closet. Pulled open another and found steps going down. I fumbled with my flashlight and tripped my way down the stairs, twisting my ankle in the process. The basement floor was heaped with junk. Ignoring the pain in my ankle, I swung the tiny light around, looking for a hiding place. A few boxes were piled by the ping-pong table in the corner. I limped over and dropped behind them. The blood pounded in my ears.

The basement door opened, and a dim bulb came on at the top of the stairs.

"Got you now, bitch," came the raspy voice. The stairs creaked as he started down.

On the opposite wall I saw a steep metal staircase leading to a bulkhead door. I grabbed a ping-pong ball that had rolled under the table.

Twelve steps. The creaking stopped.

"Come out, come out, wherever you are," sang the lizard-like man.

I threw the ping-pong ball to my right. It hit something metallic, and he moved in that direction. I leaped out from behind the table and bounded up the metal steps to the bulkhead.

"Cunt!" he growled, stumbling toward me.

I fought with the lever, forced the pin out of the hole, and pushed up the heavy door two inches. The man grabbed my right ankle and pulled my foot off the step. The door slammed, narrowly missing my fingers. I leaned over and stabbed his hand as hard as I could with the key. With a yelp he released my ankle. Then with strength I didn't know I had I pushed open the door and hauled myself out into the yard, letting the door slam on his hands. He howled in pain and surprise. I scrambled over the chain-link fence.

"Stop, you fucking bitch!"

The fence rattled behind me. He was surprisingly quick for a drunk. I dropped down behind Hazzard's pickup and peered over the fender as the man lurched down the driveway. Before I could make a run for it, a supersized SUV glided up to the curb, its low beams illuminating the bottom of the drive. I tugged on the pickup's passenger door, scrambled inside, and pulled it shut. Then I made myself into a ball on the floor and pulled a smelly tarp over me.

A car door slammed.

"Where'd that fucking bitch go?" said the lizard man.

"What are you talking about?" The second guy's voice was calm. Too calm. From the muffled sound of his footsteps, I guessed he was walking up the front lawn.

"She was in the house. This stupid chick. She was messing around in the house."

The lawn footsteps stopped. "There's no one here. Put that thing away."

"Who the fuck are you, tell me what to do. I'm gonna find the bitch and slice her open like a fuckin' fish fillet." My pursuer's silhouette appeared in the window. He was looking over the back of the pickup, his pale eyes darting about wildly.

My neck at a painful angle, I freed my feet to kick if I had to. "Why'd it take you so long to get here?"

"I've got a job, jerk. Some people are working at seven in the morning, not lying on a couch getting high."

"Fuck you, kingpin."

"We'll continue this conversation inside."

"No. You're gonna listen to *me*, man." The lizard man stepped back out of view. "I know your whole fuckin' story. It's in the book. Her own fuckin' words."

"You got nothing, you lying piece of shit. You're going to be out of business in five minutes. I don't want to have to use this, but I'll blow you away if I have to. Move."

A shadow cut through the beam of the headlights.

"Goddamn bitch," said the lizard man.

"I don't have all night, peckerhead. Give it to me or I'll go in and get it myself."

"Stay the hell out of the house."

"Why? Something you don't want me to see?"

"Stay the hell *out*, asshole!"

There was a scuffle and a door slammed.

After a minute I pulled myself gingerly up onto the seat, rubbing my neck. I found myself sitting on something hard. It was a plastic bag containing a DVD, the receipt still stuck to the plastic case. I took it out and read the title. *Back Door Boogie*. There was a small Post-it stuck to the case: "C U Friday."

Evidence Locker
Box 15
Personal diary, page 3

Dear Diary,

I made mommy sick again. last time she got sick it was from me and now today she is sick. daddy got me ice cream. he checked me for ticks I hate it when he does that. but its bad to have ticks. I'm sorry mommy. we went to carvel after and he got me a swirl cone thank you daddy.

CHAPTER TEN

Saturday

Hazzard's death got top billing in the morning papers. I spread them out on the kitchen table next to the disposable phone and extra-large coffee I'd picked up at 7-Eleven. Every cover showed the same bare-shouldered portrait I'd seen on her desk.

DEATH OVER EASY, screamed one headline. DEATH OF INNOCENCE, THUG POACHES COOK, and BATTERED, punned the others. The articles all said the same thing: the former-beauty-contestant-turned-grill-cook from Clifton, New Jersey, had been slain early Friday morning by an assailant who'd entered the kitchen by the side door during a delivery and surprised her. No cash had been taken from the register, and robbery did not appear to be the motive. The murder weapon had not been recovered. Accompanying the articles were photos of the crime scene and of Hazzard, age ten, winning first prize in the Little Miss Cranberry beauty pageant at the Jersey Shore.

Internet news stories added little to what I'd learned.

I knew from watching forensics shows that most homicides are solved within the first forty-eight hours. More than half of those had already gone by. It was clear Zahn didn't like or trust me. He had my library card, and maybe the letter I wrote, too. I couldn't exactly tell him about the two men I'd encountered at Hazzard's without revealing why I'd gone there and that I'd ignored a police barrier.

I was on my own. On my own, and possibly a suspect.

Biting back panic, I clipped out the articles. There were too many holes in the story, and questions were piling up. For instance, did Hazzard's murderer plan to kill her, or did they have a confrontation that escalated? Problem was, I lacked basic information—the circumstances of the crime. Without friends in the police department to give me information, I was stuck with what I could learn from newspapers and the Internet.

I went to my computer desk and found an old soft-cover marble notebook. Only a few pages had been used in an earlier life. I tore them out and returned to the kitchen. Then I opened the notebook to a fresh page and wrote down all the questions I could think of that needed answers. I divided my questions into categories: PEOPLE. PLACES. THINGS. In another section of the notebook I started pages for people I had come across whose lives intersected with Hazzard's in some way. The lizard man, the SUV guy. I also began a log of my activities, starting with yesterday morning. It took me almost a half hour to empty my head into the notebook.

CHAPTER ELEVEN

"Boyfriend? What boyfriend?" Rita asked, pushing a wide broom along the floor behind the counter.

"She never talked about him?" LaRue asked.

"No. You think I have all day to pry into my employees' personal lives? I'm running a restaurant here."

"Inez thinks he's married," I said, spritzing the mirror.

"Married, wonderful." Rita shook her head.

LaRue waited for Rita to move on before commenting, "Well, he wasn't the dude with the knife. She liked class."

It was five minutes after ten. The Krime Kleaners truck had just rolled away, and the three of us were whipping Sunny Side Up into shape. Rita wasn't wasting any time getting back to business. We were cleaning up after the cleaners.

When I'd arrived earlier, Rita was on the phone with her insurance agent, policy papers spread out before her in one of the booths. I'd nodded at LaRue, who was mopping the dining room floor, and we headed for the kitchen. I pushed open the swinging door and drew in my breath sharply. A day after the murder, the room's stainless steel fixtures gleamed from top to bottom and smelled strongly of disinfectant. Even though I'd expected it and felt partly relieved, I was also disappointed.

To the left of the doorway was a counter with a pass-through window and a rack for customer order slips, and beyond that were the sink and dishwasher. The left side wall was lined with storage cabinets, one lone window, and the delivery entrance. In the left rear corner was an alcove filled with cartons—the storage area—and adjacent to that along the rear wall were a six-burner stove, a grill, an oven, and more counter and storage space. The walk-in refrigerator was in the far right corner. Against the right side wall stood a freestanding refrigerator, a freezer, and two carts for dirty dishes.

In the center of the room under a hanging utensil rack was a six-foot stainless steel prep table. The table where Hazzard had been found.

I went over and ran my fingertip across the surface. A moist trail lingered. There was no way to tell that something terrible had happened here. I walked around the table and, after a slight hesitation, climbed onto the barstool facing the front of the room. This was where she had sat stirring the batter.

I studied the view before me. The wall space around the pass-through was covered with printed notices from the Department of Health. Dispensers for garnishes and sandwich picks were lined up on the table. Above the sink a small television sat on a shelf that also held some well-thumbed cookbooks and dishwashing supplies. More cleaning supplies were under the sink. A broom leaned against it. Nothing seemed unusual in any way.

I turned my head to the right but could only see the delivery door in my peripheral vision. The police thought that the murderer might have gotten in during a delivery, while the door was open. Hazzard and the delivery guy might have been in the walk-in refrigerator at the time, checking off the manifest. Maybe the killer had confronted her after she sat back down at the table.

"What are you doing?"

I turned around and saw LaRue in the doorway with the mop.

"Logicking things out. Rita's still on the phone?"

"Yeah. She's talking to the adjuster."

"LaRue, c'mere a minute."

She hesitated, then took a few steps in, her face white and stiff-looking. "Ugh, this place creeps me out."

"Tell me where you saw the blood. Was it all in here, or was there any out in front?"

"I think it was all in here. This is the only place I looked."

"Show me."

"Here." Her arm made a circle around my chair. "And spattered on the table and stuff."

"Was there a trail?"

She shook her head, thinking. "I'm not sure. It was just a mess."

"You said things were knocked off shelves. What things?"

"Well . . ." LaRue ran her fingers through her hair and scanned the room. She nodded toward the window. "Over there, you see the cookie sheets? They were on the floor, and the muffin tins. The cabinet doors were open. Might have been a few spoons knocked off the prep table. And of course the blueberries."

"What do the blueberries come in? A jar?"

"Plastic baskets. We only use fresh."

I stood up and surveyed the room. "Anything missing here?"

"The cops asked me that, too." She shrugged. "I couldn't tell you. I don't know the inventory that well."

"Can we take a look around? Let's start with the storage area."

We walked that way.

"You've got your dry goods," LaRue said, pointing to cardboard boxes. "Your napkins, your straws, your takeout containers. You've got your spices and your oyster crackers. Juices, vinegar, ketchup, all the heavy duty usage stuff."

"What's this?" I kicked a large plastic bucket.

"Frialator oil. For your French fries. It comes in five-gallon pails."

I peered over the boxes to a small clearing in the middle. "Someone could hide in there, I guess."

"Yup." She moved away, continuing slowly along the back wall, running her fingers along the shelves.

"Let me know if anything stands out."

"Yup."

I sat on the stool, trying to picture the situation as it had developed. If Hazzard had been surprised by someone hiding among the boxes and hit from behind, then the murder was preplanned. Either she was the intended target, or she was merely in the way. The killer had brained her, grabbed whatever he'd come looking for, and left. Or left without finding it. He might have been scared off.

What if he hadn't killed her immediately? What if they had argued? In that case the killer was someone she knew. That didn't mesh with someone sneaking in and hiding. She might have let him in.

I squatted down and ran my hand over the smooth floor. It smelled strongly of Lysol. It probably hadn't looked this good since the day the place opened. I put my cheek down on the faded peach tiles and looked across the surface. Faint scuff marks zigzagged the area around the stool, showing where the chair had been dragged back and forth countless times. There was no way to distinguish recent from long-ago skid marks. Not without forensics equipment, anyway. I picked up the stool and checked its feet. Spic and span, like everything else.

LaRue asked over her shoulder, "Did the cops tail you here?" She had worked her way around to the sink.

"What would they see? That I'm helping my friends clean up the Sunny Side? I hope they're working some better leads by now."

"Me, too."

"Where are your surveillance cameras, LaRue?"

"There's one by the register and one in the foyer."

"None back here?"

"No. That's a heavy steel door and there's no handle on the outside. The only people who come in this way are the delivery guys. You have to open the padlock to let them in. I'll show you."

We went over to the door, and I lifted the heavy padlock away from the ring. LaRue took a key from a nail and wiggled it in the lock until the mechanism snapped open. Yanking the door open, I found only a mounted plate on the outer surface that concealed the lock mechanism. There was nothing in the alleyway but a dumpster.

"What's delivered in the morning?"

"Dairy. Bread. Meat twice a week." LaRue took a baking pan off a shelf and put it back.

"Only twice?"

"All we do is breakfast and lunch."

"How about produce?"

"That comes in later. We get our fruits and vegetables from a local farm. Hey, Emma, check this out."

LaRue had opened one of the large cabinets beneath the window and was squatting before it. There was an empty space in the middle. All around the space were things like measuring cups and glass baking dishes.

"What belongs here?"

"A blue mixing bowl."

"Made of what?"

"Ceramic. You think the police took it?"

"Maybe."

LaRue looked back at me. "And maybe not."

A pile of napkins ruffled in a sudden breeze and brought me

back to the moment. I looked up from the counter I'd been repeatedly sponging to see Rita at the front door taking armfuls of daisies from Theodora Silk. Theo's silver Subaru Outback idled at the curb.

"Hey, answer my question," LaRue said.

I blinked. "What?"

"What'd the SUV guy look like?"

"I didn't see."

"I bet he was her BF. Big classy car, probably has a couple kids, looking for fun, no strings—"

I nodded, picking up the thread. I noticed that neither of us had mentioned Sam. That was fine. Was Hazzard's new boyfriend really new, or had Sam gotten mixed up with her when she was seeing someone else? Maybe he was banging her while she and boyfriend number two were on the outs. Maybe she had used Sam to make the other guy jealous, then dumped him. Or maybe she kept them both hanging on. Whatever the situation, somehow I felt better knowing someone else was involved. I wiped down a ketchup bottle and replaced it.

"He went to her house to get something he'd left behind," I said.

"His tighty-whiteys." LaRue's eyes grew big. "Oh, yeah, baby. What do you think, Rita?"

Rita put the daisies on the counter. Theo gunned the car and drove away.

"I think you girls should stay out of police business," Rita said. "LaRue, cut these stems, please, and place one on each table. Use the crystal vases. Wasn't that nice of Theo to give us fresh flowers to welcome back our customers?"

"Sure was." Dutifully LaRue grabbed a knife from under the counter and started hacking.

"Rita, what do you know about Jennifer's family?" I asked.

Rita gave me a dour look. She picked up the broom again

78

and headed off on an outbound sweep. "She's got her mother and a brother."

"Her brother have long hair and an anger management problem?"

"He was in the military. Lost a leg in Iraq. He lives with the mother in New Jersey."

That ruled out the lizard man. I pulled out my notebook and jotted down what she'd said. "Do you know if the family is coming here?"

Rita turned and pushed the broom back. When she saw me writing in my notebook she frowned. "I talked to the mother. She's staying with relatives until the police release . . . her daughter. They're going to have the funeral service out here and take Jennifer back to Jersey to be buried."

"So who was the dude with the knife?" LaRue mused. She began filling vases with water from the sink.

"What dude with a knife?" Rita asked.

"No one," LaRue said.

Rita emptied two crumbs into the trash and smacked the dustpan smartly against the side of the can. "Maybe you girls should stop asking questions and let the police do their job. Now, I don't want to hear any more about it. I have a business to run. LaRue, be ready to go at twelve on the dot."

She turned and headed off again with the broom. LaRue wrinkled her nose at Rita's back. I tossed the sponge in the sink and pulled the DVD out of my bag. "Maybe this is what the SUV guy was looking for. Take a look, Rue."

"*Back Door Boogie.* So?"

"I found it in Hazzard's truck."

"In her truck! Get out of town, girlfriend!"

"I think it means she had a date. A date that never came off."

"With the SUV dude?"

"That's what I'm going to find out."

I told her my idea. LaRue's eyes bugged out.

"I'm coming with you, Em."

"No, you're not."

"You're gonna need backup."

"Backup. Jesus. I don't need backup. I'm not dragging you any deeper into this, LaRue. Stay here, I'll let you know what turns up."

She put a hand on my shoulder. "Save your breath. Someone's gotta watch your six, and apparently it ain't you."

Chapter Twelve

A little after eleven we pulled up outside the Playland Adult Boutique in LaRue's Jeep Wrangler. Mannequins in the store window were dressed up as witches and cats. The cat had a chain around her neck and strategically placed slits in her bodysuit. An old Terri Clark song, "Better Things to Do," was playing on the radio.

"Break a leg, Swee'pea," LaRue said, fishing in her bag for a piece of gum.

I cracked open the car door. "Give me three words, like in improv."

"Cousin. Sad. Bergamot."

"Bergamot?"

"Yeah. As in Bergamot's going to need a new home if you go to jail."

"Gee, thanks."

"I'll wait here in the getaway car."

"Getaway car. Give me a break." I slammed the door, causing a windstorm in the pink and silver feathers of her seat covers.

I took a deep breath and walked in. A doorbell chimed, and a girl with sleek black hair and almond eyes looked up from the counter where she was clicking away at a computer. She looked about nineteen.

"Can I help you?"

I sighed heavily. "My cousin's boyfriend was in here a few

days ago. He rented a movie, but they never got to watch it. She died suddenly. Maybe you heard." I unfolded a newspaper clipping and smoothed it out on the counter. The girl pulled it toward her. She had long, hooked green fingernails in which tiny rhinestones had been embedded. Her name tag said Yoko.

"Oh, the lady from the diner," Yoko said. "Bummer."

"Yes. I'm trying to locate her boyfriend so I can drop off his stuff."

"Cool," she said, nodding.

"I was hoping you could look up his address real quick." I pushed the receipt I had found toward her.

The girl stared at me. "Are you kidding?"

"Can't you get it from his account?"

"I can, but I'm not going to. You want me to lose my job?"

I looked outside and saw LaRue watching me from the car, her feet up on the dashboard.

"Not at all," I said quickly. "I understand your position. It's just that it could be a little awkward for me to make phone calls. He might be married."

The girl was silent. I pulled the DVD out of the bag and showed it to her.

"Can you tell me at least when this movie is due back?"

She drummed her dagger nails on the counter. "It's against store policy to give out customer information. Privacy laws."

I nodded. "I'm just looking for a date here."

Yoko looked at me dubiously.

"And I really appreciate your help," I added.

She shrugged and took the DVD. "Okay, just the date." Her long green nails flew over the keys. While I waited I looked at the various toys on display behind her. I wondered if her mother knew she worked here.

"This movie's overdue," she complained. "Your guy owes us seven-fifty. And that's all I'm going to say."

I snatched the DVD back before she could chuck it in the returns bin. "Were you here when he came in?"

Yoko clenched her teeth. "I said, that's all I'm going to say."

I suppressed the urge to throttle her. When I glanced outside I saw LaRue scrambling over the Jeep's front seat, her butt in the air.

"How 'bout I call the customer and give him *your* number, and he can call you. Okay?"

At that moment the door opened and a tall, slim woman in a pink and silver feather turban, large pink sunglasses, and cowboy boots marched in and headed my way swinging a black patent leather bag.

"You degenerate hussy!" she hissed. "My detective's been following you! He saw you come out of that hotel with the DVD in your hand. You're the one who's been carrying on with my husband! Well, take *that*!" She smacked me on the arm with her bag.

"Ouch!"

"Just wait till I talk to my lawyer. The shit's going to hit the fan now, cookie." She swung the bag again.

"Ow!"

"Mrs. Bellarosa, if that's who you are, calm down or I will have to call security," Yoko said.

"Call security on *her*. She's trying to hack into my Playland account."

"Don't you threaten me, lady," I said. "Just because you and Bunky aren't getting it on anymore doesn't make it *my* problem."

"Ha! You don't know beans about Bunky!" At the "Ha!" a few feathers floated off her turban.

"Well, you sure fooled me," Yoko said to me. "I thought you were that dead lady's cousin."

"She's no cousin, she's a degenerate hussy," LaRue said. "I suppose Bunky got himself another Playland card for this purpose? If he's using our Southampton address, you can cancel that card right now. *I'm* in charge of the bank accounts in this marriage, and I'm not paying any overdue charges he racked up carrying on with *her.*"

"No, Mrs. Bellarosa, he's using the regular card."

"Let me see that." LaRue leaned over the counter and swiveled the computer monitor to face her. "Well, he's a bigger bozo than I thought." She turned to me with a haughty look. "You'll hear from my lawyer in the morning." Then she marched out of the store, molting along the way.

"Hey, wait a minute!" I ran out of the store after her, but she was in the Jeep before I could get there. The door slammed and she took off down the street, tires screeching, her "In Goddess We Trust" bumper sticker getting smaller and smaller. Two blocks down, she pulled over to the curb and opened the passenger door.

I trotted up and stood there, panting. LaRue grinned wickedly.

"Hop in."

"Did you get it?"

"Did I get it, she asks. Does a bear poop in the woods? Of course, I got it." She chucked the feathered seat covers into the back. "Salvatore J. Bellarosa, seventy-six-oh-one North Ocean Avenue, Patchogue. You want his phone number?"

CHAPTER THIRTEEN

I googled Salvatore Bellarosa and learned the names and ages of his wife and son and the family's previous addresses going back twenty-five years. Links also surfaced for Sally's Cesspool Service, identifying it as a family-owned residential service provider with dispatch locations in Bohemia and Port Jeff. Bellarosa was also mentioned in a chatty message board entry as having provided prompt service in draining a Mastic customer's cesspool in 2002.

I programmed Sally's address into my cell phone's GPS system. Then I trotted downstairs and rapped on Mrs. Porter's door. After a few moments the door opened. Mrs. Porter stood there in a Bat Boy T-shirt, black leggings, and pink slipper socks. What little hair she had was tied up in a topknot. She lit up when she saw me. From deep inside the apartment I heard a television audience chant, "Wheel! Of! Fortune!"

"I'm on my way into town, Mrs. P. Do you need anything?"

"Oh, thank you, dear. An onion would be useful. And something good to read. *You* know." Her eyes twinkled.

I nodded. Her apartment smelled like soup. "Anything else?"

"Well, if a box of Mallomars jumps off the shelf at you, I won't complain."

I found Pearl Battley hunched over the children's desk at the Port Jefferson Free Library, punching her keyboard animatedly, her white bun bobbing.

"You missed all the fireworks," she said without looking up.

It took me a second to leap onto her train of thought. "Last night?"

She nodded. "After you left, Manny lit into Inez. You know how full of himself he is, strutting around town like a self-appointed mayor. Well, he started in with something along the order of, whose arm did you twist to get on television."

"Oh, brother."

"Inez hasn't lived here very long, by Port standards. That in itself is enough to make some people take a dislike to her."

"That, and the fact that she's half Puerto Rican, half Jewish."

"And her great-grandparents weren't Bayleses," Pearl said, referring to an early shipbuilding family. She looked up at me and rested her chin in her hands. "The way she's so tuned into what's going on—it's too much for people like Manny. He thinks she has an 'in' with the police and media."

"He said that?"

"Oh, yes. And that's when the Roman candles went off. Inez has quite the temper."

"Sounds like sour grapes to me. Manny just wanted to be on the news himself."

"Ah. You have hit the nail on the head, Emma." Pearl moved a stack of books to the table behind her. "Inez said she just happened to be at the right place at the right time, which was the wrong thing to say. Manny's feathers were quite ruffled. He looked exactly like a wild turkey."

"Then what happened?"

"Well, the party broke up. Charlie left with his coffeemaker. Theo left—she had a headache. She has always been rather frail, in my opinion. That nice young fellow Egon brought in to take over the business—Egon's finally ready to retire, thank goodness—he left. Egon and I were the last to leave." She looked at me apologetically. "What a gossip I am, Emma. I know you didn't come into the library to make conversation. Why don't you tell me why you're here?"

"Do you know where Tony's from?" I kept my voice casual.

"Oh, goodness, you'd have to ask Egon. Did you meet him at Rita's? Nice young man. From what I've heard, he's very accomplished in management. He owned a restaurant before he bought into the Greenhouse. I'm not the best person to ask, though. All I know is, Egon has been much more relaxed since Tony came into the picture. Now, tell me how I can help you, Emma."

"Oh, that. I need a new library card."

"Did you lose the old one?"

"Yes."

"That's really a matter for the circulation desk, dear."

"I know. But if I give you my password, can you get into the system? I'd rather do this with you."

Pearl looked puzzled. "Of course." She punched the keys, her head bobbing up and down between the keyboard and the monitor. "Maybe someone returned your card to the lost and found. Could that be? When's the last time you used it?"

"A few weeks ago. Actually, if you can give me a date, that would be great."

"Isn't your birthday coming up soon? I know that's always a big occasion for you."

"Thirty-five this year."

"Ah. Well, my dear, the best is yet to come. Happy, happy birthday. Okay, here we go. Trace, Emma R." She peered at the screen, revolving the mouse on the pad. "You say you last used your card three weeks ago?"

"Uh-huh."

She frowned. "That's odd."

"What is?"

"Your record shows that you borrowed three books last week,

on October seventh."

"That can't be. I haven't even—"

"Oh, my." Pearl's face turned white. "Look at this, Emma."

I went around the desk and read the titles on the screen:

Unsolved Murders of the Twentieth Century
Waiting for Forensics—Cold Cases Revisited
Undetected: Getting Away with Murder

I felt the blood drain from my face.

"Emma," Pearl said. "I am not the sort of person to break a confidence. Only twice in my life have I deliberately done so, and only because it was necessary. This time I am breaking more than a confidence—I'm breaking the law. But you are like a daughter to me, and I must tell you something." She took a deep breath. "The police were here this morning asking for access to patron library records."

I felt myself slip into a deep, cold tunnel. My voice sounded far away when I spoke. "What were they looking for?"

"I didn't speak to them, the director did." She gazed at me steadily. "There were two detectives—a tall blond fellow and a bald one with a scar on his forehead."

"Zahn and Bonomo," I muttered. My throat felt so dry, I couldn't swallow. "Did the director give them the records?"

Pearl snorted. "Of course not. You know how strict we are about protecting our patrons' privacy." Her face grew serious. "Are you in trouble, Emma?"

"That's the million-dollar question, isn't it?"

"You are frightening me, dear."

"When's the last time I used my card before that?"

"September twenty-first." She looked even more like a white mouse than usual, her face tight and scared.

I touched the back of her chair for balance. "Pearl, I can't tell you anymore right now. But you mustn't worry about me."

"How can I promise that? Now I am frightened for you. Mistakes have been made from—misperceptions. Things that were not thought out correctly."

"I know."

"And evil. There is evil in the world." Pearl clutched her sweater around her.

Our eyes locked. "Remember when I was Harriet the Spy? When I used to creep around in the book stacks, taking notes on people?"

"Of course, I do, dear."

"And you'd be sitting at this desk, and I'd come and tell you that this person's an English teacher and has two dogs, and this person is doing a term paper on Apollo 13, and that person likes chocolate?"

Pearl nodded. I squatted down next to her chair.

"I still do that stuff. It's the way I am."

She opened her mouth, but I went on quickly.

"Somebody was not very smart this time. They've made a couple of mistakes already, and I'm going to find them out."

Tears sprung to her eyes. "I can't tell you how long I've been fighting for photo ID cards. And now look."

"I'll be fine. I have friends helping me. You've helped me."

Pearl looked at me for a long moment. "This is real life, Emma, not a book. Choose carefully those you trust."

I didn't see Tony until my nose collided with his shoulder, and then I saw stars first.

"Hey, hey, hey." Tony held me at arm's length and looked at me with those Antonio Banderas eyes.

I rubbed my nose, blinking. The houses across the street wobbled as if under water. "Hey, yourself. What are you doing here?"

He nodded at the Greenhouse van parked at the curb. "Our

delivery boy had a dental emergency. I'm making the rounds. You?"

"I was returning some books." I smoothed my hair back, composing myself.

"You don't look so good."

"Gee, thanks."

"I didn't mean it like that. I meant, you look like you're going to pass out. Are you?"

"I hope not. I've got a whole afternoon of errands ahead of me."

"Such a busy lady. And here I was going to ask you if you'd had lunch yet."

"Got to skip it today." My vision cleared. Tony had on a royal blue V-neck shirt that revealed a glimpse of gold chain and muscle underneath. He was wearing jeans and I wanted to check out the fit, but it would have looked obvious, so I refrained.

"Tara's has T-bone steaks on the menu today. I could go for one of those and a cold Smithwicks." He raised an eyebrow. "What do you say? You look like you could use a meal."

Could I ever, I thought. I gave in and stole a quick look at the jeans. My goodness. Like hot fudge on a scoop of ice cream.

"Tell you what, Tony," I offered. "Let me take care of some things, and I'll meet you there for supper."

CHAPTER FOURTEEN

Traffic was heavy as I made my way down to Sally Bellarosa's in the Cutlass. It's only fourteen miles from Port Jeff on the north shore to Patchogue on the south, but at one o'clock on a Saturday afternoon it can take forever. I hit all the red lights on Route 112, some more than once. I drummed my fingers on the steering wheel, the big engine rumbling contentedly. Cars poured into and out of a continuous stream of strip malls, each with its own pizzeria, bagel shop, dollar store, and Miss Somebody's Dancing School. If anyone was following me they would have seen a blond wearing white-framed Jackie O sunglasses.

When I turned onto 83 South, the road opened up and I gave her some gas. I felt crazy with impatience. On the seat beside me was the DVD. The missing movie was probably giving Sally conniptions. I wondered if he had torn Hazzard's house apart looking for it.

I flipped open my cell phone to my GPS and muted the sound. Then I took the throwaway phone and pressed the digits for the Bellarosa residence, but held off completing the call while I sat at a red light with an SUV blaring rap music on my left and a Beemer crooning tropical lite on my right. When we started moving again I hit *send*. On the fourth ring a man picked up. I listened to him bark hello four or five times before disconnecting. He could have been the SUV guy, but I wasn't a hundred percent sure.

I stopped at the 7-Eleven for the items for Mrs. Porter and a baloney sandwich and a bottle of raspberry iced tea for myself. I could feel my blood sugar dropping, and it would not do to pass out now. I gulped down my lunch through the next few stoplights.

South of Sunrise Highway the road narrowed to two lanes. Old-fashioned lamp posts and well-tended Victorian homes sprouted up on either side. Turning up the sound on my phone, I heard the GPS announce my destination.

As I approached 7601, I tapped the brakes but didn't stop. Sally's house was newer than its neighbors, a two-story gray colonial with teal shutters and a wraparound porch. At the top of the driveway sat a dark green van with SALLY'S CESSPOOL SERVICE printed on the side. Behind it was an Inferno Red Chrysler 300 with a My-Child-Was-Citizen-of-the-Month bumper sticker. Her car. A black Dodge Durango with tinted windows and a GUT DEER? decal was parked at the curb. His. I memorized the plate numbers as I passed.

Two doors down I pulled over and adjusted my mirrors so I could watch the Bellarosa house. It was a typical Saturday on Long Island. Cars were coming and going from soccer practice. Across from the Bellarosas a man squatted on his roof, hammering shingles. A kid sat on the curb, picking at a scab. A circular saw whirred in a garage. A squirrel scampered across the street, looking for acorns. I jotted down the two license plate numbers in my notebook and snapped a picture of the Durango with my cell phone camera. It could easily have been the same car I saw at Hazzard's. On the other hand, a lot of Long Islanders drive gargantuan SUVs.

I raised my windows and hit redial on the throwaway phone.

"Hello?" Same voice as before.

"Hi, this is Coral at Playland Adult Boutique?" I torqued my voice up half an octave and put a question mark at the end of my sentence.

"Yeah?"

"Is this the Bellarosa residence?"

"Yeah."

"You have an overdue DVD. It was due back this morning? We have a customer on wait list for it, and we were wondering when you could bring it back?"

There was a pause. "Uh, I'll get it back to you today."

"Thank you very much, Mr. Bellarosa." I hit *end* and adjusted my mirror so I had a full view of his front door. He hadn't even asked what the title was. I was betting he was very glad he had answered the phone and not his wife.

Two minutes went by. Then the door opened and Sally Bellarosa stepped outside. He stood on the porch a few moments, smacking the palm of his hand with his fist. I snapped a quick picture. Bellarosa was in his late thirties. He was about six feet tall, muscular with wavy black hair, and he was wearing a Long Island Ducks jersey, gym shorts, and sneakers. Apparently making up his mind, he strode purposefully to his car and slid in. I started my car at the same time he did, to mask the roar of the engine. Sally made a quick U-ie, drove a few feet, and stopped. In my mirror I saw the front door open and the Citizen of the Month hop down the front steps, eating an apple. He ambled to the driver's side window and leaned over. Because of the tinted windows, I couldn't see much of Sally except for his beefy arm on the window frame.

"C'mon, Dad," the kid whined. "Everyone else is."

Sally barked a brief retort and then his fist popped out and knocked the apple from the kid's hand. It bounced down the street as the boy watched in shock. Nice. Sally took off up North Ocean. I made a U-turn and followed him at a safe distance.

Instead of heading to Hazzard's, as I'd expected, he made a left to get on Sunrise Highway, and I almost slammed into the car ahead. So much for making assumptions. I let a couple of cars get between us and followed him onto Sunrise.

He got off at the Lincoln Avenue exit and drove for several blocks. I kept two cars between us at all times, the way they do in the movies. Then Bellarosa made a right into the parking lot of the Sudzo King Laundromat. I followed him in and parked a few spots away.

Sally lifted the rear door of the Durango and rummaged through the cargo area. Whatever he was looking for wasn't there, because he slammed the door down, went around to the passenger door, and leaned in. After a few seconds he emerged holding a half-filled plastic bag. I took some pictures. Sally wadded up the bag and marched into the Sudzo King with me right behind.

The place was packed. Sally strode down the center aisle of washers, toward the back. I grabbed an empty laundry cart and pushed it after him.

At the end of the row, he rounded the corner. My cart and I rounded it right behind him. As I did, the laundry attendant, an old woman with a rag tied around her head, leaning on a mop, thrust out her chin at me.

"You need change?"

"Uh, no, I'm good," I said over my shoulder.

"Change over there." She pointed at the front door. "You gotta put tens and twenties. Damn kids broke the machine, now it don't take fives no more."

"Thank you." I looked around wildly. Sally had disappeared. I reversed my tracks and darted over to the next aisle. Sally was down at the far end, emptying his bag into a dryer. He slammed the dryer door and turned suddenly in my direction.

Quickly I bent and tied my sneaker. When I stood up, he was gone.

I dashed up the aisle and stopped in front of the dryer. A

load of laundry was circling in the window, socks and shirts and pajamas, Sally's unknown contributions a part of the mix. My spirits sank. From the back of the room I felt a pair of eyes boring into me and glanced back. The laundry attendant was leaning on her mop, watching me.

Through the window I saw the Durango backing out. I hurried to my car and jammed the key into the ignition.

The Cutlass vroomed backwards obediently. Then as I wheeled forward, it did a funny thing. The engine went chooglachoogla-choogla, coughed a few times, and died. The next second I was nearly thrown out of my seat by a loud bang, followed by a puff of black smoke from the rear end of the car.

Through the windshield I saw Sally pulling onto the side street. In despair I cranked the starter again. Nothing happened.

"You got a gummed-up carburetor there," someone called out. A man in a flannel shirt leaned against his car with his arms folded, watching me. "Give'er a minute or two, maybe she'll clear up."

"I don't have a minute or two," I called back. "Isn't there something I can do?"

"You ain't going nowhere yet." He walked over to the car. "Unless you can fly. The carb's clogged."

"How do you know that?"

"S'only thing makes that choogling noise. You prob'ly got some old gas gummin' up the works. When's the last time she had a tune-up?"

"I have no idea."

"Prob'ly don't drive it enough." He leaned on the roof, peering in. "You gotta drive these old things all'a time to keep'em clean. All'a time. Well, just look at them velour seats. Woo-hoo. What year is she?"

"A 'seventy-three. Actually, I'm in kind of—"

"You don't mind, do ya?" He stroked the seat back and whistled. "She's a beaut, this one. I never seen the 'seventy-three close up. Always liked the Colonnades, though. Real beauts. I had a 'sixty-nine Cutlass once with a four fifty-four, but she's been gone now, oh, I'd say 'bout—"

"Look, I'd really love to chat, but I'm in a hurry."

"Well." He straightened up, tucking his thumbs in his pockets. "She oughta be about ready, by now, maybe. Give 'er a turn."

The engine leaped into blessed operation.

"Take 'er slow, now," the man said, pushing the air with his palm.

I zoomed out of the lot. Sally couldn't have gotten far. Almost immediately I spotted him on the other side of the bridge. My tires squealed as I turned the wheel to the left as hard as I could. The sucker had a turning radius like an ocean liner.

Instead of getting back on Sunrise, Sally drove straight ahead into the parking lot of Attias Indoor Flea Market. I prayed the Cutlass wouldn't stall. Every time I slowed down, the engine made a popping sound.

The parking lot was a zoo. Sally found a spot in a far corner and I followed suit. A minute later I was entering the clash of smells and lights and ballyhoo that was Attias.

Sellers bombarded me, hawking everything from French fries to French perfume and stereo speakers to sneakers. Sally made a beeline for the Gold Junction, where he received a hug from the chain-laden woman behind the counter. I hid behind a revolving rack of hair extensions while he and the vendor haggled over a series of thin gold chains that all looked pretty much the same. To my mind, it really didn't matter which one he bought. His wife was going to hate him anyway when she found out about Hazzard. Finally Bellarosa settled on a chain, paid for it, and moved on.

His next stop was a stand selling mirrors shaped like

silhouettes, baby rattles, and other familiar items with hand-painted messages like HAPPY SWEET 16 AMY on them. He spoke briefly to the vendor, who dug through a box labeled Customer Orders and pulled out a two-foot-long mirror in the shape of a bowling pin with the painted message SPLIT HAPPENS. Sally looked it over carefully, rubbed out a smudge, and paid for it.

Next he headed to the rear of Attias where the restrooms were. He was walking fast, and I had a hard time keeping up without trampling slower-moving customers. When he disappeared into the men's room I busied myself at a nearby electronics concession. On eight portable televisions, a veterinarian was demonstrating how to brush a cat's teeth. His model was a fifteen-pound buster who looked less than thrilled to be held down and have his gums lathered with poultry-flavored toothpaste. I figured I'd end up in the emergency room if I subjected Bergamot to that treatment. While I watched I kept an eye on the hallway that led to the restrooms, but Sally didn't reappear. I stopped a man on his way out.

"Anyone else in there?"

"Nope."

I pushed past him into the hallway. A door at the end said AUTHORIZED PERSONNEL ONLY. I opened it. On the other side there was bright sunshine and a garbage dumpster with two crows pecking away at its contents.

CHAPTER FIFTEEN

Maybe she'd been pressuring him to make a commitment. Or maybe she'd threatened to expose the affair to his wife. It made sense he'd dump evidence of their relationship at the Sudzo King.

Other factors pointed to Sally as the killer. He knew where she worked. He was strong enough to overpower her. And he was at his own place of business by seven a.m., which meant he could have gotten to her before then.

On the other hand, would a guy who had the balls to threaten me on the phone run out the back door of Attias?

Maybe, if he had enough to lose. Sally's fear of exposure had to have been a factor on some level. Suppose Jennifer had used that to her advantage? What if she'd called him up one day and said, "Look, you want me to keep my mouth shut, how about paying my rent this month?"

I sipped my coffee, trying not to spill any on the seat of Mrs. P.'s car. The small parking lot at Brookhaven Airport was full of cars, but most of the traffic was in the air above me, where a bunch of little planes was buzzing around like flies.

What puzzled me was how I fit into the picture. I didn't know him from Adam. If Sally had killed her and left my library card at the scene, how had he gotten hold of it in the first place? From Hazzard? Had she told him about me? That would have meant bringing up Sam, her former—or concurrent—boyfriend. Which introduced another possible motive for murder: jealousy.

Had she shown Sally the card? Or had he found it after she was dead?

I got out of the car and tossed my cup into a trash can. For the moment I put my thoughts aside to deal with the task at hand. I was here to grovel, and I would do it well.

Ned's hangar, which he shares with my Uncle Sherman and Sherm's pristine Beech Baron, is up at the north end of the airport, past the town tie-downs, near Dowling College's aviation school. After checking in with the gate guard I drove cautiously past the rows of parked aircraft, stopping whenever a plane taxied by, and parked by Ned's hangar next to his black Mustang GT convertible and its UPUPNWAY plates. I hadn't called ahead. I knew he would be around. During waking hours he's either flying, getting ready to fly, getting back from flying, or tinkering with his plane. The other seven hours he sleeps.

Ned was in his hangar. He had the canopy of his marigold yellow airplane open, and he was leaning into the cockpit, lost in thought, a toothpick dangling from his mouth, when I walked up and stopped just outside the hangar. A lawnmower buzzed by overhead. In the background, faint authoritative voices came out of the radio propped up on his workbench.

"Hey," he said without lifting his head.

"Hey."

"You're just in time, Em. Come here, I need your help."

"What?" I planted my feet. I like to keep as much distance between myself and those winged tin cans as I can.

"I want you to look at this. I misplaced my reading glasses and can't see a damn thing."

I walked over hesitantly and looked into the back seat compartment of the airplane. There wasn't much there but a cushion, a bunch of dials, and a stick sticking out of the floor. They call this plane an Extra. Extra what, I don't know. Extra small? Extra flimsy?

"What am I supposed to be looking at?"

"That." He pointed to a piece of plastic attached to a thin metal rod that was probably holding the whole airplane together. "It's a prototype for a hands-free snap-on snack holder I invented. Do you see two screws in the hinge, or did I drop one?"

"Maybe you should invent a snap-on eyeglass holder."

He arched an eyebrow. Until a few years ago Ned had worked in the city as a designer of cat toys. Feline recreational engineer, he called it. During a midlife crisis he reinvented himself as an entrepreneur, creating and launching Ned's Runway Pies, now sold in airport vending machines all over the country. The pies come in eleven flavors, like Mandarin chicken and banana cream, and are dispensed in insulated zipped pouches that look like runways. Ned's idea was to provide easy snacks for pilots who have their hands full. Sales took off after enthusiastic reviews in the snack trade journals, and the vending machines began to show up not only in pilots' lounges, but in major hub airports like Atlanta and Cincinnati, where the pies were gobbled up by the traveling public, who weren't being fed anymore by the big airlines. In two years Ned's Runway Pies netted their inventor millions of dollars and gave him the freedom to quit his job and become an airport bum full-time. Now he has all day to invent pie accessories.

"I see two," I said. "Does this thing come in colors?"

"Yeah. Black and black. See, you position it near your mouth, like this. Take a bite whenever you want. No hands. It clips onto the plane—panel, visor, wherever."

"Handy."

"I'm trying it out this afternoon, soon as I fuel up."

"Can you even swallow upside down?"

Ned smirked. "You'll find out in a few days."

"Ha."

He leaned over again to fiddle with his snack holder, and I sat down in his golf cart to wait for the right moment. This was a delicate matter. It had to be handled just so.

"So," Ned said without looking up, "I take it you're here to ask for an extension."

"Come on, Ned. Have I ever asked for an extension?"

"Why else would you be here three days before your birthday? Not because you love airplanes so much."

"Did it ever occur to you that maybe I just dropped by to say hi?"

Ned began whistling "Liar, Liar" by the Castaways.

"You are such a pain in the butt," I said.

He reached under the panel and yanked something, still whistling.

I frowned and tried again. "Good riddle you guys came up with this year."

"That was me and your dad, principally. Pike's been out of commission with both legs since the jump, and Sherm—well, you know Sherm."

"Well, it's clever."

"We thought so."

I could see the corners of his mouth turn up as he bent over the Extra.

"So, how's the search going?" he asked.

"It's going swell."

"Great."

I sighed. "Do you read the news at all, Ned? Did you hear what happened in Port Jeff yesterday?"

"The murder? Yeah, I heard. Another sicko. I put newspapers under the plane to change the oil and the headline stared me in the face. Beauty contestant, right? Pass me those pliers, Em."

"Well, the thing is, I knew her. I've managed to get pulled in, a little bit." I zoomed the cart forward two feet, handed him the pliers, and zoomed back. "The woman who was killed worked at the diner I go to."

"No kidding." He gave me a quick look and bent his head again.

"Yeah. So I've been kind of helping out."

"Helping the police?"

"Sort of." I hopped out. "I need to stop the clock for a couple of days while I take care of something important."

Ned made a few adjustments to the snack holder, unsnapped it from the rod, and put it in his shirt pocket. He tossed his toothpick into a cardboard box sitting nearby and looked me in the eye. "That sounds like an extension to me."

"It's not. It's a stop and start. Entirely different thing."

"How so?"

"I will suspend looking for my present during the time the clock is stopped. When we start it again I'll pick up exactly where I left off—with three and a half days."

"How do I know you're not going to think about it during that time?"

"I'm not, believe me."

"Watch your back, Em." Ned got behind the wing and pushed the plane out of the hangar. He picked up the tail and walked with it until the plane faced the runway. Then he put it down again. "Here's my take. You can argue the point, of course. When I'm working on a new invention, like my snack holder here, I think about it even when I don't consciously have it front and center in my mind. It's percolating all the time. You're in a similar situation. Those wheels are going to be turning. Shouldn't we deduct for that?"

I frowned. "How much are you going to deduct?"

"I don't know. Depends on how active your brain waves are, whether you're awake or sleep—"

"Oh, come on, Ned."

"What if the solution comes to you out of the blue? I think that's grounds for disqualification."

"Ned!"

At that moment the fuel truck pulled up and a kid jumped out.

"Hullo, Mr. Trace. Going up to practice your sequence?"

"You bet, Marty." Ned attached a ground wire to the plane. "Five gallons in each wing, please."

"Middle tank, too?"

"No, let's keep it light today."

"You going along for the ride?" the line boy asked me, dragging the hose over. Seeing my face, he added with a grin, "I guess not."

He started the pump and I went into the hangar to wait. On the wall, Ned had hung photos and aviation mementos he'd collected over the years. A blue T-shirt with part of the back cut out was tacked up above the workbench, the words written on the fabric faded by time.

NED TRACE
FIRST SOLO FLIGHT
BROOKHAVEN AIRPORT
SHIRLEY, NEW YORK

Next to it was a photo of the sixteen-year-old Ned wearing the shirt and a big shit-eating grin, holding a certificate, his arm on the cowling of the little Cessna behind him.

I moved down the row and paused in front of the last photo. At once the terror of the memory it evoked washed over me. Somehow I was drawn to it every time I was here.

The photo depicted a 1979 Bellanca Super Decathlon with red and white stripes on the wings and tail, parked by an open hangar. In front of the plane were two teenagers, a boy and a girl. He wore a black T-shirt and jeans, had a shock of dark hair across his face, and a confident smile. His arm was around the girl's shoulders. She was six inches shorter, rail thin, wearing jeans and Keds and a pink sweatshirt with a picture of Secretariat on it. She was squinting into the sun, her mouth an angry line.

My father had taken that picture. At the time he took it I hated him, I hated Ned, and I hated all the other idiots who were standing around smiling at me. I had just climbed out of the Decathlon after my first flight, which would also be my last. Scowling was the only way I could keep from bursting into tears.

"Watch this." His voice through the headset was ragged with excitement. In the background the engine droned.

I squeezed my eyes shut. "Take me down," I whispered.

"What?"

"Take me—"

"Put the mike to your lips."

I felt his eyes on my back. Fingers trembling, I let go of the cabin wall with my left hand and adjusted the tiny foam microphone on my headset. The fingertips of my right hand stayed on the moving stick, although I had no say in its direction.

"I want to go down." My voice seemed to come from outside of me, from somebody else. But there were only the two of us in the airplane.

He laughed.

"We're going down. Scaredy cat."

"I am not."

"Yes, you are. 'Take me down, take me down,' " he mimicked in a high voice.

"Shut up."

"You're not my Minute Mouse anymore."

His words stung. "Am, too."

Minute Mouse was the name he'd given me back when I was little, when he was Courageous Cat and we hung out together and hatched plots. I opened my eyes to take one last look at the Earth I was leaving forever. But Earth was not in the windscreen, only the bluest of skies, as blue as the morning glories in my mother's garden, through the blur of the propeller.

"So long, Minute Mouse. Rest in peace." He faked a few sobs.

"I said, shut up! You are such a jerk."

The nose of the plane was tilted way up. I could tell because my butt in its seat pack had slid all the way back against the seat rest. He was always talking about flying by the seat of his pants. Now I knew what he meant. Without moving my head I glanced down at the straps that encased me: the five-point safety harness that went around my hips and over my shoulders and was tethered to a silver buckle between my legs, and beneath it the parachute harness that locked across my chest and included a "D" ring on my left breast to pull if we had to eject. So many straps, and not one that could save me.

"Ready?"

I was not, but there was no point in protesting. I was only fifteen. He was three years older and in control.

Beneath my left hand the throttle moved back, and the engine quieted. Through the headset it sounded like my dad's old lawnmower. Or the fan in my bedroom on a summer night. We tilted up even more, the nose of the plane pointing unnaturally high. My feet beside the pedals felt a change as the left pedal was depressed to the floor and the right came up. He was doing all this from the back seat. He'd put me in the front so I'd have the better view. Lucky me. The stick lurched to the right, out of my hand.

"C'mon, break," he said.

Why was he telling the airplane to break? I got a sick feeling in my stomach as the plane wobbled in the air as if it had forgotten how to fly. Then the left wing dropped, and the shadow of the metal brace dividing the windscreen passed over my lap and face. Horror filled me as I looked straight ahead at the bay thousands of feet below.

Almost immediately the water began to rotate clockwise, slowly at first and then faster, a nearby piece of shoreline circling with it like a sock going round in the dryer. Behind me he crowed in delight. I wet my pants, just a little. My last thought as we plummeted toward the bay was of a shipwreck my biology teacher had told us about—the schooner that had sunk here more than a century ago. I pictured codfish swimming in and out between its rotting masts, oblivious to the missile headed their way.

I screamed good and loud.

CHAPTER SIXTEEN

Something shiny on the hangar floor caught my eye. I picked up the object from where it had fallen among some quart containers of engine oil and put it in my pocket.

Ned was outside, signing a fuel receipt.

"So?" I asked.

"I have to think about it."

"That's your answer? You have to think about it?"

"I know something's up, Em. It's not like you to change the rules in the middle of the game."

"I already told you what's up."

He put the pen back in his pocket and gave me a long look. Then he said gently, "Let the guy go already. There are reasons it didn't work out. Next time you'll find someone who cherishes you for who you are."

"Did I ask for your advice?" I drew my breath in sharply. "You know what, Ned? Forget the whole thing. Just forget it. I'm sorry I came."

He stepped back, surprised. I strode to the Cutlass and climbed in. I turned the key in the ignition, but instead of turning over, the engine emitted a distant, whiny sound. I let go of the key and leaned my head on the steering wheel.

A shadow moved across the dash. I rolled down my window and blinked at Ned through a mist of tears.

"Leave me alone."

"What's the matter, Em?"

"Nothing."

"Where'd you get this piece of shit you're driving?"

I wiped my nose with my sleeve. "Why don't you mind your own business?"

"I swear, you are the most exasperating—come back inside and tell me what's going on."

When I didn't move, he turned and walked away. After a minute I got out of the car and went into the hangar. Ned snapped off the radio. We sat on the beat-up couch in the corner and he handed me a warm ginger ale. I drank half of it before I was able to speak.

"Listen, you can't talk about this to anyone. Not even Dad. Okay?"

"Okay."

"I'm involved in this murder in Port Jeff."

I took a breath and jumped in, firing out facts and ideas in a rapid chaotic way. I covered the bad blood between Hazzard and me, how the police suspected me, the phone call, the lizard man, Sally, and everything else I could think of. Ned chewed on a toothpick all the while, not saying anything. Eventually I ran out of things to say.

"I know what you're going to say," I finished. "You're going to tell me this is dangerous and to stay out of it. I did, at first. But somebody is trying to make trouble for me, and I don't think that person will back off until the police arrest someone."

"Do you have a good lock on your door?"

"Yes."

"Better yet, do you want to stay at my place for a while?"

"I can't. All my work's at home, and my cat needs me. I'll be fine there."

He was quiet a moment. "Two questions come to my mind. One, what is the lizard man selling? And, two, what is Sally buying?"

"Aren't they the same thing?"

"Not necessarily. The lizard man might or might not know the value of what he is selling. He might have other things to sell, besides what he's selling to Sally. And Sally might be in the market to buy any number of items, none of which he wants to spell out to the lizard man. Think of it this way. You buy milk, but you don't buy all the milk the supermarket has to sell. You also buy other things besides milk. And sometimes you buy them in different stores."

I frowned, trying to take it all in. "How did the lizard man get into the blackmail business?"

He shrugged. "Opportunity knocked."

"So you don't think he's the killer."

"I don't think so. But I've been wrong before. Do the police know about him?"

"I have no idea. He wasn't mentioned in the news. I have no idea who the police are looking at, besides me."

He got quiet again.

"This murder would seem to be premeditated," he said finally.

"You mean the three library books. Yes."

Ned tossed his toothpick into the box on the floor. "Too bad you don't have a bud at the Suffolk County Police Department. It would be nice to have a look at the autopsy report. Among other things."

That reminded me of something. "I met a friend of yours. Pete Zahn."

He started. "Who?"

"The detective handling the case."

"Zahn? Handling the case?" Ned whistled and shook his head. "Well, how do you like that? Detective, you say?" His face had gone pale.

"I take it you two haven't been in touch."

"Not since . . . now, this is interesting."

I waited.

"How do you know I know him?" he asked.

"Because he asked me if we were related."

"I wouldn't have thought . . . of course, that might explain
. . ." Ned rubbed his chin, looking into space.

"He might try to have the case reassigned," I suggested.

"Why would he do that?"

"Conflict of interest. If he knows one of the parties personally—"

"Oh, no. No, no, no." Ned laughed harshly. "He'll stay on it.
No question about it. He'll stay on it like a dog on a scent."

He frowned and dug out a new toothpick. I waited but he
didn't say anything else. I went back to the main subject. "So,
aren't you going to tell me to quit what I'm doing?"

"I'm not going to tell you that. You're a grown woman. Obviously, this is something you need to do. What I will say is, think
carefully about the risks you take. Tell someone you trust where
you'll be at all times, and always make sure you have an out."

I finished up the last of the soda. "Sensible advice. I'm
shocked."

"Why?"

"It's just that I wouldn't expect it from someone who does
what you do."

"What, flying? Flying's like anything else, Em. It's all about
risk management. Learn all you can, understand the risks,
remain aware of your situation, and plan accordingly. *You* manage risk every time you take your car out on the highway." Ned
threw the soda cans into the recycling bin. "Speaking of which,
let's take a look at what's going on in that clunker."

He was under the hood of the Cutlass when a familiar-looking
plane taxied by carrying two people sitting in tandem. The
woman in the front seat looked to be in her early fifties. She
was leaning forward, peering out little-old-lady style. The man

in the cool aviator shades behind her waved cheerfully as they passed.

"You see that guy?" Ned waved back. "He knows more about aerodynamics than anyone I've ever known. You fly with him, and you really learn your stuff. And he's patient—he'll spend all day talking to you until you get it. Terrific person. That's one of his aerobatic students going up for a lesson."

"Does he do this all day long?"

"No, he's an art teacher in Riverhead. Recognize the plane?"

I looked at the blue and white body, the high wings, and the fan of blue stripes on the tail. "A Decathlon?"

"A Super D. Like the one you and I flew in, only this one's a 'ninety-five model built by American Champion. They've stayed faithful to the original design."

Ned went back to tinkering under the hood. I watched the Super Decathlon taxi down to the end of the runway, make a half-circle, and park in a little area off to the side. The plane looked like a toy from here. My hair blew across my forehead and I brushed it away. The wind and sun felt good on my skin. Ned whistled as he fixed the car. It was starting to feel like an all-right day after all.

He slammed down the hood. "Okay, start her up."

I got in and cranked the starter. The Cutlass roared to life.

Ned leaned on the window track. "Give a shout if you need any help. And Em, don't worry about the bet."

I waved him away. "I'll keep you posted."

He slapped the car. "That's my girl."

"Oh, Ned, I almost forgot." I handed over the eyeglasses I'd found in the hangar. "Get yourself a spare pair."

Ned walked away, smiling. I put the car in reverse. Through my rearview mirror I saw the little blue plane glide over to the end of the runway and align itself with the center line. I watched with a mixture of feelings as it began its takeoff roll and slowly gathered speed, until the image left my mirror. Turning my head, I watched the little plane leave the ground, climb steadily into the blue, blue sky, turn toward the west, and disappear from view.

Chapter Seventeen

The lost and found was a pink plastic basket in the rear of the Sudzo King. I picked through the top layer of laundry until I found what I wanted: two blouses, a bra, and a pair of panties. They smelled like Bounce. I quietly uncrumpled my plastic bag so I could stuff them in and sneak out before the laundry attendant saw me.

"You was here earlier."

I jumped. The old woman was right next to me, hands on her hips, peering around my arm at my fistful of clothing. She frowned at me suspiciously, and I suddenly noticed she had a glass eye.

"What you looking for?"

I pointed to the basket. "My husband put my things in the wrong dryer by mistake. Lucky for me someone turned them in."

She jerked her chin forward. "That's from today, what you got in your hands."

"Did you see who put them here?"

She stared at me as if it were the most preposterous question she'd ever heard. Her frown repeated itself in double and triple chins, right down her neck. "How would I know? I got a job to do. I wash the floor three times a day. Three times. The whole floor. I'm not looking at who's putting or taking from the lost and found. People go to the wrong dryers all the time."

"I see."

The attendant stepped even closer, close enough for me to smell her breath, and locked my eyes in her gaze. Unable to help myself I looked from her real eye to the glass one and back.

" 'Cept," she said.

"Except what?"

" 'Cept maybe I know. It all depends."

I stuck a twenty in the pocket of her smock.

"Try to remember."

She pulled the bill out and took her time examining both sides.

"It was a woman," she said finally. "Two little kids. Noses running, racing those damn metal trucks all over the floor, making marks. Her. She put the clothes."

"Anything besides this stuff?"

"I got nothing to hide."

"Thank you." I backed away and turned to leave. Her voice followed me.

"Rings. I always look. You're not wearing any rings."

I looked back. She nodded, satisfied, her glass eye glinting.

"That wasn't your husband," she said.

CHAPTER EIGHTEEN

I handed Mrs. Porter her Mallomars, her onion, and the latest issue of the *Weekly World News,* which featured stories about vampire llamas, babies born without bones, and the aphrodisiacal qualities of Bavarian dingle loaf. I also suggested she get the Cutlass tuned up.

"I don't want you getting stuck somewhere. If you make an appointment with your mechanic, I'll bring the car in."

"You're a sweetheart, but my nephew will be here tomorrow. It used to be his car, and I'm sure he'll want to take care of it. Did you just get home?"

"Yes, why?"

"I thought I heard you on the stairs earlier. Oh, dear. My hearing's gotten so bad."

At the top of the second flight of stairs, I stopped to listen. I heard dishes clattering and a radio talk show issuing from the unit below mine.

The only people who have my key are LaRue, my parents, and Mrs. Porter, none of whom had any reason to use it today. I opened the door and looked around, feeling a little silly. Bergamot gravitated to my ankles and followed me around the apartment. The outfit I had picked out for tonight—a sea green sleeveless blouse and black faux suede pants—was spread out on the bed where I'd left it. Nothing seemed out of place.

I had an email from Ned saying that he'd flown the Baron down to Atlantic City with Sherm and would be back on

Sunday. The rest of the mail was junk except for a funny note from Mom telling me that the downstairs ladies' room at the Pike Place Market was a scream. Dad had also forwarded me an announcement about opening day for the fall horse racing meet at Portland Meadows. I started to write back to Mom, but abandoned the attempt.

I half-wished I hadn't made a date for tonight. All I really wanted to do right now was curl up on the couch and watch *Sleepless in Seattle*.

The Tara Inn was mobbed. A dozen motorcycles were parked at the curb, and a few bikers and others were hanging out, smoking and talking.

I opened the door to cheerful mayhem. "Big Shot" by Billy Joel was playing on the jukebox. The television set was tuned to the local university football game, and a bunch of customers, three deep at the bar, raised their glasses and roared as a touchdown was scored by the Stony Brook Seawolves.

I found a free seat at the bar and sat down to wait for Tony. The specials were individually written on paper plates stapled to the walls: Alaskan king crab legs, chicken teriyaki, marinated T-bone, one-pound lobster, broccoli and cheddar poppers, Cajun rib eye, fried macaroni and cheese.

The bartender, a young guy in a tie-dyed Tara T-shirt, plunked a napkin in front of me.

"Howdy. What can I get you?"

"Blue Point Oatmeal Stout."

I watched a little of the game. It was a conference event, Stony Brook versus Syracuse. With twelve minutes to go in the fourth quarter, we were trailing Syracuse by thirteen points, but the Seawolves looked mean and the Orange looked anxious, so I was hopeful. I flipped open my phone and called LaRue.

"Well, you have fun, girl," LaRue said when I told her about my date. "What happened with Bellarosa?"

I told her how I'd trailed him to the Sudzo King and then lost him, but wound up with what I believed were Hazzard's undies and things.

"He had to get rid of them before the police find them. It's the only explanation."

LaRue popped a bubble. "You gonna show them to X-Ray Eyes?"

"Pffft. He'll blow a gasket."

"Maybe he'll stop following you."

The crowd at the bar erupted in a roar. Syracuse had turned over the ball at their own twenty-five-yard line. When I could hear myself again, I said, "He might go after me even harder. Zahn and Ned are acquainted, I found out."

"No kidding."

"Yeah. Some bad history between them."

"A woman?"

"I don't know yet."

LaRue was silent except for the cracking of her gum.

"This could work for us," she finally said. "Maybe he'll turn the case over to someone else."

"I'm not so sure. Did you get the pictures I sent you from my cell phone?"

"Bellarosa? Yeah. I don't recognize him."

The bartender placed my beer before me. I took a cold gulp before continuing. "Do me a favor, LaRue."

"Shoot."

"Have a conversation with your craft buddy Theodora tomorrow. Nose around a bit and see what you can find out about their new surveillance system. Ask her if it does intermittent or continuous filming."

"Intermittent or what?"

"Or continuous. Does it snap pictures at intervals—say, every ten seconds—or film continuously?"

"Okay. I have a good excuse for calling her, anyway. She never finished telling me how to make that wreath."

"Perfect. And LaRue. Find out if there's a camera on the street side."

"Roger that."

Laughter erupted behind me. I turned to look and almost fell off my barstool. Not six feet away, in full Technicolor and surround sound, the lizard man was exchanging high fives with a bunch of guys standing near the pool table. His stringy hair was in a ponytail, and he was wearing motorcycle boots, jeans, and a black sweatshirt that said IF MEAN PEOPLE SUCK, BE MEAN TO ME. His friends were slapping him on the back, and he was lurching about, bowing and making rolling motions with his hand. He had duct tape on his hand where I'd stabbed it with the key.

"Gotta go." I snapped the phone shut and pulled my hair forward to hide my face. In the mirror over the bar I saw the lizard man slither up beside me and signal the bartender.

"How's it shakin'?" he said, looking my way.

I nodded and huddled over my pint while he ordered seven Budweisers. When he backed away with the bottles I motioned to the bartender.

"Who is that guy?"

He pushed my change across the bar and leaned over confidentially. "Can you spell loser? He only comes in when he has a little money. Tends to get rowdy, hits on the female customers. I'm not telling you what to do."

"Thanks for the tip. What's his name?"

"Clifford Bisbee. 'Biz the Lizard' they call him." The bartender held up a fifty-dollar bill. "He just paid for all those Buds, so I guess he's got some money burning a hole for a change."

I watched Bisbee in the mirror. His back was to me as he held court with his friends, who laughed at every word out of his mouth. I sipped my beer, thinking. The battery icon on my cell phone was down to one bar. I could probably get one more picture out of it.

"What's your name?" I asked the bartender as he passed.

"Ralph."

"Ralph, step over this way for a sec. I love your shirt. Mind if I take a picture?"

"Not at all."

He posed in front of the liquor display, grinning. I got everything in the background, including the Lizard's reflection.

"Great. Thanks a bunch."

"Now you have to post it on Facebook," said Ralph.

I smiled and glanced down at my phone to see if I'd missed a call from Tony. It was almost seven. Five more minutes and he was history. In the meantime, why waste a good investigative opportunity?

In improv we'd learned how to channel characters from TV shows by focusing on their three main character traits. I looked into my beer and channeled Pinky Tuscadero from *Happy Days*. Taking one last swallow, I kept an eye in the mirror. When the Lizard turned my way I shrugged out of my sweater and dropped it carelessly over the back of my barstool. His eyes went to my bare shoulders. Bingo. I shoved my empty glass across the counter and leaned toward the bartender.

The raspy voice was close to my left ear.

"What are you drinkin', little lady?"

The bile rose in my throat. I turned and looked into his pale gray unblinking eyes.

"Honey, all I drink is Oatmeal Stout."

"Get her another," he barked to the bartender.

Ralph glanced at me warily and moved away behind the bar.

"Why, thank you, kind sir," I said to the Lizard. His skin was leathery and slack. He was older than I'd thought at first, or maybe he was just ill from living a crappy life. His eyes showed no recognition.

"Name's Cliff." He extended his hand. "Biz, to my friends."

I grinned, barely touching him. "A pleasure."

"Just call him Richie Rich," one of his buddies called out.

"Can it, Fleece," Bisbee said over his shoulder.

"I'm Patty," I said. "Say, you work over at the True Value, don't you?"

"Me? Nah. You must be thinking of some other good-looking guy."

"I saw you there last week. I did! They had a sign up looking for help."

"Not me. I only work on days that don't end in 'y.' Bust my butt, too. What's a matter, you outta work?"

"Yeah. I just got paid for my last gig, that's why I'm celebrating."

"What's your line?" His eyes moved up and down my body, weighing and measuring. He took a swig, blowing beer breath over me.

"Driver, courier. Security. Like that. Why, you got a lead?"

"You got the right guy, sweetheart," another guy called out, waving a bottle. "Stick with him, you'll be in the black."

"Yeah?" I looked brightly at Biz. "Is that right?"

"Shut up, Grabowski," he snapped. My beer arrived and he pulled a bill out of his wad to pay for it.

"Biz's got the magic touch," Grabowski went on. "He'll make all your troubles go down the drain."

"Boy, I sure could use a magic touch," I returned. "Every job I get turns to Teflon. Nothing sticks."

They all roared except Biz the Lizard.

"I'm looking off the books," I confided to him. "I like to keep things free and easy, know what I mean? Like this job I just had in Cee-Eye. It's over, I'm gone." I clapped my hands in a scissor motion. "Poof!"

"Poof, yeah."

"Something'll come along. It always does. But I like to know I got some paper flowing."

"Why don't you go work for a rabbi?" another guy interjected. "They make good tips."

Har-har-har.

"Branchik, why don't you go crack yourself up?" The Lizard wiped his mouth with his sleeve. "I'm trying to have a conversation with the lady."

"Humorous friends you got."

"A barrel of monkeys."

I took a gulp and thumped the bottle down on the bar. "So, Biz, that's the story."

"What kind of gig you got in Central Islip?"

"Running interference for a friend of a friend."

"Uh-huh." He took a long swallow of his beer, watching me sideways. His neck was weathered to the point of scaliness.

I decided to shut my mouth. He seemed to be making some sort of decision, and I let him reel in the line at his own pace. I turned my attention back to the football game in time to see Syracuse fumble and turn the ball over to Stony Brook with three minutes left in the quarter. The Seawolves were now trailing by six. They worked their way up to midfield and punted back to the Orange. The bar was so noisy I knew no one could hear what we were talking about.

Bisbee finally leaned over and hooked his boot over the bottom rung of my barstool, barricading me against the bar. He grabbed a napkin and pushed it toward me. It was hard not to look at the duct tape. "Gimme your number. I might have something."

"What kind of something?"

"Returning merchandise. You work nights?"

"I work anytime. But I don't do—"

"S'all clean. All clean. No drugs, no pics. But I gotta check you out first." He eagle-eyed me, rubbing his chin. "How do I know you're not a cop?"

I burst out laughing. What a moron. "Me? A cop? No, Biz, I gotta check *you* out. How many clients we talking about here?"

He didn't answer immediately but his face gave him away. My heart did a little jump. This was bigger than I thought. This was more than just Sally. The crowd at the bar burst into a deafening roar as the Seawolves's cornerback intercepted the ball and ran thirty yards into the end zone with fourteen seconds to go and tied up the game. The extra point put us in the lead.

He jabbed at the napkin with his finger. "I'm not gonna talk here."

I wrote down the number of Able Editing and shoved the napkin back. "Here you go, honey."

"Hey. I know where I seen you before."

I froze, pen in hand. The Lizard wrapped his bony fingers around my wrist and leaned forward, jamming his thigh against my leg. A wave of beer breath washed over me.

"I never forget a face. Especially one as pretty as yours. I been sitting here trying to remember and it just now came to me." Slowly his lips curled upwards, showing a few gaps where teeth should have been. "Bluebell's parole party."

I let out my breath. "Bluebell—?"

"Yeah, yeah. Last summer. Down at the beach. *You* remember."

I thought fast. "Oh yeah, Bluebell. How's she doing?"

He gave me a funny look. "How's *he* doing."

Oh, shit. "That's what I said, Biz—*he*."

"Pretty good. Getting tractor trailer driver training."

"Well, good for Bluebell. The guy deserves a break already. About time."

Bisbee scratched his chin. "Yeah."

"Hey, Biz," Grabowski called over, "we got a new name for you. Biz the Wizard. 'Cause you're a financial genius."

"Grabowski, I told you to *shut the fuck up.*" Bisbee let go of my wrist and lunged toward Grabowski. Two of the wait staff and the big guy at the door closed in on him while simultaneously in the last seconds of the game Syracuse's quarterback threw a Hail Mary that was plucked out of the air by Stony Brook's safety. The bar went wild and I escaped in the confusion, unhooking my sweater from the barstool as I left.

CHAPTER NINETEEN

Sunday

"I got an idea," LaRue said, popping a stick of gum in her mouth.

"Oh, no, not again." I rolled up my window. "No more ideas."

We were parked in the harbor lot with the engine idling. There was a chill in the air. A cold front had come through overnight, and a thick layer of stratus clouds had spread out overhead. As I gazed up through the windshield of the Jeep, a fat raindrop hit the glass.

"Just listen, Em. We check out the bowling alleys, like you said. We find out where Sally bowls."

"And then what? Go back on his league night and leave a note on his car? 'I saw what you did and I know who you are.'"

"We go back on his league night, yeah. I go inside and pretend like I work there, throw away people's empty cups and bottles. I keep an eye on Sally. He and his buds probably get those pitchers of beer with the plastic cups. When he's not looking I grab his cup and bring it out to the car. We split. Then you bring the cup to Zahn so he can get his fingerprints and DNA and stuff."

I stared ahead of me at the harbor. A metal ring clanged repeatedly against a flagpole. Seagulls swooped and circled or sat tall on the pilings. The tops of the two striped stacks looked like they were holding up the clouds.

"Where am I while all this is happening?"

"In the car."

"What makes you think Zahn's interested in Bellarosa's DNA?"

She popped a bubble. "You're gonna convince him."

"I don't like this idea."

"Why am I not surprised."

More raindrops hit the glass. They achieved critical mass and started rolling down in crooked streaks. "We could deliver the cup to Zahn anonymously."

She nodded. "We could."

"I like your idea, LaRue. I just don't want to see it backfire."

"You said yourself we gotta smoke him out."

"I know."

"He the dude, man."

I tapped the latest issue of *The Record* in my lap. There was a paragraph on page six about the museum break-in. According to the report, Charlie Steigbeagle had arrived on Friday morning at nine o'clock and found the door slightly open. The only thing that appeared to be missing was an old map of the area from the shipbuilding days that had been on display. The glass case had been smashed and the map removed. "What about this? You think there's any connection?"

She shrugged. "All the shit that happens every day? I wouldn't jump."

"It just seems weird, is all."

"You're weird."

"Shut up."

LaRue put the car in reverse and backed out. I pulled my breakfast out of my bag and started eating it.

"Where to first?" she asked. "Patchogue, and work our way back?"

"Sure," I replied, my mouth full. I scanned the list we'd put together. There were seven bowling alleys within ten miles of

Sally's house.

LaRue signaled right. "Okay if we stop by Nanny's and drop off the craft stuff?"

She always brought Hoyt's leftover floral supplies—ribbon, foam, beads, and the like—to the nursing home where ninety-seven-year-old Bianca Fusticola lived. Egon had always thrown them out until he looked out the window one day and saw LaRue in her waitress uniform running up the street after the garbage truck.

I nodded my assent and cracked open my marble notebook. I was getting some ideas about the next steps to take, and I wanted to write them down while they were fresh in my mind. Crumbs dropped into the crevice of the binding.

"What are you eating?" LaRue asked.

"Fluffernutter."

"You're gonna rot your teeth. You know how much sugar's in that?"

"Mmmm-hmm. All natural."

"You have enough sugar there to last a week."

"Sugar is brain food, LaRue. I'll bet you didn't know that. Want a bite?"

LaRue wrinkled her nose and pulled over in front of the Sunny Side. We hopped out and dodged raindrops and traffic crossing the street to Hoyt's. She led the way around the side of the building to where two bags of floral detritus leaned against the wall. We grabbed a bag each.

"Camera's under the front awning," she said.

"I saw that."

We trudged back to the car and loaded the bags in the back. If we'd done nothing else right during the Buddha bust, at least we'd parked our cars halfway up the block. Maybe Sally hadn't been as smart.

It was a five-minute drive to the nursing home. On the way I left a message for Inez telling her that if a call came in for "Patty," to let me know. Patty is the code name we use at Able when we have a difficult client and don't want to advertise the identity of the editor doing the job. All of us editors have been Patty at one time or another.

The stately white pillars of the Distant Shores Nursing Home stood out among the oaks and maples on Route 347. We parked on the side of the two-story building. A line of wheelchairs faced us through the window of a Florida room. There was no movement in the room, and it took me a few seconds to realize that people were sitting in those wheelchairs.

I tore my eyes away. The drizzle turned to a downpour as we hurried inside with our bags. Distant Shores's lobby was large and comfortable in an old-fashioned parlor kind of way. Green sofas and matching fringed lampshades ringed the room, which was anchored by bowls of potpourri and large paintings of woodland scenes that had been hung just a little too high. In the rear of the lobby, several wheelchairs were arranged around a television set that was broadcasting a Sunday morning religious service.

The girl at the welcome desk pointed us to a corner where a good-looking young guy with dreadlocks was writing on a dry-erase board. He took one look at LaRue's overflowing box and grinned widely.

"Oh, cool, more craft stuff. You guys putting in a whole new setup down there?"

"What?" LaRue asked.

He squatted down next to the bags and whistled. "Wait till Ellen sees this. The rec therapist is like in heaven. She doesn't get much of a budget for supplies."

"Well, enjoy," LaRue said.

As we got back in the car I couldn't help but look again at the wheelchairs in the Florida room. I couldn't tell whether their occupants were awake or asleep. The sight depressed me.

"Promise me, when I'm ninety-five, you won't put me in this place."

"This is one of the good ones," LaRue said.

Shirley Bowl, our first stop on the Bowling Alleys of Long Island tour, was just opening for the day. We breezed in and quickly located the wall of champions. On display were plaques and photos of high bowlers and winning leagues. We scrutinized the faces, but Sally wasn't there. We crossed Shirley off the list and headed west to Patchogue Bowl, and from there to Sayville Lanes. Both stops netted gutter balls. At East Islip Bowl we struck gold. Sally's photo was in a group of four behind the shoe rental counter. A sign under the picture read:

WERE PROUD OF OUR HIGH ROLLER'S
MARIE LAVIN 236
MICHAEL DAVIS 262
SALVATORE BELLAROSA 255
HOWARD GIMPLE 242

Bingo.

We moved down the counter to where the fall league schedules were taped to the wall. The lone employee on duty, a middle-aged man with a shaved head, was spraying shoes and whistling "The Impossible Dream" from *Man of La Mancha*. He paused briefly mid-verse as we passed him.

LaRue and I scanned the first few lists. The Lady Rollers, the Vipers, and the Ball Burners bowled on Mondays. On Tuesdays it was the Pin Stripes, the Banana Splits, and the Gutter Gals. The Wrecking Balls and the Pin Heads hit the lanes on Wednesdays, and so on.

"Can you make out the names?" LaRue whispered.

"Not from here."

The shoe-spraying man moved toward us. His name, Louis

Pizzetti, was embroidered in script over his left pocket. "Can I help you ladies?"

"We want to see our friend bowl but we don't know what night he's here," LaRue said.

"You know the name of the team?"

We shook our heads.

"What's the last name?"

"Bellarosa."

Pizzetti moved along the row of lists, his muscular arms folded in front of him like Mr. Clean. "Bellarosa, Bellarosa. Salvatore or Gina?"

"Salvatore."

He extended one arm, pointing. "Monday, seven o'clock. The Ball Burners."

LaRue shot me a look that said, *Huh.*

"Appreciate your help," I said.

The man turned away to pick up some rags on the back counter. "No problem."

"Hey," LaRue said as we headed for the exit. "I just realized something."

"What?"

"You know where we are?"

"Yeah, East Islip."

"But do you know where we *are*? Oh, my Goddess, Em." She pulled on my sleeve, her eyes wide open. "We are *right* down the street from Porky's. I could go for some ribs. You?"

I held open the door for her. "You know I don't eat that stuff, LaRue."

"Give in. Just once."

"It's too much—meat."

She popped open her umbrella. "Well, how 'bout we go there anyway and you can order mac and cheese and I'll get myself a St. Louie and baby back combo."

"Fine."

"With a little pulled pork."

The rain was still coming down as we hurried across the parking lot.

"Here's my theory," I said when we were in the car. "Hazzard had a little blackmail business going. Sally was one of her targets. I don't know what she had on him, but she seduced him and blackmailed him. The Lizard—"

"Wait a sec. You think there were others?"

"Uh-huh. When I was talking to the Lizard, I let him believe I was someone who could arrange meetings or make deliveries. I got the impression he had more stuff to sell and was willing to cut someone in. I think Sally scared him. Bisbee realized he'd bitten off more than he could chew."

"You're crazy, you know that? You could get yourself killed."

"That's why I have you, remember?"

LaRue keyed the ignition and pulled out onto Montauk Highway. We drove for a while in silence, listening to the rhythmic squeak of the windshield wipers. I checked my cell phone for the umpteenth time for a message from Tony. I wished I could let it go. I'm like the kid who keeps touching a bruise to see if it still hurts.

"What makes you so sure Sally's the killer and not one of the other blackmailees?" LaRue finally asked.

"A few things. That night at Hazzard's, I heard Bisbee call Sally the kingpin. I didn't give it much thought at the time, but I think Bellarosa was Hazzard's main target. He was the cash cow. He had the most to lose and was the first one Bisbee called. He's strong, too. He could easily have overpowered Hazzard. And volatile—if you saw the way he knocked that apple out of his kid's hand. He also could have left the house early and done her in on his way to work. One of his offices is in Port Jeff."

"That's a lot of 'could haves.' "

"That's why we're coming back tomorrow night. To turn the 'could haves' into 'dids.' "

"Why didn't he kill the Lizard, too?"

"Maybe the Lizard still had something Sally wanted."

Traffic ground to a halt in Bay Shore. There was no parking on Main Street, despite the weather. LaRue parked in the municipal lot behind the restaurant, and we popped our umbrellas and headed toward the aroma of Porky's famous barbecue sauce.

"What I don't get," LaRue said, "is why Sally picked you to frame."

"I don't think he knew anything about me except what he learned from Hazzard. She was on the lookout for money-making opportunities. Maybe she bragged about her scheme to Sally. Maybe she waved my library card in front of his face."

"Or that letter you wrote."

The bluesy music and bustle of the eatery greeted us as we stepped in the door. We were seated at a table near the front, under a portrait of singing pigs. Steaming platters of ribs and chicken passed by at eye level. All around us people were laughing and enjoying themselves, which only made me feel more depressed.

I ordered a mac and cheese and a Smithwicks. LaRue ordered her combo platter along with cole slaw and sweet potato fries, and a Diet Coke to wash it down. Our food appeared before us in record time.

"How can you eat all that in the middle of the day?" I asked.

"You're so annoying, you know that?"

LaRue dropped a rib bone she'd cleaned off on top of the pile she was building. We ate for a few minutes without talking. Or rather, she ate and I stirred my macaroni around. Every few seconds I looked over at my cell phone parked by my fork.

"Did he call?"

"No."

"Why don't you just call him already?"

"I did, and he hasn't bothered to return—look, I'm finished with this dating crap. Who needs it? I have a great apartment, great friends, and a great job. I have all the freedom and potential happiness I want."

"So there."

"Right, so there." A wave of nausea passed through me and I put down my spoon.

LaRue pointed her fork in my direction. "The truth is you're afraid to call Tony. You're afraid he changed his mind about you and he's going to give you a line."

"Wouldn't *you* be?"

"No. He seems like a really good guy, Em. Egon wouldn't sell his business to someone who wasn't trustworthy. Tony's probably been busy and that's why he didn't call. But he will if you don't have the balls to call him first."

"Well, I'm—"

"Not going to. I know." LaRue sighed again. "Swee'pea, I will never figure you out. You're so brave about some things and so wimpy about others. You'll go after sleazeballs with knives, but you won't climb three feet up a ladder or call a guy you like." She slurped the ice at the bottom of her glass with her straw.

I pushed my chair back. All of a sudden the walls seemed too close. My palms were clammy and I felt faint.

"LaRue, this is not a good—"

"I'm sorry. I'm sorry." She gripped my wrists. "Forgive me? I'm an idiot. I didn't mean any of that. Wait, I'll get this wrapped up. Don't leave."

"I'm not." I stood up dizzily. "I'm not mad. I just have to get some air." The music faded as if someone had suddenly turned down the volume. Darkness appeared at the edges of my vision.

Her mouth moved. "Are you okay?"

"I'll meet you at the car." I dropped a twenty on the table and lunged toward the door. Outside I leaned against the building and tilted my head up, letting raindrops fall into my eyes and mouth. After a few seconds I felt better. I took a deep breath and headed slowly for the car, not bothering with my umbrella.

He was there when I turned the corner, but by the time I saw him it was too late. He grabbed my left arm and twisted it behind me, pulling me violently against him.

"Don't say a fucking word," Sally Bellarosa said between clenched teeth, "or I'll break your arm. Now walk. This way."

He shoved me forward, away from Main Street. Away from people. I stumbled, my head still fuzzy.

"Wh—where are you taking me?"

In response he jerked my arm higher, and I winced in pain. Pieces of wet hair fell across my forehead. A hundred yards ahead I saw a lone pedestrian hurrying between the parked cars, his face hidden by his umbrella.

"What do you want? Cash? Let go. I'll give you what I have."

"I don't want your cash."

"I've got fifty bucks."

"I don't want it. Keep moving."

Sally pushed me roughly, his breath on my neck. I stomped suddenly on his foot and he loosened his grip.

"Help!" I screamed, jerking away. "Somebody help me!"

He yanked me back and spun me around, slamming me sideways into a parked minivan, my left shoulder impacting the metal with a thud.

"I liked you better as a blond," Sally said, crushing me against the van with one hand.

"I don't know what you're talking about."

"You've only been stalking me the past two days, you lunatic. What the fuck's going on? It's about the book, isn't it?"

"Let go, or I'll—scream."

"Yeah? And when the cops get here you gonna tell them how you been following me? What do you think they'll say?"

"You've got the wrong person, mister. I just came out of—"

"I know where you came out of." He leaned over me, a sneer parting his lips. Stubble covered his chin and his hair was stuck to his forehead. He looked like a wet Rottweiler. "Now I want to know who you are."

I stalled. If he'd had a weapon, he'd have used it by now.

"Let go, and I'll talk," I said.

Sally loosened his grip but stayed close. I turned slowly to face him, my back against the van, my arm throbbing painfully. I wondered who'd tipped him off.

"I think you know who I am. I'm the person you called the other day. From the pizza place."

"What the hell are you talking about?"

"Let's call the cops. I think they'll be very interested in your story. While we're at it you can tell them how you got a hold of my library card. I'd like to know that, myself."

Sally shook his head. "Jesus Christ, she's a fucking lunatic. What are you talking about, library card? Lou didn't tell me I was dealing with a fucking lunatic."

Lou. The guy in the bowling alley. He'd been in earshot when LaRue had suggested Porky's.

"Where's your sidekick?" Sally growled.

"On her way."

He put his fist under my chin and jerked it up. The back of my head struck the window of the van with a loud crack. Rain dripped in my ears. I tasted blood.

"Give me the book."

"Wha—"

"The book. Give it to me now, and I'll leave you in one piece."

I felt something warm spreading sideways on the back of my

head. Dark spots appeared again on my periphery, and I knew I was going to pass out.

"Give me the book!" he roared.

I began to slip down the side of the van, the world rushing away from me. Somewhere far away a cell phone rang. The last words I heard Sally say sounded like he was talking under water.

"If I see you again, you fucking lunatic, I'll kill you."

CHAPTER TWENTY

A woman wearing gold hoop earrings shined a flashlight into my eyes. "What is your name?"

I opened my mouth to answer, but was distracted by a humming near my left ear. There were several voices in the room, talking softly. I wasn't sure where my hands were, under the covers or over.

"How come it's doing that?"

"She's awake. Thank Goddess. Doing what, Em?"

"Who is President of the United States?" the woman asked.

I blinked. People kept talking. I couldn't distinguish between the voices, and it was difficult to speak. The humming continued. A mosquito? With effort I formed my mouth into an O.

"How come—it's doing that?"

The light snapped off. "Will you be taking care of her?"

"Yes."

"She'll need stitches. We'll take a couple of X-rays to make sure there's no fracture, and set her up for a CT scan. I'm going to—"

"Why a CT scan?"

"To check for bleeding in the brain. Swelling. She was unconscious when you found her, you said?"

"Yes, but not too long. I was right behind her."

"That's good. But I'm keeping her overnight for observation. She'll be in recovery later, if you want to wait."

"Yes."

"You'll find a coffee shop downstairs."

"Thank you."

"Set me up in two."

The ceiling began to roll by, and the lights were very bright. I shut my eyes.

"How are you feeling, hon?" a male voice said. It came from above and behind me.

"Okay."

"Good. We're going to take care of that nasty cut, and then you'll rest. That's a good friend you have. She probably saved your life. Do you remember what happened?"

My head was swimming. I made a small gagging sound.

"Grab a basin, Hank."

We stopped and moved and stopped again. Hands rolled me onto my side. My head pounded, and my back was very cold. Cold metal touched my cheek. Someone held me so I could throw up, then washed my face gently. Before I dozed off again I felt my hair being lifted up.

"What day is it?" the doctor asked, looking up from her chart.

I squinted to bring her face into focus. "You're wearing the same earrings as before, so I guess it's still Sunday."

She smiled. "It is. I'm Dr. Fala. You have a concussion. When you hit your head on the car window, you suffered a scalp wound. It caused an impressive amount of bleeding that scared your friend, but you didn't break any bones. That cut and where you bit the inside of your cheek may bother you later."

"Where am I?"

"Good Sam. You just came up from recovery."

"Came up?" I looked around me. I was in a semi-private room. There was no one in the next bed. I turned the bracelet on my wrist. E TRACE GOOD SAMARITAN HOSPITAL.

"You'll go home tomorrow. First I want to make sure

everything's copacetic."

She returned to her chart. There was a strong medicinal smell coming from my hair. I felt the back of my head and found a bandage.

"Just a small shaved area," the doctor said without looking up. "The rest of your hair will cover it. I always hated sewing, but my mother would be proud of me for the beautiful stitches I made you."

"How many?"

"Seven. For luck."

"Some luck."

"You were extremely lucky, Emma. I don't need to tell you that this could have ended up much worse. Now, I've given you a painkiller and something for your cheek. The painkiller will make you drowsy." She stopped writing and looked up. Her expression was serious. "There are two policemen in the hallway. I've managed to keep them at bay so far, but they're not leaving until they speak to you. How are you feeling?"

"Okay, I guess."

"Your friend said you almost fainted in the restaurant. Has that happened before?"

"All the time. I have to eat every two hours."

"I'll check your blood sugar while you're here." Dr. Fala went back to writing. "You're the first person who didn't ask me what 'copacetic' meant." She looked up and smiled. Then the smile faded and her fingers brushed her cheek. "What's this?"

I touched my face. "Oh, that. That's from a couple days ago."

"How did it happen?"

"Something fell off a building onto me. Metal."

She peered closely at the scrape. "Are you sure?"

I understood what she was thinking. "It was an accident."

The doctor sat back. "You've had some week. Are you practicing to be a superhero?"

"Yeah."

When I said nothing more, she stood up. "All right. Buzz the desk if you have any problem."

Dr. Fala left and Team Zahnomo entered the room.

"Well, Emma, we meet again," Zahn said. "Not under the pleasantest of circumstances. How do you feel?"

"I'll live."

He sat down in a chair next to the bed. Bonomo stood against the wall. I eased onto my side to face them. My head hurt a lot less in that position.

"So, I was reading the reports today," Zahn went on, "and there was a nine-one-one down in the Third Precinct involving you and an unidentified assailant who'd fled the scene. One LaRue Fusticola made a statement. It piqued my interest, shall we say."

I'll bet, I thought.

Zahn pulled out his pen and notebook. "You want to tell us what happened?"

"I was attacked by Hazzard's boyfriend."

"Where?"

"Behind Porky's. I left the restaurant and he was there. He marched me to the parking lot and slammed me against a car."

"How did he know where to find you?"

"Don't know. He's got eyes on me."

Bonomo put his hands in his pockets and watched me intently.

"Doesn't he talk?" I said to Zahn.

"Never mind him. I take him along to sniff out the best pizza."

Bonomo chuckled.

"Tell us about the boyfriend," Zahn prompted.

The room swam before me, and I closed my eyes for a moment. "Well, I found a DVD, a skin flick, that went back to him, and then I went to his house and followed him—"

"Wait a minute. You found a DVD? Where?"

"In Hazzard's pickup truck. I was hiding there while he was talking to this other guy—the Lizard. They were making some kind of deal. When they went inside the house, I escaped." It was hard to keep things straight. The effort of telling the story was exhausting.

"Her house?"

"Yes."

"When was this?"

"Friday night."

Zahn wrote something down. "What were you doing there?"

I raised myself on one elbow, picked up my water glass, and drank its contents down to the bottom before lowering my head back to the pillow. "She had a letter of mine that I wanted back. Something I had written in the heat of the moment. I was so angry at her for breaking up my relationship with Sam. You guys were tailing me, and I was afraid you'd find the letter first."

"Did you go inside the house to look for it?"

"Yes, but I didn't find it."

"Was anyone else inside while you were there?"

"The Lizard. That's why I left and hid in the truck."

I thought he'd press me for more details, but he didn't. Zahn scribbled on his pad and looked up. "Go back to the other part, the boyfriend's house. You said you were there."

"Yes."

"Was that the same night?"

"No, the next day. Saturday. I followed him to a laundromat where he got rid of a bunch of Hazzard's clothes he'd been carrying around in his car."

The detective frowned. "Hazzard's clothes?"

"A bra, a pair of panties, and two blouses—a pinkish one and

140

one with a paisley pattern." I looked from Zahn to Bonomo. The two detectives floated in circles and overlapped like a Venn diagram. "I'll give them to you. They're in my car. In the trunk."

"What about the DVD?"

"That's in there, too."

Zahn sat back in his chair and looked at me with interest. There was a flash of something in his eyes, I wasn't sure what.

"You're riding around with these things in the trunk of your car?"

"Detective, I was afraid. Once I realized he was trying to frame me for murder, I did what I had to. Haven't you ever been afraid? Ever in your life?"

Zahn was silent for a moment. "Why do you say he was trying to frame you?"

"I think he planted my library card at the murder scene." I remembered Bellarosa's confusion when I mentioned the library card. Was it an act? "After you left my house on Friday, I got an anonymous phone call saying the police had the card. He disguised his voice, so I can't swear it was him, but putting two and two together—"

"Why didn't you tell me about it before?"

"I would have if you'd given me a chance."

"Did the call come in on your home phone or your cell?"

"My cell. I don't have a landline."

"We'll take a look at that if you have it."

"It's in my bag."

"I've got it," Bonomo said. He reached down and handed my bag to me. I dug out my phone and gave it to Bonomo, who gave it to Zahn. I was glad the throwaway phone wasn't in there.

"The call came from the pay phone at Anthony's," I said. "The pizza place down the block."

I had never seen Zahn pause so frequently, but now he did again—with my cell phone in mid-transit to his lap.

"It's not rocket science," I said. "I did star-six-nine. You can look all the way up my street from that phone. He could easily have been watching my parking lot while you were there."

Bonomo said, "Why do you think he wants to frame you?"

I made an offhanded gesture. "Probably something to do with Hazzard's little blackmail scheme, don't you think?"

Now Bonomo was silent.

"Don't tell me you don't know about that. The little business Hazzard had on the side, collecting dirt on people and selling it back to them?"

"How do *you* know about it?" Bonomo asked.

"From the Lizard. Now, I *know* you both know the Lizard. Clifford Bisbee. I'll bet he has a record a mile long."

"What were you doing talking to Bisbee?" Zahn asked.

I touched my head gingerly. It was hurting quite a lot. I decided to go with the simplest answer.

"He hit on me in a bar. That was the next day, the day after I saw him at Hazzard's. It was the Lizard who actually fingered Bellarosa as the kingpin."

"Who?" they both said.

Now it was my turn to be confused. "Sally Bellarosa. Her boyfriend."

"Jennifer Hazzard's boyfriend?" Zahn asked, trying to cover his confusion.

"Yeah. Cesspool Sally. Who did you think we were talking about?"

I bit my lip and looked from one to the other. Bonomo took his hands out of his pockets.

"Would you pass me the water pitcher, please?" I asked.

Bonomo poured me a glass of water, and I drank half of it.

"Bellarosa thinks I have the blackmail book," I went on, closing my eyes. "That's why he attacked me. But actually Bisbee has it. That was going to be my next step, getting it from him.

But now that you're here, you can do it. I don't really want to get hurt again."

There was a prolonged silence.

"What else do you know about the blackmail book?" Bonomo asked.

I knew then that I was way ahead of them. Neither one had a clue.

"I suspect it lists Hazzard's targets." I opened one eye. "There are multiple targets, possibly including me. Bisbee is looking for a point person to make deliveries and collect payment. I was going to accept the job, but, as I said, now that you're here, I think I'll respectfully decline."

Zahn looked at me for a few moments without speaking. He'd been scrolling through my calls, and now he dropped the phone in his lap. "What does he look like?"

"Bellarosa?"

"Yeah."

"You want his home address, too?"

"A description will be fine," he said tightly.

I ran down Bellarosa's main features and watched Zahn write as I spoke.

"Are you going to arrest him?"

"That depends. Are you going to press charges?"

"Hell, yeah."

He shrugged.

"What's that mean?"

"Bellarosa's going to tell me you've been stalking and harassing him. Calling him under false pretenses. He's going to call you on it."

"That's a bunch of crap, Detective. The guy committed a felony. He attacked me."

"You both broke the law. If I arrest him, I have to arrest you, too."

"So, you're just going to let him go?"

"We'll talk to him," Zahn said. "I'm sure he'll cooperate."

He put the notebook and pen back in his pocket and glanced down at my cell phone.

"You have a few messages."

"Let me see."

I pressed recent calls and saw that Tony had called at around the time I'd left Porky's. Mom had called, too, and Ned. LaRue must have gotten the word out.

"Family," I said. "I'll listen to them later. If you don't mind, I'm a little tired right now."

Zahn stood up. "We're finished—for now. If you hear from Bisbee again, call me immediately. Don't do anything without talking to me."

"Okay."

"I mean that, Trace. You came close to buying the farm today. At least I know where you'll be for the next eighteen hours." I saw that odd flash in his eyes again. "We're going to take that stuff out of your car." It was not a request.

"Be my guest."

"Feel better," he said and walked out with Bonomo.

Chapter Twenty-One

"Yes. Yes, I will," I said into the phone. "Love you, too, Mom."

I hit *end* and sank onto my side. "She's a basket case."

"I love your mom," LaRue said. She looked like she was going to cry. "Swee'pea, I'm so sorry."

"For what?"

She gazed ruefully at my hospital gown and my sticking-out hair and stitched-up bandaged head.

"For calling you a wimp. For not realizing—for not leaving the restaurant with you. Everything. This is all my fault."

"Don't be ridiculous."

"It's true. If it wasn't for me getting my stupid ribs wrapped up to go, none of this would have happened. If I hadn't of opened my big mouth in the bowling alley, Sally would never've found you."

I stared at my clothes piled neatly on a chair, my sneakers side by side at the bottom of the pile. I tried to imagine myself not being here to put them on.

"He was looking for me, LaRue. He would have found me sooner or later."

"You know what I thought when I came around that corner and saw you lying in the puddle? I thought you'd been hit by a car. Just lying there—not moving. And the blood. And no one around." She spread her hands and dropped them in her lap. "You scared me half to death, Em."

"And I didn't even have what Sally was looking for." I paused for a few seconds to explore the inside of my left cheek with my tongue. It felt like gristle where I had bitten it as I fell. "It doesn't make sense, LaRue. If you logic it out."

"What do you mean?"

"Why did he think I had the blackmail book? If Sally set me up for a murder he committed, why didn't *he* have it?"

"He had to get out of there fast after he killed Jennifer. Or he didn't know where she kept it."

"No. He wouldn't have killed her without first getting that book in his hands."

"Maybe he did and someone took it from him."

"Maybe." I twisted the blanket between my fingers. "LaRue, something's bothering me about all this, and I don't know what."

LaRue thrust her arms into her jacket sleeves. "I for one am glad you're in the hospital tonight. At least I don't have to worry about you for one night."

"Would you do me a big favor? Bring my laptop when you come back. And a couple of *Northern Exposure* DVDs. They're in the basket next to the TV."

"Sure. Anything else?"

"I left my black and white notebook and a phone in your car."

After she'd gone, I turned slowly onto my other side and faced the window. The rain had cleared, and the sun was going down, sending hard slats of sunlight through the blinds, into the room. Dust particles were suspended in the light like small galaxies. I stared at them a long time, trying to make sense of their swirling patterns. Every time I thought I had a handle on them, they shifted. Finally I gave up and fell asleep.

A cone of light flooded in from the hallway, illuminating my bed table with its dish of congealed chicken à la king. The room was dark except for the light from the television. The volume had been turned down, but I could still make out a nasal voice speaking in clipped tones.

"Coming 'round the far turn now it's Fantastical in first place. So-and-So is behind him at the rail, with Jessie Bear rallying for third. Then Remember Me, Corduroy, and Absolutely Sure. Goodnight Moon is still six lengths behind in last place. Forty-four and three at the half mile—"

I shifted onto my right side, swimming in a world of Tylenol with codeine. Dad slept slumped over in the chair, arms folded across the chest, which rose and fell with his breathing. I touched his sleeve, and he awoke with a start.

"Hey, Pumpkin, how're you feeling?" He leaned over and kissed my forehead.

"I'm okay, Dad."

He clicked on the lamp. "Stitches bothering you?"

I made a small nod. His hair looked as if it hadn't been combed in six weeks, nor cut in three months. As if reading my thoughts, he combed his fingers through it.

"LaRue called me," he said. "I was working on a scene and didn't get the message until five."

"How's your screenplay coming along?"

"Pretty well. I may yet meet my deadline." He furrowed his brow. "You know, I don't like that neighborhood, honey. You really shouldn't—"

"Dad, it was lunch time. There were tons of people. And LaRue was with me."

Dad looked skeptical. *But not Sam.* He didn't say the words aloud.

"Anyway, it didn't happen because of the neighborhood."

"No?"

"The guy who jumped me thought I was someone else. Someone he was looking for. Does it matter? The police have him now, anyway. Or they will shortly."

Pain filled his eyes. "Sometimes I worry about you, Emma Rose. Things like this happen, and you're . . ." He let the sentence trail off, but I knew what he meant to say: *All alone.* The unsaid words echoed in the room.

"I'm not five anymore, Dad. I think I can handle things." An annoying whine had crept into my voice.

He avoided my eyes. "I have to go into the city tomorrow and meet with Harry." Harry's his agent. "It's the only day he's available."

"It's okay, Dad. LaRue's taking me home."

There was nothing more to say. He looked miserable. I could see his eyes speaking the words, *Sam, Sam, Sam. If not me, then it should have been Sam.*

My eyes spoke back at him, *Not Sam. Not any man who does to me what Sam did.*

LaRue had brought me season four of *Northern Exposure.* I spent some time arranging the extra pillows I'd rounded up so I could sit up comfortably. When I was done, my stitches floated in a valley between pillows. I popped disk one into my Mac-Book, which was balanced on my lap. While it was booting up I listened to Tony's message again.

"Hey, about last night, Emma. I'm really sorry. I was making a last-minute run for Egon and got a flat on the Sagtikos. I tried calling you, but, ah, I kept getting your voicemail. *Keep* getting it. Give me a buzz, okay?"

He said the word "flat" in a can-you-believe-it tone. I didn't. I punched delete and shut the phone. I'd call him later. Maybe.

LaRue had reported that the Sunny Side had provided the police with videos from the twenty-four hours preceding the crime. Egon had not turned over any videos because there had been none. The new surveillance system was of the continuous filming type, but the system was not working properly. Nothing had been recorded from Wednesday night until Saturday morning. The technician had been in twice over the weekend to look at it, and it was working fine now. The problem might have been a faulty wire, a common problem in new systems. The wire had since been replaced.

"Did Theo tell you that?" I asked her.

"Tony did. Theo was out when I called."

My relief was tempered by a nagging feeling that somebody somewhere was not telling the truth.

"Aren't you happy?" LaRue asked. "No one saw us."

The *Northern Exposure* episode I watched was called "Nothing's Perfect." Chris, the radio-DJ-slash-guru in tiny Cicely, Alaska, runs over a woman's dog with his truck and proceeds to fall in love with her. The woman is a grad student obsessed with the mathematical concept of pi, which she believes holds the answer to all of life's mysteries. She thinks that if she takes pi to ten or twenty million digits, she'll find something really incredible—a sign.

As the story developed, I relaxed. The soft voices of nurses in the hallway discussing the merits of highlighting floated into the room and blended with the voices coming from my computer.

Zahn would talk to Bellarosa. He'd find the murderer. The Lizard would relinquish the blackmail book. Jennifer would be buried, and life would go on. The police would forget all about me, and I could go back to being an editor with a cantaloupe-eating cat.

Near the end of the *Northern Exposure* episode, to even the score for causing the deaths of both the pi lady's dog and her parakeet, Chris sacrifices his Harley by sending it over a cliff. He reads a few lines from Tolstoy: "Truth is like a lizard. It leaves its tail in your fingers and runs away, knowing full well it will grow a new one in a twinkling."

With any luck, not *this* Lizard, I thought, as the camera pulled away and Danny Kaye sang about arithmetic over the episode's final shots.

What? A thought intruded from the edges of my mind and wriggled there, like a fish just out of reach. Maybe it meant something, or maybe it was just the product of a mind on meds. I'd check it out tomorrow. If I was right, maybe I was barking up the wrong tree.

Evidence Locker
Box 15
Personal diary, page 38

Dear Diary,

I can't tell Grandma about daddy. Girls like me go to h-ll. I know I am going to h-ll. I always think I'll go out the window and hide on the roof when I hear him coming, but I never do.

Chapter Twenty-Two

Monday

"Uh-oh," LaRue said, her foot on the top step.

I put down my plastic bag-o-stuff and came up behind her to see what she was uh-ohing at. My apartment door was open. Not all the way—just an inch. But it was an inch too much.

I pushed past her and listened at the door.

"Meow," Bergamot said at the low end of the crack.

"I definitely shut this door last night," LaRue said.

"You didn't lock it?"

"My keys were in the car. I was carrying all your stuff and trying to keep Bergy from getting out. I know I shut it. I heard it click."

"How did you get into the building?"

"Your downstairs neighbor. The lady with the topknot."

"While you left the car running?"

LaRue pulled a stick of gum out of somewhere and popped it in her mouth. Bergamot meowed again. Louder.

"Someone's going to get in your Jeep one day and drive away, LaRue."

LaRue jerked her chin toward the door. "We going in?"

I pushed the door open. I remembered then what Mrs. Porter had said the other day about hearing someone on the steps. The door had been locked that time. Maybe whoever it was had had to come back. Grandma Bea's rocking chair was moving gently.

The computer and TV were still in their places.

"It's too bad they didn't actually bust the lock," LaRue said as we carried my stuff in. "Maybe ol' X-Ray Eyes will believe you this time."

"If nothing's missing I'm not even going to call him."

Bergamot lassoed my legs with his tail and escorted me to the kitchen. The Fluffernutter sandwich fixings from yesterday were still on the kitchen table, next to the ghost pumpkin. I put the jars of peanut butter and marshmallow fluff back in their place of honor on the counter and dumped the standing coffee into the sink. It didn't look like anything had been taken.

I felt Bergamot's eyes boring holes in my back, so I refilled his water bowl and added a few shakes of Meow Mix to his food dish. He stuck his nose in the food, shot me a disdainful look, and disappeared around the corner.

My desk was its usual cluttered mess. Nothing appeared to be missing. I put my laptop on top of the pile of papers and plugged it in.

My extra apartment key was still taped to the underside of the desk. I removed it and put it in my pocket. Then I opened the top drawer and pulled out the folder of newspaper clippings I'd been collecting since the murder and stuffed it into the I LOVE LIBRARIES tote hanging on the back of the chair. I dumped in my black and white notebook and throwaway phone, too. And stuff I'd printed out from the computer. I would sleep on top of this bag if I had to, but I was not going to let it out of my sight.

I pulled three clippings from the folder and spread them out on the coffee table.

LaRue appeared in the doorway with my pillow. "Your antique silver dollar's still here."

"Come here, LaRue."

I pushed the *Daily News* article across the table toward her.

"What do you see in the photo?"

LaRue put the pillow at the other end of the couch and sat down. "Main Street."

"What else?"

"Hoyt's. Yellow tape. Cops. People." She looked at me curiously.

"This picture was taken on Friday morning at exactly"—I referred to my notebook—"ten thirty-eight. Now look at the pics from *The Post* and *Newsday*. These were taken at seven twenty and seven forty-two, respectively. Anything stand out?"

LaRue bent over them. "The new camera system?"

"Look at the side of the building. How many bags of craft supplies do you see?"

"Six in the *Newsday* pic, and—" Her eyes shifted. "Six in *The Post*."

"Look again at the *Daily News*."

LaRue's eyes flitted back and forth between photographs. She was quiet for a moment. Then she said slowly, "Two. There are two bags in that picture." She lifted her head. "What happened to the other four bags?"

"Exactly."

"How do you know when these pictures were taken?"

"I found them online while I was waiting for you to pick me up. Then I emailed the photographers and asked. All their photos are time-stamped."

LaRue stood up and started pacing.

"Could the bags have been picked up by the garbage collector?" I asked her.

"No. Garbage goes in the dumpster. And it doesn't go out on Fridays."

"How about an art teacher? Maybe Egon gave them to someone."

She shook her head. "Egon knows I always take that stuff to

Nanny's. What made you pick up on the bags?"

"The new surveillance camera points to the side of the building, so that's where I looked. It would have recorded someone removing the bags—if it had been working. How convenient that it was on the fritz." I put the articles back in the folder. "Here's another weird thing. Tony told me that the vandals swept up the broken pottery."

"That's weird, all right." She nodded thoughtfully. "I thought it was funny there were only two bags. The last time I took craft stuff to Nanny's was back in August. There should have been more." She gave me a sharp look. "Remember that kid at the nursing home who asked if we were redoing the store? It sounded like he already got a delivery from Hoyt's."

Our gazes met. LaRue went to make a phone call, and I fluffed my pillow and lay down on the couch. Part of me wished I were back in the old days. Sam was a rock at times like this. I could spill everything to him, and he'd tell me what to do.

I stood up dizzily, retrieved my computer, and set it up on the coffee table. The medical examiner's report had come out this morning and confirmed Hazzard's death by blunt instrument. Her body had been released, and the funeral was set for tomorrow. There was nothing in the reports about a missing bowl, surveillance videos, or blackmail. Nothing about Sally Bellarosa.

Zahn had to have talked to Sally by now. Right?

And the Lizard? You would think.

To get my mind off the case, I checked my Facebook page and found some early happy birthdays from friends. The messages were an uneasy reminder that I had just two days left to find my present.

"Inez wants to know if the Helping Hands should stop by," LaRue said.

"No! I mean, tell her no, thanks."

"I did. I'm not sure the message got through. But you can tell her yourself when she gets here."

"Gets here?"

"In a half hour. I have to go home and give Petey his medicine. Inez is taking the afternoon shift."

I pulled myself up onto one elbow. "LaRue, I appreciate what you're doing, but I don't need all-day babysitting."

"Like hell you don't."

"I've got my computer, my phone, and I even have milk in the house."

Goddess that she was, LaRue came and stood over me with that wry goddess smile, the sun a halo around her red hair. "Forget it, Swee'pea. As long as Sally Bellarosa is out there somewhere, your friends are going to be right here with you, ready to defend." She did a kickboxing move over the coffee table, missing my nose by inches.

After she left, I punched the number of the Distant Shores Nursing Home into my throwaway phone.

"I'd like to speak to the young man who helps the recreational therapist," I said to the stern-sounding woman who answered.

"We have three recreational aides."

"I want the one with dreads who was working yesterday."

Her fingers clattered on a keyboard. "Andre's not in yet. What is this in reference to?"

"The craft supplies I brought over. I think I left my sweater in one of the bags."

"I'll put you through to the therapist, Ellen Trapp. Who is calling?"

Rats. "Rhoda Lavone."

"One moment."

There was a click, and I was listening to "Climb Every Mountain" from *The Sound of Music.* In a few seconds a woman answered cheerfully. I repeated what I had said to the front desk.

"I can check. I keep all my art supplies locked up downstairs, otherwise they'd disappear in two seconds. What was your donation packaged in? A box or a bag?"

"Leaf bags, a bunch of them from Hoyt's Greenhouse."

"Oh. How many?"

"I'm not sure, five or six." At least I'd confirm the number, if not who'd brought them. "You know, I don't need to bother you with this. I can wait for Andre."

"Oh, it's no bother," Ellen said. "I'm glad to do it. I'm heading into a brief meeting now, but I'll go down afterwards. Where can I reach you?"

I had one more call to get in before the changing of the guard. I was almost positive now that Sally wasn't the killer. His confusion about the library card and demand for the blackmail book had given me doubt. But before I could move forward, I had to find out once and for all if he'd made the anonymous call.

Whoever picked up the phone at Sally's Cesspool Service didn't say hello immediately. I heard loud pop music and male voices laughing in the background, and a voice close to the phone said, "Shoot him on sight!"

I jumped. "Hello?"

"Shoot him on sight, I tell ya! Or make him buy ya a beer." More laughter. Then the voice said, "Sally's Cesspool, hello."

I pinched my nose with my thumb and forefinger. "This is Rhoda Lavone, and I want to know why you guys aren't returning my calls."

"Whoa, there. Let's back up a step, Mrs.—?"

"Lavone. Who am I speaking with, please?"

"Sal Bellarosa here. Head honcho. Nice to meet you, Mrs. Lavone. Let me get the book in front of me, and we'll see what's what. You say you called us and didn't get a call back?"

My voice shook. I hoped he didn't hear it. "We were in a really bad place with the cesspool here, and my husband's friend recommended you guys. So I called. I even left a message I'd be home on Friday at one o'clock if someone could please come over. No one even had the *courtesy*—"

"When did you call us, Mrs. Lavone?"

"Thursday. Twice." Sally didn't respond, so I barreled on. "It's too late now. I got somebody else. But I am not at all happy with your customer service."

"I'm sorry, Mrs. Lavone," Sally said. I heard pages flipping. "Your message didn't come through. I'm looking at Friday now, and I couldn't have been there at one, anyway. I had an appointment in Deer Park. But I'd like to make it up to you with a coupon for a free service visit during the next three months."

"Never mind," I said. "I'm not going to need cesspool servicing for a very long time."

I shut the phone and tossed it onto the coffee table. My nose reinflated gradually, like couch cushions when you stand up.

There was a brisk rat-a-tat at the door and in stepped Inez, clutching a plastic bag. She was wearing a raspberry dress with puffed sleeves, her black pumps, and lipstick to match the dress. It was her first time in my apartment, and her eyes skittered all over the place before falling on me. Bergamot shot over to her and wound his furry orange chubbiness around her shins.

"Don't you rip my pantyhose, kitty cat!" Inez wagged her finger at him. "No, no, no! Watch those claws! Oh my God, why is he doing this? I don't even like cats. They give me the jim-jams."

"Maybe he's interested in what's in the bag."

She shut the door and strode over to the couch. Bergamot beat her to it and jumped on top of me.

"You look terrible, hon," Inez said, leaning into my face.

"Thanks, Inez."

She put a cool hand on my forehead. I smelled roast chicken and Calèche. "You're as white as a sheet. Did you eat anything today? You look like you didn't eat."

Bergamot craned his neck toward the plastic bag. I clamped a hand on him.

"Yes, I ate. I had a bowl of Cocoa Puffs."

"You gotta keep up your strength, hon." Inez turned and clickety-clacked to the kitchen, Bergamot at her heels. Her voice traveled back. "I got you a nice rotisserie chicken from the King Kullen. And a little potato salad. Why this maniac is still on the streets is beyond me. The poor girl is dead three days already. And what are the police doing about it? That's what *I'd* like to know. Where do you keep your serving platters, hon?"

"Over the stove. So, who's minding the store while you're here?"

"Henry. He's staying until three, that's when I gotta git."

"The owner? I thought he only showed up for parties."

"It wasn't easy, hon, believe me. *Gantseh k'nacker.* Such a big shot, he hates to get his hands dirty. But I told him my friends come first."

I heard drawers and cabinets opening and shutting and cutlery clinking. In the background Bergamot started a rhythmic meowing while Inez kept up the patter. "So her mother and brother are in from Jersey, Jennifer's, and they're staying at the Hampton Inn. The breakfast is very good over there. Nice and fresh. Did you read today's paper?" She appeared in the doorway, brandishing a knife. "*Absolutamente nada* about the murder weapon. Only that she got clocked. With what, I want to know? *They* know, but they're not telling."

"Maybe they're hoping the killer will make a mistake."

Inez disappeared. The knife clinked. "That Detective Zahn, he keeps everything very close to the vest. Very close. Listen, cat—what's her name?"

"Bergamot. And it's a him."

"Listen, Bergamot, you're being a pain in the patootie. Now, here's some nice chicken that really belongs to your mother." The meowing stopped. "You know that job I gave you Friday, hon? Ferrette? She's having conniptions."

"Why? It's not due till tomorrow. Tell her she'll have it."

The fridge door opened with a sucking sound. "You don't know this client, hon. She saw me on the news, and now she's calling me ten times a day."

Inez appeared with a plate of food. There was chicken, cole slaw, potato salad, marinated tomatoes and mozzarella, buttered rye toast, and a pickle. It looked like something straight out of a food magazine. She set the plate on the coffee table along with a Boylan root beer.

"Why, Inez, this is beautiful. I don't know what to say."

"Don't say anything, hon. Just eat. Get your strength back." She watched me pick up my fork. "Do you want more butter? I didn't know how much to put."

"No, this is fine." She continued to hover. I took a bite of chicken and a swig of root beer. "Inez, have a seat. You're making me nervous."

"You know that call you were waiting for? It came in. A guy asking for 'Patty.' "

I looked up, wiping my mouth with my napkin. "Oh?"

Inez stood there with her hands on her hips. She had my Michelangelo's "David" apron on over her dress, which was pretty comical, but I didn't laugh.

"He says he wants to talk to 'Patty.' Says he's from the hardware store. True Value." She arched her eyebrows.

"He's just a guy I met. I didn't want to give him my number."

"Don't you just-a-guy me," Inez said. "He sounded like a sneak thief."

"A sneak thief?"

"A nogoodnik. A creep. Who is he?"

"What did you tell him?"

"I said I'd give you a message. He didn't want to leave a message. He left his number."

I suppressed the impulse to jump up and down on the couch for joy.

"Can I have his number, please?"

Inez cocked her head. She looked exactly like a robin, albeit one with explicit human male anatomy on her apron front.

"Didn't you get in enough trouble yet?"

My throwaway phone rang and I hit the green button.

"This is Ellen Trapp at Distant Shores." It was the recreational therapist. "I went through all the bags, and I didn't see your sweater. It was all gems and beads, things like that."

"Oh, dear. How many bags were there?"

"Six from Hoyt's. I can double-check, but I don't think your sweater's here."

Out of the corner of my eye I watched Inez zip around the living room opening windows.

"When does Andre come in?"

"In about an hour."

I thanked her and hit *end*.

Mother Robin flew back to the nest. "I know you're up to something, hon. What is it?"

"Inez, what do you know about Tony?"

"Egon's Tony? He ran an Italian restaurant in Nassau County. The kind where you make reservations."

I scooped up the last of the potato salad. "Where does he live?"

"I don't know. But the fella's got money." She shot me a knowing look. "Did you see what he's driving?"

"No. What?"

"A Nissan Three-Fifty-Z. Very hot car."

"Don't you think it's odd that he got out of a successful restaurant to buy into a little floral business?"

"Maybe he was ready for a change," Inez said. "You don't think Tony has anything to do with that poor girl, do you?"

A gust of wind blew my clippings into a flurry of newsprint. I moved to sit up, but Inez waved me back and gathered up the papers. She went into the kitchen and returned with the ghost pumpkin, which she set on them as a paperweight.

"I know what you're up to," she said. "You're trying to solve the case, aren't you? I can see you got everything on that poor girl's murder right here. That's why you got that concussion. And the creep who wants to talk to 'Patty,' he's part of it, too."

I nabbed the pickle with my fork. "You're right, Inez, but that's all I can tell you. May I please have his phone number?"

Inez looked doubtful, but she reached into the bosom of her dress and handed me a folded piece of paper.

There was an ominous thud in the kitchen, and Bergamot appeared in the doorway with a drumstick hanging out of his mouth. This time Inez didn't stop me as I jumped up. The two of us ran to the kitchen, she clickety-clacking in her heels and me hobbling right behind. Some chicken was still on the platter, and might be saved. The carcass was on the floor, adorned with little teeth marks.

I pointed to a cabinet. "Plastic containers, top shelf."

What I later remembered about what happened next was its Mad-Hatter-Tea-Party feel, an incongruous confluence of events that made no sense at the time. Inez opened the cabinet and three books tumbled out, glancing her on the shoulder before hitting the floor, *smack, smack, smack!* What were books—?

The front door slammed shut from the wind.

Inez yelled, "Ouch!"

Mrs. Porter stood next to me, smiling and holding a meat-loaf.

I picked up a book and stared at the title.

Undetected: Getting Away with Murder

"Holy crap," I said.

"Did I come at a bad time?" Mrs. Porter asked.

"Are you the landlady?" Inez asked.

"Oh, no," Mrs. Porter said. "I live downstairs, in 1A. Were you ever a Rockette? You look like you danced at Radio City. You have legs like a dancer."

I looked from Mrs. Porter to Inez and back at the book.

"I always wanted to be a Rockette," Mrs. P. said.

CHAPTER TWENTY-THREE

Tuesday

Andre confirmed without hesitation that four bags had been delivered from Hoyt's at about nine on Friday by a dark-haired man with a smudge of gray at the temples. Tony.

I'd played out the scenario in my head several times and couldn't rule him out. Early Friday morning Tony could have parked behind Hoyt's. When the bread man arrived at the Sunny Side Up, he could have crossed the street, sneaked in, and killed Hazzard. Afterwards, having disabled Hoyt's cameras, he could have smashed the blue bowl, swept up the pieces, chucked them in with the craft supplies, and delivered the bags to Distant Shores. Logistically speaking, he could have done all that. It was awfully hard to believe, though.

The tumbling library books bothered me. I'd walked around the whole place trying to figure out what was missing and never once considered that something had been planted. Someone had balanced the books atop six jars of marshmallow fluff I'd bought on sale. When I'd left Zahn a message that the Lizard had called, I'd also mentioned the books. But somehow I couldn't bring myself to tell him what I'd learned about Tony.

"Sucks," said LaRue when I told her the next morning. It was five a.m. and we were in Sunny Side's kitchen, waiting for the new cook to show up. I wanted to have another look around.

LaRue opened the side door to take out the garbage, and a

little gray cat with a notched ear limped up and looked beseech-ingly into our faces.

"Oh, poor baby," LaRue said, bending over. At the impend-ing hand, the cat backed up.

"You know this cat?"

LaRue nodded. "Every morning he comes. Jennifer used to feed him. I guess I'll take over now."

She poured some milk into a bowl and set it down outside the door. "Where did he go? Here, kitty."

"He'll be back." I moved through the room. I had a tingling feeling in my skin, as though I were on the verge of discovery. Maybe that bonk on the head had done me good. I squatted next to the storage cabinet where the blue bowl had lived.

LaRue pulled pancake ingredients out of the fridge and set them on the table. Twilight appeared in the service entry win-dow.

"It's so quiet in here," LaRue said. "Weird."

I circled the room, surveying as before the oyster crackers, the buckets of Frialator oil, the countertops, stove, and grill. I ran my hand down the side of the refrigerator. I studied the hanging utensil rack and watched LaRue's red hair bob as she stirred the batter.

Maybe I was looking at the scene all wrong. I was looking at it as an observer would, not a murderer. I stood behind LaRue. Opposite her was the pass-through to the dining area, the television, the cookbooks.

"What did you just say?" I asked.

"Nothing."

"Yes, you did. You said something about it being quiet."

LaRue jerked her chin toward the television. "When Jennifer was here, she always had the TV on."

"She did?" I walked over to the television and reached up. The buttons were hard to reach. Hazzard had been a good three inches taller than I was. "Where do you keep the remote?"

"In that drawer. She always turned on the news to keep her company. Said she couldn't work without it."

I clicked on the television. The screen stayed black. In the corner of the screen the words *Component 1* appeared in white. Under a pile of papers next to the television was a DVD player.

"Did she ever watch movies?"

"Just the news."

"The television is set for DVD."

"Really?" LaRue hopped off the stool and came over.

"Does Rita watch movies back here?"

"I don't think she even knows there's a DVD player."

I frowned at the white letters staring calmly back at me from the screen. *Component 1.*

"When you called me on Friday, you didn't mention the news being on."

"You're right! It wasn't."

"Bring me that stepstool, Rue."

I climbed up and looked around on the shelf. Next to the DVD player was a dusty pile of old westerns. I pressed "Open" on the player. The drive slid out, empty. "There's nothing in here now. But someone was watching a DVD. Did the police ask you about this?"

She shook her head. "You think it was that movie you found in her truck?"

"Why move it to the truck?"

"No clue."

"I think it must have been a different one. Since Hazzard was dead, she couldn't have removed it."

LaRue said, "Then, the murderer must have."

I lifted my eyebrows and smiled. "Stupid murderer forgot to change the input setting back to *Cable*."

CHAPTER TWENTY-FOUR

Inez had updated the vomit-colored counter with new signs. One had the word WHINING in a red circle with a line through it. Next to it was a small plaque printed in elegant script.

SUPPOSE WE REFUND YOUR MONEY, SEND YOU ANOTHER ONE FOR FREE, CLOSE THE STORE, AND HAVE THE MANAGER SHOT. WOULD THAT BE SATISFACTORY?

A small oval sign near the billing area said:

IF YOU STARE AT ME ANY LONGER I'LL HAVE TO CHARGE YOU.

Behind the big beaver-gnawed desk sat Henry Greenberg, Able's owner, who was punching the keys of a huge calculator at lightning speed. His bald head shone under the fluorescent light. He didn't look up.

"Hon, how's your head?" Inez rushed out from behind the counter.

I deposited my rubber banded job in the bin. "Much better, thanks."

"My father used to say, '*A mentsch tracht und Gott lacht,*' " Inez said. "A person plans and God laughs. You gotta watch your step, hon. Don't forget, there's a killer on the loose." She pulled me to the end of the counter, away from Henry. "I gotta tell you something. The word around town is that Jenn broke up your relationship with Sam."

"Where'd you hear that?"

"The frozen food aisle at Waldbaum's."

I glanced at Henry. "Inez, if the guy who asked for Patty comes through, we'll have all the answers by the end of the day."

Inez waved her hand. *"Az di bobe volt gehat beytsim volt zi geven mayn zeyde."*

"What does that mean?"

"If my grandmother had balls, she'd be my grandfather," said Henry.

Chapter Twenty-Five

"Don't look now," LaRue said, "but Sam just walked in."

We were standing in line in the sanctuary of McKenzie's Funeral Home, elevator music wafting over us as we waited to pay our respects. Hazzard's mother sat in a folding chair near her daughter's casket, clasping a sunflower. Ronk was still driving around, looking for parking.

Tony was notably MIA.

"Breathe," LaRue said.

"Is he coming over?"

"He's signing the register."

"How does he look?"

"He looks like Sam. Swee'pea, relax. You knew you were going to run into him sooner or later. Hey, I got an idea. Let's sit in different places for the service."

"Why?"

"Surveillance. We can text each other if anything happens. I'll sit by Brenda, in the back. You?"

I scanned the rows. Most of the seats were taken. "There's a seat next to Theodora. But I'm turning my cell phone off."

"Okay. We can use hand signals."

"Hand signals?"

"If I pull on my right ear, it means someone's coming into the room. If I pull on my left ear, someone's leaving. If I cough, someone is watching you. If I blow my nose, look out, police. If I take out a cigarette—"

"LaRue, I'm not going to remember all this."

"Write it on your arm. If I take out a cigarette, meet me in the lobby, *right now*. If I hold up my cell phone, get the hell out of here."

"Hang on, I'm looking for a pen. I thought you quit smoking."

"I did. You got one?"

I pushed up my sleeve. "Yes. 'Right ear'—damn, it's not working."

"Here, use my Sharpie. Right ear, someone's coming. Left, someone's going. Cough, someone's watching. Blow nose—"

"Hold on. Cough—"

"Police. Cigarette, lobby. Cell phone—"

"Got it." I put the cap back on.

"Good. Here he comes. Act natural."

LaRue blended into the group talking to Hazzard's family.

"Hello, Emma," Sam said behind me.

I pulled down my sleeve and turned around. For a long moment we looked into each other's eyes. His looked sad, but it could have been the light. He needed a haircut—his brown curls were getting that commas-gone-haywire look I used to tease him about.

"Hello, Sam."

"How are you? How's business?"

My smile felt tight. "Business is fine. I just finished reading a book proposal for someone in Psych on the correlation between shoplifting and birth order."

"Spankowitz? He's somewhat of a nut case, but brilliant." Sam stuffed his hands in the pockets of his tweed jacket. "Did you enjoy it?"

"It was okay. How go things in Elizabethan literature?"

"Not too—badly." He stopped himself from saying "bardly," an old joke between us. "One young fellow—we were having a discussion in class about whether or not the man from Stratford wrote the plays, and he came out with the *most* amazing insight. He theorized that the plays were written after Shakespeare's death by a royal committee and compiled into the First Folio. He will go far, that young man, very far. Yes. And I'm teaching a seminar on lost words of the English language. It's been a lark." Sam folded his arms across his chest. "Well. Here I am blathering away about the university, and we've got *this* mess."

"Did you get my phone messages?"

"Messages? Oh, you mean—yes. Yes, I did." His gaze shifted. "I meant to call you back, Emma. But you know how it is. There's so much paperwork at the start of the semester."

Sam made an awkward little bow and backed away. I looked down at Hazzard's mother, who returned my gaze with eyes that held all the sadness in the world. I touched her shoulder.

"I'm so sorry."

She picked up the stem and held it to her breast. "Jenny was my sunflower. Why would someone want to hurt her?"

The funeral home had surrounded Hazzard's head with flowers to conceal both the injury and the medical examiner's work. She looked peaceful in her casket. A peaceful blackmailer. I looked down at her for a long moment, but she gave nothing away.

I slipped into the seat next to Theodora. We nodded hello.

"Some crowd," I observed.

"It's the drama." Theo rubbed her pendant with bony fingers. "It brings them in."

I looked around to see who was sitting where. In the back row LaRue and Ronk were head to head in conversation. A few rows ahead of them sat Inez in a slim black dress with pink roses. She was waving and chattering and powdering her nose in a tiny gold compact. Egon sat with Pearl Battley near the front. Sam sat across the room next to Rita, who was dabbing at her eyes.

Mae Wah from the China Kitchen sat in front of me. Seeing her made me remember my birthday present. One more day.

Theo prodded me with a finger. "What do you think of the sprays?"

"The what?"

"The flowers around the casket. I did all the arrangements. Roses, pink poms, snapdragons, and heather."

"Nice. How's it going with the new boss?"

Theo snorted. "I've been working for Egon for twenty years. We have a system that works just fine. Nothing's going to change that."

"Does Tony want to change things?"

"What do you think? I told him the first day, you stay out of my flowers, and I'll stay out of your ledgers. He got the message. Egon's not retiring yet, anyway." Theo looked at me as though I were a piece of moldy cheese. "I saw you talking to your ex," she added. Despite the offhand tone, I detected a low-wattage light in her eye. "Any chance of a reconciliation?"

I was saved from having to answer by the appearance at the podium of a minister who began extolling the virtues and pure heart of Jennifer Hazzard, whom he had never met. I scanned the room. LaRue wore a sad little smile while Ronk leaned back with her eyes closed. Inez sat up straight like a Doberman Pinscher. Sam looked down at his lap, and Rita was still dabbing at her eyes.

The minister announced that Jennifer's friends and associates might come up and say a few words. A woman with a curly perm got up and gave a blow-by-blow description of how Hazzard had helped carry their bowling team, the Gutter Gals, to victory this past season. I wondered if bowling had brought Hazzard and Bellarosa together.

Rita was next. "I thought that Muffin was all the dog I'd ever need. Since—this happened, Jennifer's dog, Bruce, has been staying with us, and he is just the *sweetest*—"

I heard a cough and turned around. LaRue was pulling on her right earlobe. I consulted my wrist. Someone coming in. Okay. I looked at the door. No one coming in. LaRue pulled her right earlobe again.

"What's the matter?" Theo whispered.

I looked at LaRue. At my wrist. I frowned at LaRue. The woman sitting behind me frowned at *me*. I faced front.

"Are you two talking in code again? What's that stuff all over your arm?"

I wanted to smack her. "Nothing," I said, pulling down my sleeve.

Sam stood at the podium and cleared his throat. I caught the scent of mountain air aftershave and made an involuntary peep as Tony sat down in the row in front of me next to Mae Wah. He glanced back. In two seconds my hands were clammy and my heart was thumping like popcorn in the microwave. Holy moly. I fixed my eyes on Sam as if he were the most fascinating person in the world.

But for some reason I couldn't hear a word Sam was saying. There was some kind of disconnect in my brain, a voltage overload that had zapped my sense of hearing. I could see his mouth moving as he rocked back and forth, hands in his pockets, formulating some long sentence that I was sure was grammatically correct.

Sam looked in my direction and his eyes rested briefly on Tony, then on me. There was a momentary blip in the rocking motion before he continued with whatever it was he was saying.

Tony's head was bent over. Then he turned and handed me a piece of paper on which he'd drawn a sad-faced flat tire and the words LOW WITHOUT YOU. I stuffed the paper in my bag and ignored his gaze. When the service ended I'd exit the end of the row toward the wall and lose him in the crowd.

The minister was back at the podium, wrapping up. I made my move as soon as it was prudent.

Tony met me in the aisle and grabbed my arm. "Don't run off. Please." His hair was mussed, although it wasn't windy out. After letting his eyes probe mine briefly I managed to break the connection.

"I waited for you over an hour."

"I feel terrible, Emma. I assumed there'd be a jack in the van and I could put on the spare. It was hell getting a tow truck."

"Why didn't you call me?" We moved aside to let people by. Everyone headed for the exit, except us.

"I was stuck half a mile from the exit ramp. There are no phones on the parkway."

"Haven't you heard of cell phones? They're all the rage."

He nodded, averting his eyes. "I'd been using mine all day long. It was out of juice."

"Your phone was *dead*? You had a flat tire *and* a dead phone?" My voice shook. "That's the lamest excuse I ever heard for breaking a date."

"You're absolutely right."

"It's unacceptable."

"I know."

"Stop agreeing with me."

The sanctuary was empty except for the two of us and the funeral director, who stood by the exit, nodding encouragingly, his hands clasped. He probably needed the room for the next group. Tony said, "At least let me make it up to you."

"How?"

"Let me come over tonight and make you dinner. You don't have to do a thing but sit back and relax. I'll bring everything with me, from soup to nuts. How does that sound?" He lifted

174

his eyebrows.

The last time I'd had a man in my apartment, not counting Zahn, was Sam, on a Sunday morning in May shortly before we broke up. We'd pretty much stopped making love by then. I had a lingering image of Sam sitting at my kitchen table with *The New York Times,* a cup of black coffee in his hand and a scowl on his face.

"What do you say—sixish?" he asked.

I tried to picture Tony bonking Hazzard over the head. No way. My heart wasn't buying it.

"Okay," I said at last. "You're on."

The fresh air was invigorating after the cloying scent of the funeral home. Tony disappeared into a knot of people in the parking lot, and I inhaled deeply. LaRue and Ronk were waiting across the street in the Lexus. I started to cross, then spotted the rear end of a familiar car parked a block away. I signaled to Ronk to wait and jogged over to it.

The passenger window slid open as I approached.

"Hello, Detectives," I said.

CHAPTER TWENTY-SIX

Bonomo, in reflective sunglasses, tilted his head up.

"How's the head?"

"Still attached." I peered in at Zahn, who was quickly folding up what looked like a floor plan. "Did you get my message?"

Zahn didn't look at me. He put the folded paper in his pocket. His mouth was tight. "You have your car?"

"No. My friends drove me."

"We want to talk to you, but not here."

"We're about to go grab some lunch," Bonomo said. "How about joining us?"

"All right, but I have to tell my friends."

"Climb in first."

The back seat was full of cardboard boxes and crap.

"Just shove them over," Bonomo said.

I texted LaRue.

Something I have to take care of. Don't wait.

A few seconds later came her reply.

10-4 good buddy.

"Okey-doke," I said. Zahn pulled out and headed west on Main Street, toward Stony Brook. I watched the scenery roll by and thought about Sam. I was thinking particularly about his reaction to Tony in the funeral home. That blip of hesitation. It pleased me, it did.

We pulled into a sports bar called The Bench, north of the university. "Big Big Man" by the Beat Farmers was playing on the sound system. Zahn asked for a table in the corner. I pretended to study the menu while I watched the detectives. Bonomo frowned in concentration. He looked like he was either choosing boxes for a football pool or wasn't ready to admit he needed reading glasses. Zahn gave the menu a cursory glance, folded it, and looked everywhere but at me.

"How's the steak?" Bonomo asked.

"Good," Zahn said.

"What do you suggest, Emma? Have you eaten here before?"

"A few times. I've only ever gotten the chicken fingers. They're good."

Bonomo nodded and shut the menu. A perky waiter came by to take our order. He chitchatted with us about how well the Stony Brook Seawolves were doing. I noticed that Zahn wasn't joining in. He sat there tapping his fingertips together.

When the waiter left, I said to Zahn, "Did you talk to Bellarosa? Did the clothing belong to Hazzard?"

Zahn trained his X-ray eyes on me. "Did I talk to Bellarosa? You want to know if I talked to Bellarosa?"

"Well, yes—"

"Is that what you're asking?" Two bright red spots appeared in his cheeks.

"What he means," Bonomo broke in, "is that we routinely follow up on all leads. We can't discuss them with you, though. It would compromise the case. You understand."

I nodded. "I actually wanted to ask you—both of you—about the DVD that was in my trunk, whether it was what it said it was. Because those labels can be changed. It would just take some warm—"

"Why do you want to know that?" Zahn snapped.

"Because the TV at the Sunny Side is set to play DVDs."

The tension in the air was thick enough to slice.

"The TV at the Sunny Side," Zahn repeated in a clipped voice.

"Uh-huh. The one in the kitchen."

"And when did you notice that?"

"This morning."

Zahn looked like he was ready to spit bullets. "This morning, she says. Now, how many days has it been since Friday—four? How many people have been in and out of there since then? Can you tell me that?"

"Pete," Bonomo said.

"I don't know. No one's touched it, though."

"How do you know that?"

"Because no one watches that TV, except Hazzard. Watched."

Zahn smacked the table with the flat of his hand. "What do you think this is, Trace? Are we collaborating here? Are we playing junior detective? Little Miss Amateur Investigator is here to help the big boys solve the case, is that it?"

"No, I'm just trying to—"

"I know what you're trying to do." Zahn grabbed the edge of the table with both hands and leaned forward. His blue eyes bored into mine. "You Traces are all alike. You're all goddamn experts at sticking your noses where they don't belong. Every single one of you."

I sat back, stunned. The waiter with his tray of drinks froze three feet from our table. Bonomo waved him over and he silently placed glasses in front of us. Bonomo reached out and switched his iced tea, which was in front of me, with my Coke.

"You know, Detective, I'm only trying to follow your instructions. You told me to let you know if I found out anything. Well, I found out a few things."

"I told you to let me know if Bisbee called you."

"You also said you wanted the truth. The whole truth. Not just the parts I thought were important."

I bit my lip. Maybe I'd gone too far.

Bonomo cleared his throat. "I don't know about you two, but I'm hungry. I had a bowl about this big of corn flakes this morning. I wanted eggs, but my kid cleaned them out. Now that he's on the track team, he makes omelets on practice days."

Ominous silence.

"I didn't call Bisbee."

"Damn right," Zahn said.

"I've been flat on my back for two days."

"And how's *that* slowed you down?"

"Will you two cut it out?" Bonomo said. "This isn't getting us anywhere."

"Fine," I said. "You're right, Detective. This is your case, you're running the show. I'm out of here." I stood up. Our waiter emerged from the kitchen with our food and stopped in mid-stride. The people at the next table stopped talking and looked at us.

"Sit down," Zahn ordered. "We're not finished."

"I don't have to put up with this—this lack of respect."

"You're going to hear me out, Trace. After that, if you want to leave, you can leave."

I focused on the door ten feet away and willed my feet to move. Then I looked at Bonomo. He nodded slightly toward the seat.

I sat. The waiter delivered our meals.

"Now," Zahn said, "let's straighten out a few things. I do want the truth. All of it. That doesn't change the rules I play by. And it certainly doesn't change the rules *you* have to play by if you're playing my game."

I felt a little thrill of inclusion, but said nothing.

"Number one. I'm in charge of this case. Not you, not him, not anyone but me. I make the decisions. I ask the questions. Understand?"

I nodded.

"Number two. We're dealing with a complex legal system here. There are rules. What we can submit as evidence depends entirely on whether we've obtained it lawfully. If we don't have a court order signed by a judge entitling us to search and seize property, and we don't have reasonable cause to suspect someone, we can't just haul off and take whatever we want and expect to use it later."

"Does that include books that fall out of the cabinet onto my head?"

"It includes everything. And you should have called us as soon as that happened."

We ate for a few minutes in silence. I knew I should tell Zahn about the bags Tony had brought to the nursing home, but I couldn't. I had to be sure about Tony first. Maybe there was another explanation for what he did.

"And another thing," Zahn said. "You just suffered a violent attack. You could have been killed. Do you have any idea of the danger you're putting yourself in? You're not trained to defend yourself against what we know to be a vicious killer with no conscience."

I swirled a chicken finger in the hot sauce. "It would look bad for you if I got killed, wouldn't it."

"It would be worse for you."

"Consider, too," Bonomo said, "that if the killer gets wind we're onto him, he might get spooked. He could make a move that spoils the case."

"Like move the evidence."

"Or kill someone else."

Zahn put his fork and knife across his plate and tossed his

used napkin on top. He pulled out his Blackberry and looked at it. "Tell me about the call from Bisbee."

"I didn't talk to him. He left a message at my office. Inez gave it to me."

"Inez Lipchitz?" Zahn looked at Bonomo. "Crap. This is exactly what I'm talking about. What does Inez know about it?"

"Nothing," I said. "I just told her, if a guy calls for 'Patty,' it's for me."

"Who's Patty?"

"No one. It's a made-up name."

"Did he leave his number?"

"Yes."

Zahn drummed his fingers on the table.

Bonomo said, "Pete. Are you going to ask her, or am I?"

Zahn's eyes locked with mine. The tug-of-war going on behind them was almost palpable. At last he spoke.

"Trace, there's something we want you to do for us. We need your help, and you need our protection to do it. Neither of us can do it alone."

"What do you need me to do?" I asked.

CHAPTER TWENTY-SEVEN

The phone rang twice before he picked up.

"I see what's going on," the Lizard said in his raspy voice.

"Is that you, Bisbee?"

"Huh? Who's this?"

"It's me, Patty, calling you back, Biz." I looked out the Taurus's rear window at Zahn and Bonomo standing outside the 7-Eleven. Bonomo was eating an ice cream cone.

"Patty." The Lizard horked a few times. "I thought you was someone else. What took you so long?"

"I got tied up. What's up? They hiring at the hardware store?"

"What? Oh, yeah. They hiring."

"Well, good. I'm almost outta beans." I leaned on a cardboard box. "So let's get together and talk."

"You kiddin'? We're settin' up the drop right now."

"I got to see proof, Biz. Insurance. You show me the book or whatever you got, we talk, then I take the job."

"That's bullshit," the Lizard said. "I don't do bullshit."

"Well, I do. It's my life, and I'm not ready to stop living it. What phone are you using, anyway? How do I know this isn't your personal phone?"

"It's a throwaway. You think I'm stupid?"

A device in the front seat of the Taurus beeped.

"What was that?" Bisbee said. "Where are you?"

"Home. That was my microwave. Can you meet me at four?"

"Yeah. Uh, no, I got another appointment. Five."

That was cutting it close. "I have plans. Four-thirty."

He paused to let his pea brain process that. "Okay."

"Where?"

A flick of a match and more horking. "You know the E-Z Self Storage on Patchogue Road?"

"Yeah."

"Go there. Meet me at building 'M.' The one with the elevator."

"Do I need a code to get in?"

"I got a code. My friend works there. Good place to do business, you know? Safe and secure." He gave me the code and chuckled. It sounded like an oven rack sliding out.

"Don't forget," I said. "Bring proof. No proofy, no dealy."

When the detectives got back in the car, I handed Bonomo his phone and repeated the conversation.

"Okay," Zahn said. "Now, listen carefully."

CHAPTER TWENTY-EIGHT

I punched the code into the keypad and waited while the metal gate rolled slowly to the side. Then I eased the Cutlass Supreme through the opening. Once inside, I stopped again to get my bearings while the gate rolled shut behind me.

The E-Z Self Storage Center consisted of a series of long, low, windowless buildings with garage-type rolling doors, each building casting an identical stripe of shadow in the late afternoon sun. A large black "A" had been painted on the nearest building. Beyond a series of flat rooftops I could make out the second floor of a two-story structure—the only one like it in the facility. That had to be "M."

I pushed the button on the remote Zahn had given me and shoved the device under my seat. Slowly I guided the Cutlass along the narrow road past buildings "A," "B," and "C," sitting forward a little to keep the transmitter from digging into my back. My heart was thrumming so loudly that I could hear nothing else, and the metal steering wheel was coated in sweat.

The police were here, somewhere, watching me. All I had to do was talk to the Lizard, get him to show me the blackmail book, and they'd move in and take over. Easy peasy, right?

Out of the corner of my eye I saw a pickup truck loaded with mattresses in the row between "G" and "H." A man stood in the truck bed, digging through boxes. I drove past at a steady five miles per hour. People were putting their deck furniture in storage for the winter, or taking snow blowers out. Zahn had given me explicit instructions not to slow down or look around me. I was to head straight to my destination.

It had taken a half hour to outfit me at police headquarters. The same pregnant desk sergeant who'd greeted me last time, Sergeant Morales, led me to a small office where a cream-colored denim shirt hung on a plastic hanger. A cable, two small electronic devices, and a large square adhesive bandage were arranged on the table. Morales locked the door and I took off my shirt.

"This is your transmitter," she said, plugging one end of the cable into one of the devices. "It will allow the detectives to see and hear everything that is happening." She opened the bandage and taped the device to the small of my back, pressing the bandage around the edges to make sure it stuck. I put on the shirt and started buttoning it. She put out a hand to stop me.

"The middle button is your camera." Morales guided it through the buttonhole. She reached behind her for a lens cloth and lightly wiped the button's surface. "It's also a microphone. Don't touch it or hold anything in front of it. Face your target when you speak, and try not to move too much. But don't freeze up, either. You want to look natural."

"How do I turn it on?"

"You don't. It's already on. What you're going to turn on is the transmitter." She handed me the second, smaller device. "Here's your remote. When you reach the site, push the button once. Then hide the device either in your glove compartment or under the seat. I'm sure Detective Zahn will tell you what he wants you to do with it."

I smiled now at her unintended humor and made a right turn into the row next to "M." No vehicles were parked there. The Lizard must have left his car somewhere else and walked. I drove maybe fifty feet, shut down the engine, and got out.

The absence of rolling doors in the first floor told me that all of the units were accessed internally. In the center of the wall was a lift and a steel door that probably led to a stairway. I did a casual three-sixty, as instructed by Zahn, and strolled over to the door. Still acting casual, I opened it.

The stairwell was dank and smelled of mothballs, pee, and old bicycle chains. It was also dark. I found a light switch timer on the left-hand wall and gave it a crank. The stairs blossomed into gummy, yellow-stained unloveliness.

"Bisbee?" My voice echoed. "Are you up there?"

I climbed the stairs slowly, stopping halfway to call his name again and to wipe my sweaty palms on my pants.

It was dark at the top, so I hit another light switch timer and found myself in a long hallway full of doors. Five-by-fives. On the other side of the stairs was another hallway just like it. There was no activity in either direction.

"Hey, Bisbee, where are you, man?"

Maybe I'd arrived first and he was outside now, waiting. I trotted downstairs again, but all I saw was the comforting sight of Mrs. Porter's Cutlass. I had a compelling urge to get in and drive away. To call out to Zahn, "Get me out of here, I've had enough of this game."

But it wasn't a game, and if I left I might screw up an entire police investigation.

As I turned back grimly, something on the cement curb outside the lift caught my eye. Three small brown spots, like the three stars of Orion's Belt. I squatted down for a better look. Then I unbolted the lift door and rolled up the corrugated inner grate.

There were only some cables inside, so the lift must have been left upstairs. I ran upstairs and tugged vainly on the door. Then I remembered that both doors had to be fully closed for these lifts to operate. I cursed myself for being an idiot, ran downstairs, closed the grate and the door, and ran back up. I yanked the lift door open.

At first all I saw was a wooden dolly shoved into the corner.

Then I saw two worn snakeskin boots sticking out from behind the dolly.

The third thing I saw was a river of blood flowing out from under the dolly toward the cement floor where I stood.

I opened my mouth to scream. Nothing came out. I stood there, no air coming in, no air going out, until loud footsteps pounded up the stairs.

"Stand back!" Zahn ordered. "Don't touch anything!"

He grabbed my shoulder and pulled me back roughly. His gun was drawn. Bonomo and another man and woman dressed in street clothes ran up right behind him. The man shone a powerful flashlight over my face, over the mess in the lift. I whirled away from the brightness and felt strong arms grab me and pull me in. Then I sobbed and sobbed, deeply, into Bonomo's sweater, while he held me.

CHAPTER TWENTY-NINE

It was six-thirty before Zahn was finished with me. Bonomo delivered me back to headquarters for a clothing and equipment exchange and dropped me off at home.

I'd spent an hour and a half sitting in the Cutlass while the photographer and other technicians went back and forth from the crime scene van to "M" with evidence-gathering paraphernalia and Zahn paced in front of the building, talking into his cell phone. The whole building and the roadway around it had been sealed with yellow tape. The Cutlass and I were inside the tape, so I couldn't leave until Zahn said I could.

"When you spoke to Bisbee did he indicate he was meeting someone earlier?" Zahn asked me through the car window.

I nodded. "At four o'clock. He didn't say who."

"How about this blackmail book? Do you know what it looks like?"

"No. I've never seen it. Why, is it gone?"

Zahn straightened and spoke into his phone.

I leaned out the window. "Try his boots."

"Hold on, Gus." Zahn dropped the phone by his side. "What?"

"He keeps his knife in his boot. Maybe the notebook, too."

"He should have taken that knife out of his boot today," Zahn allowed.

★ ★ ★ ★ ★

Tony's silver Nissan was parked in front of my building when I got there. At least he'd stuck around after getting my message. I caught my reflection in the driver's side window as I walked by—what a mess.

Mrs. Porter answered my knock cheerfully. "Come on in, Emma. I've been talking to your nice young man." Her grin faded. "What's wrong, dear? Did something happen to the car?"

I shook my head. "You'll have it back tonight, Mrs. P. The police brought me home."

Tony's face appeared over her shoulder. "The police?"

I sat down heavily in a chair by the door and traced its carved finials with my fingers. My eyes flitted to the television set, which was tuned to *Jeopardy!* without the sound. The room smelled like soup again. Through the kitchen doorway I saw a table with two teacups and plates and a partially eaten cake between them.

"When did you get here?" I asked Tony.

"About an hour ago. Before you called. Mrs. Porter has been nice enough to let me keep my ice cream in her freezer." He stepped around Mrs. Porter and touched my arm. "What happened?"

"There's been another murder."

Mrs. Porter covered her mouth with her hand.

"Oh, no," Tony said. "Who?"

I looked at him. "A sleazoid named Clifford Bisbee. Ever hear of him?"

"No. Should I have?"

I shrugged. "He's got a record. The police think he has something to do with Hazzard."

"Did he kill her?"

"I don't think so."

The kitchen looked cozy. There were several lamps scattered

about the living room, but it was still too dark in here. Too many shadows.

"Would you like a cup of tea, dear?" Mrs. Porter asked. I nodded, and she padded off in her scuffs.

"Thank God you're all right." Tony squatted down in front of me. "Where did it happen? Although I guess more to the point would be, what were you doing there?"

"I'll tell you later."

"Let's see what the television has to say." Mrs. Porter handed me a teacup. She switched to the local news channel and turned up the sound. The stabbing at the E-Z Self Storage Center was breaking news. The camera panned the wall of building "M" and landed on Mrs. Porter's incandescent Cutlass.

"There's my car!" She turned around brightly. "My car's on TV!"

So much for using the Cutlass for my undercover work.

"Before you got here," Mrs. Porter went on, "we were talking about the murder. The first one, I mean. I was just telling Tony my theory."

"You have a theory, Mrs. P.?"

Her eyes twinkled. "Remember the story about the woman who killed her husband with the frozen leg of lamb? She roasted it and served it to the policemen who questioned her. And while they ate it, they said, why, the murder weapon is probably right here, under our noses! I think that's what happened in this case. The killer hit Jennifer Hazzard with a frozen chicken and *ate* the murder weapon."

CHAPTER THIRTY

Bergamot was sitting on a kitchen stool watching Tony cut up onions when I got out of the shower. Vegetables from two cotton canvas grocery bags were spread out on the counter, along with a bottle of Chardonnay and two wine glasses I didn't recognize. Booker T. & the M.G.s was playing on the boom box.

"I was going to make veal medallions with wild mushrooms in red wine," Tony said, wiping his hands in a towel, "but after the day you've had, I thought you might want some comfort food. So I ran out and got some pork chops while you were in the shower."

He'd even brought along his own corkscrew, a cute, three-piece gadget with which he now extracted the cork in about two seconds.

"What's that?" I pointed to a pot that was plugged into the wall. I wore a long-sleeved jersey to cover up the leftover Sharpie that I couldn't get off with toothpaste.

"A rice cooker. I'm going to throw in brown rice, the pork chops, onions, carrots, a few seasonings, and some broth, and let it cook itself." He steered me to a chair. "Sound good?"

"Very."

"We'll have the veal another time."

He handed me a glass of wine and went back to chopping. I was quiet for a minute, sipping, my fuzzy slippers perched on the rung of the chair. It was weird having him in my kitchen, chopping in rhythm to the music. But a good weird. The terrible sight of the Lizard's boots began to recede.

"You don't have to talk about it," Tony said, reading my mind. "Just relax."

"I can't talk about it, anyway."

"Are you on some kind of secret mission?"

"Sort of."

"Can I at least see your secret decoder ring?"

I laughed. "If you can find it."

Tony laughed, too. I liked the way he laughed. He pushed vegetables off the cutting board into the rice cooker, placed the chops on top, and added herbs and seasonings with abandon.

"You need a good pepper mill," he observed.

"I don't cook much. I'm more of a microwave kind of gal."

"Still, there's nothing like fresh pepper."

Bergamot jumped down from the stool and rubbed against Tony's legs. Then he leaped up to the counter and from there to the top of the fridge, where he crouched like a vulture, his eyes fixed on the rice cooker.

Tony turned on the cooker and swept the peelings into the garbage before sitting down.

"You owned your own restaurant, didn't you?" I said. "I can tell."

"Half owned it." He twirled the base of his wine glass. "Luce. In Garden City. Have you heard of it?"

"No. I live a sheltered existence, food-wise."

"Well, according to Zagat, it's got a rating of twenty-six."

"Is it still there?"

"Oh, yeah. Took eight years to build up that business to where it is today—a dinner destination for the very rich."

"So how come you left?"

Tony got up and brought back two napkins. He folded them into neat triangles and put one beside my plate. "Well, the short version is that I was ready for a change. I was in a rut, both personally and professionally. I was working at Luce seven days a week, tired all the time, not seeing my kids."

"Oh, you have kids?" Now it was my turn to swirl my wine.

"A boy and a girl, eight and ten." He rubbed his beard. "Don't get the wrong idea, Emma. My marriage is over. We're separated."

"Ah. Your kids are with her?"

"Most of the time."

"Ah," I said again, nodding. *Crap. Crap crap crap.*

"How about you? Do you have kids?"

"Me? No. Uh-uh."

"Ever been married?"

"No."

"Why not?"

I took a sip of wine. "Not in the stars, I guess."

He pulled a slim wallet out of his back pocket, unfolded it, and handed it to me. It was a photo holder with snapshots of his son and daughter at the beach. The children looked bright and happy.

"Those were taken a year and a half ago. They look older now."

"What are their names?"

"Angela and Zach."

"They look just like you."

He smiled and replaced the photo wallet in his back pocket.

"That sometimes changes as they get older."

We sipped our wine and listened to the steam puff through the vent in the rice cooker. There was a lot I didn't know about Tony. A lot I wasn't sure I *wanted* to know.

"Running a business is hard enough even without working seven days," I said finally. "Couldn't your partner relieve you on some of those weekends?"

Tony gave a short burst of laughter. "Now, there's an idea.

No, he was too busy. But this will be different." He poured more wine in my glass. "I have a good feeling about this move, Emma. I like Egon and I like how he runs his business."

"Egon's a good guy," I agreed. "He's been friends with our family for years."

"Really? I'm glad to hear that." A dimple showed in his left cheek when he smiled. "You've had a terrible day, Emma. I know how upset you must be. And yet, I can't help but feel really happy to be here—just to be near you. Is that strange?"

"I don't think so."

He touched the back of my hand with his finger. A current passed through me. "Are you okay with this?"

I blinked. "There's so much weird shit happening, Tony. I'm—I'm a little mixed up right now."

"Weird shit happening to me, too."

Tony enclosed my hand in his and pulled me to my feet. He gathered me close and kissed me, his lips soft and warm. I cupped my hand behind his head and kissed him back.

The rice cooker was bubbling merrily when I led him into the bedroom and let him undress me, and the day that had gone to hell turned around then. I knew it wouldn't take much before I wanted him inside me. I enveloped him and held him tight while the afternoon's horror fled through the blinds, through the crack between the windowpanes, into the whistling wind and the night sky. He smelled delicious. I was with him, and safe.

When it was over I held and squeezed him inside me, encouraging him for later. That made him smile. We lay that way for a while, not talking. I rubbed his back lightly, wondering if for Tony, too, it was more about the intimacy than the physical release.

We went out to the kitchen and ate supper sitting close together and finished the bottle of wine. Then we made love again, more slowly this time. I loved the way he held my hands against the pillow over my head. I hadn't turned on any lights in the apartment other than in the kitchen, so the house seemed vast and dark and unknown, with only the sound of my grandmother's clock ticking in the living room and an occasional car to interrupt the stillness.

I must have dozed off, for when I opened my eyes it was twelve-o-three. Tony squeezed my shoulder to let me know he was awake, too.

"You know what?" I said. "It's my birthday."

"It is? Then I'll be the first to say happy birthday. How many kisses?"

"Thirty-five." He leaned over to plant them in various spots. I picked his head up. "Will you stay with me tonight?"

"You couldn't get me to leave."

Later I got up to go to the bathroom. When I'd crawled back in bed, Tony said, "You've lived in Port Jeff a long time. Can I ask you something?"

"Sure."

"What do you know about Theodora?"

The question surprised me. "Theo? We're not exactly buds. Why do you ask?"

"Last week, Egon held a staff meeting announcing that I was coming on board, and I said a few words. I expected some wariness. That's normal. It takes people a while to develop trust. I got a warm welcome from everyone except Theo, who was actually hostile. I can't seem to get a handle on it."

I nodded. "Don't take it personally. Theo's always been an odd duck. Suspicious of people, you know? We went to high school together. Graduated the same year, in fact."

"Is that so?"

"Yes." I thought back. "I know her mother died when she was very young, and she was raised by her dad and grandmother.

195

The grandmother—Theo's mother's mother—was a Silk. She could trace the family ancestry back to when the town was still called Drowned Meadow. I don't know if she's alive anymore. She'd be in her nineties."

"Oh, she's still kicking. She's in the nursing home on Nesconset Highway."

"Distant Shores?" I paused a minute, thinking. "I didn't know that. Anyway, Theo's dad showed up at school plays and concerts, that sort of thing. Strange guy who didn't mix with people, sat alone in the back of the auditorium. When we had the fifth grade trip to the Museum of Natural History in New York City, he stayed in the parking lot the whole time, smoking. He moved away in high school. Theo stayed here with her grandmother." I put my arm across his chest. "I don't know much else. She didn't have close friends. Kids shunned her because she was just too strange."

"Kids can be mean."

"True. One year my mother felt sorry for her and made me invite her to my bowling party. I was eleven. Theo didn't even bowl. She just hung around the edges the whole time. I was so angry at my mother, I didn't talk to her for two days."

Tony rolled onto his back and looked at the ceiling. "Well, this helps. It helps a lot. Thanks."

"You're welcome. Now I have a question for you."

"Shoot."

I steeled myself. "Do you remember bringing some bags of craft supplies to Distant Shores on Friday?"

"Sure."

"Any reason why? LaRue usually takes them over there once a month."

"I know all about that, believe me. When Egon gave me the grand tour, he specifically told me not to touch LaRue's craft bags."

"Then, why *did* you?"

"Because Theo asked me to."

A jolt went through me. "Theo did?"

"Yes. Apparently the nursing home called and told her they were running low."

Evidence Locker
Box 15
Personal diary, page 82

Dear Diary,

They read Robert Frost's poem, "Birches," in English today. There are so many good parts but here's a part I like. "I'd like to get away from earth awhile and then come back to it and begin over."

Also this part—"You may see their trunks arching in the woods years afterwards, trailing their leaves on the ground like girls on hands and knees." I like that. I never knew poems could be like that.

I miss being in class and hearing what the teacher says. But Grandma gets me the homework. She tells them she is mailing it to me. Today she got me Robert Frost from the library. I tore the plastic cover off—I'm keeping the book! Ha-ha.

He stays away from me now. Grandma and I don't know what we will do when it is born but for now I am writing my name in the birch trees at night.

CHAPTER THIRTY-ONE

Wednesday

"Whadda we got here?" LaRue asked, setting down her coffeepot.

Outside Sunny Side's window civil twilight embraced the shops on Main Street. I'd been up for hours already, working out my plan.

"They brought Sam in for questioning." I turned the screen of my laptop toward her.

LOCAL MAN STABBED TO DEATH
PROF QUESTIONED IN BLACKMAIL SCHEME

"They think he was the blackmailer?" LaRue asked.

"Target."

The article reported Bisbee's murder at the E-Z Storage and described him as an unemployed laborer who lived two blocks from recent murder victim Jennifer Hazzard. Police declined to say whether the crimes were connected, although witnesses had seen Bisbee entering and leaving the Hazzard house. Detectives were looking into his recent activities, which may have included a blackmail operation targeting local residents.

It went on to say that Samuel Benjamin, a Stony Brook English professor and possible blackmail target, had been questioned and released.

LaRue cracked her gum. "And welcome to round seven of 'Who's Got the Blackmail Book?' "

"You believe this about Sam?"

"The guy has secrets, Em."

"He's not a murderer."

"I'm with you on that. What about—?" She jerked her chin in the direction of Hoyt's. I'd told her what Theo had asked Tony to do.

"I want to check that out before I start running off at the mouth again."

She lowered her voice. "Rhode Island's like four hours away by ferry and car. She did a presentation that morning, remember?"

LaRue was right. Theo would have had to drive half the night to get back and kill Hazzard, then drive back to Rhode Island for her presentation. The ferry didn't even run during the night. She would have had to drive around the city.

LaRue looked over at the other booths. "I got to refill my other customers. What do you want for your birthday breakfast?"

I picked up the menu. "How are the pumpkin pancakes?"

"Good. Omigod, the Queen of Fluffernutter's gonna have pumpkin pancakes?"

"I just like how they sound."

"All righty, pumpkin pancakes coming up."

"Wait a sec, LaRue, I changed my mind. I'll have a plain bagel with cream cheese. Lightly toasted. And a large orange juice."

"Ha."

When LaRue was gone, my thoughts returned to Sam. What if the police *did* suspect him? What if he *was* on Jennifer's blackmail list?

Both possibilities were . . . well, possible.

He knew where she worked and the hours she kept. He could

have gotten hold of my library card. And he *could* have kept a copy of his key to my apartment and planted the books there.

With his teaching schedule, he could even have made that phone call.

Hypothetically, from Zahn's vantage point, Sam could have had it in for me for some bizarre reason. But the idea that he'd done any of this was ridiculous. The man was infuriatingly non-confrontational.

I stared out the window, trying to wrap my mind around the idea of Sam being blackmailed.

All of us have secrets. Maybe we got drunk and embarrassed ourselves at a party. Maybe we stole a magazine off the drugstore rack, or forgot to tell the spouse about the dent in the car. But how many of us made a mistake so enormous, so repugnant, so far outside the mores of society that we'd do anything—pay money, even commit murder—to keep it a secret?

Bellarosa certainly had a lot to lose if his wife found out he was sleeping with Hazzard—his home, the respect of his kids, maybe even his business. What did Sam have to lose?

The sun rose and cast a painful glare on the Greenhouse awning. I ate my bagel slowly, watching two seagulls peck at a smashed pumpkin on the sidewalk. The library didn't open for another two and a half hours. My plan was on hold until then.

A woman across the aisle from me was sharing a plate of pumpkin pancakes with her little boy.

"Mommy, can we pick pumpkins today?" he asked, swinging his feet.

"Sure, sweetie pie. After we go see Mrs. Maldonada, we'll take a ride out to the pumpkin farm."

"After we go see Mrs. Mal-Do-Nada?"

"Yes, honey. Eat your breakfast."

The boy picked up his juice. "I'm going to get the biggest,

gigantic-est pumpkin in the whole world! Big enough to sleep in!"

I put down my bagel. Sleep in? Well, how-*dee*. Just like that, I knew where my birthday present was. A slow smile started in the pit of my stomach and worked its way up to my face. I got up, leaving a ten on the table.

It was a glorious day, windy and crisp, as I drove east toward my ground pass. I cranked up the music and sang "Got to Get Better in a Little While" with Clapton at the top of my lungs. Ten minutes later I swung into the gravel lot at Sandy's Farm Stand. Sandy was stocking the display with squash and Briermere pies. Under his engineer's cap I saw a smile of delight.

"My favorite birthday girl's back!"

"You betcha I'm back. Oh, you fellas are clever. Very clever. Almost got me this time."

Sandy tipped his chin up and laughed.

"The only thing I haven't figured out is where the spuds are." I climbed up on the hay bale next to the giant pumpkin. "You don't grow potatoes."

"Ah, but my next-door neighbor does, down the road."

"Close enough." Around the pumpkin stem was a faint circular incision. I wrapped both hands around the stem and tugged. " *'Over the eyes that cannot see.'* That's your neighbor's potatoes." I wiggled off the top and peered inside. " *'Under the ears that cannot hear.'* That's the Indian corn growing out back. Nice, tall, deaf Indian corn. And this"—I pushed up my sleeve, thrust my arm into slimy pumpkin seeds, and pulled out a plastic-wrapped bundle—"is my present. *'In the belly of an eastern icon.'* "

Sandy applauded. "You are one smart cookie, Emma dear. Always have been."

"Is it what I think it is, Sandy? A Bose music system?"

"Open it up."

I did. It was.

"I thought you had it figured out last time you were here," Sandy said. "Good thing I kept my mouth shut. Let me get you a towel."

"And a snap-and-seal bag, if you have one."

CHAPTER THIRTY-TWO

The Blue Sky Diner at Brookhaven Airport was buzzing with activity. Sausages sizzled on the griddle, and the counter stools were taken by an assortment of flyboys and aircraft mechanics.

"Last Sunday," one of the grizzled pilots was saying, "I'm landing at Sky Acres, and I'm on downwind for three-five, and this guy gets on the radio and says he's on the forty-five for a left downwind for *one-seven*."

"Oh, my God," two or three of the others said.

"I'm lookin' and lookin', and I don't see the idiot. Finally—you listenin' to this, Alfie?—I see him way the hell out there, going in the wrong direction. Meanwhile I'm turning base behind a Citabria—"

I signaled to Jane, behind the counter.

"Morning, Emma, what can I get you?"

"Have you seen Ned?"

"Long gone. Did you try the hangar?"

"I'll take a look, thanks."

"I hope you made him pay for your breakfast, Coodie," the guy named Alfie said, and they all laughed.

A young guy wearing amber reflecting sunglasses and a crisp blue shirt held the door open for me. "Want a ride over?"

"You know Ned Trace?"

"Doesn't everyone?" He grinned, pointing to a golf cart parked at the curb. "Hop in."

He took the radio and clipboard from my side of the seat and chucked them in the back tray. We whirred along, sunshine pouring into the open golf cart.

"I have to make a quick stop at the FBO first," he said.

"FBO?"

"Fixed Base Operator. It's also the flight school where I work." He nodded at the building across the parking lot from the diner.

I looked at his shirt pocket. MIKE GREEN, CFI, CFII. HAVEN FLIGHT SCHOOL. "You're an instructor?"

"Yup."

"You're kidding."

"No, why?"

"Because—" *Because you look like you're twelve.* "Because you don't look like an instructor."

"I have almost all my ratings. I'm working on my ATP now."

"What's that?"

"Airline Transport Pilot. I want to work for the airlines." He handed me a business card with his name and a dozen initials after it. "I'll take you over as soon as I turn in the paperwork on my last student. We always have breakfast after his lesson. Interesting guy. Works part-time at the animal shelter."

"Does he want to work for the airlines, too?"

Mike laughed. "No, he's seventy-two."

"You have a seventy-two-year-old student?"

"Sure. Anyone in good health can learn to fly. Take yourself, for example. You could start lessons today and have your private by next summer."

"I don't think so, Mike."

He pulled over to the curb in front of the flight school and jumped out.

"How about a discovery flight? Want me to check my schedule?"

"Mike, I'm sure it's a hell of a lot of fun, but I'll pass."

After he went inside I looked around the cart. There was a radio on the floor like the one Ned had. I clicked it on. A computerized voice talked about wind direction and pressure at sea level. It was strangely comforting to listen to. I clicked it off as Mike hopped back in.

"Now, see, I assumed you were interested in flying, or why would you be hanging out with Ned Trace, the King of Upside Down?"

"He's my uncle." The amber mirrors flashed in my direction as we zipped past a group of hangars. "Ned's my dad's youngest brother," I explained. "We're close in age, but technically I'm his niece."

"Are you the one with the birthday bet?"

"You know about that?"

"They've got a pool going here at the airport. When's the big day?"

"Today."

"Well, happy birthday." Mike stopped short in front of Ned's hangar. "So, am I rich?"

"Depends on how you bet."

"Against you."

"Sorry, Mike." I held up my snap-and-seal bag filled with pumpkin seeds. "This is my ticket *not* to ride."

Ned wasn't around. I got out and told Mike not to wait. When he was gone I wrote on the bag of pumpkin seeds, "See you at La Casa!" and hung it on the hangar door handle where Ned would find it. Then I strolled over to a grassy area where a bunch of planes were parked. They looked very small, very old, and very tired. I pressed my nose against the side window of a high-wing plane and looked inside. It looked a little like the interior of my father's old Ford, but with more dials on the dash. Maps and papers were piled on the passenger seat. A bungee cord was wrapped around a small steering wheel.

I cupped my hands beside my face so I could read a small sign taped to the panel. KEEP LOOKING AROUND, it said. THERE'S ALWAYS SOMETHING YOU'VE MISSED.

CHAPTER THIRTY-THREE

My arms full of yearbooks, I made my way upstairs to the children's section and found a seat near the play area. Behind me two toddlers were building a tower of blocks. Pearl Battley was helping a child at the computer. I cracked open the yearbook for my high school graduating class and flipped to the T's.

Emma Rose Trace. There I was, looking timid and a little defiant, my thick hair gelled into waves that didn't know whether to curve in or out. I turned pages until I found a photo of the only club I'd joined in high school, the independent film club. Four of us had posed next to a *Harold and Maude* poster in the advisor's classroom.

I turned back to the S's and scanned the faces until I found Theodora Silk. Other than the passage of years, she looked pretty much the same back then. Same frizzy bangs, same hangdog expression. She wore an old-fashioned blouse with puffed sleeves, the kind most teenage girls wouldn't be caught dead in, in any decade. I found her again in the community service club, raising a wall for a Habitat for Humanity house, and again in the arts and crafts club standing next to LaRue, a sophomore then with big hair.

I wasn't sure what I was looking for and hoped something would hit me. Maybe this was a complete waste of time. But I had to start somewhere, and that meant going back.

Theo had asked Tony to deliver the bags. That meant I had

to consider the possibility that she was the murderer. And if she was—if she'd been desperate enough to strike twice—what would stop her from doing it again?

I turned to the yearbook from our junior year. Because it was such a small high school, they took individual portraits of all the students, but printed the senior photos larger than the rest. I noticed that Theo's portrait had a paler background than the pictures around it. Flipping through the pages, I found several others with the same pale background. They must have been retakes. Either the students hadn't liked their original photos, or they'd been absent on picture day.

I noticed that Theo appeared in neither the community service nor arts and crafts club photos that year. Out of curiosity I opened the sophomore year volume and found her in both clubs, as well as the Future Homemakers. I bent over her face with a magnifying glass.

Pearl stood over me.

"Their photos were stolen," she said cryptically.

I looked up, confused. "What?"

She tapped Theo's picture. "The Silks. Last Thursday. Their photos were taken during the break-in at the museum."

It took me a minute to remember the news story. The Charlie Steigbeagle find. "I thought a map was missing."

"That's what everyone thought. Yesterday, when Charlie was straightening up, he noticed that two photos of the Silk house were also gone."

"The walking tour photos?"

Pearl nodded. Many of the old shipbuilder's homes from the seventeen- and eighteen-hundreds, Theodora's among them, had been incorporated into a series of self-guided walking tours of the Village.

"Were any other photos taken?"

"Just the Silks'."

I made a note in my black-and-white notebook to call Charlie.

"Pearl, can you tell me anything about Theo's grandmother? I know she was a Silk. But I remember the father had a different last name."

"Theodora's father? Yes, he did. Let me think a minute. It was such a long time ago." Pearl frowned at the floor. "Villers. That was it. When Theodora was a child, she hyphenated it, Silk-Villers. But she dropped the Villers at some point."

"We always thought of her as a Silk. That's what she wanted."

"That's what her grandmother wanted," Pearl said. "It was very important to Ida to maintain the Silk name and presence in the community. Especially once her daughter died and there was only Theodora to carry on. I suppose the girl's father knew what he was in for when he married into this matriarchy. There would be no Villers legacy by any stretch."

I wrote down the name. "Do you know where he moved to?"

"Yancy Villers? Oh, dear. I want to say he had family in the Midwest. Ohio or Iowa. I could be mistaken. Ida was a strong woman. She stayed on to take care of Theodora."

I nodded. "I remember her coming to our high school graduation. She wore a big hat with flowers on it. The only other part of that day that sticks in my mind was the iced tea. It was too sweet."

Behind us the tower of blocks came crashing down, and we both jumped. Pearl congratulated the kids on their stupendous crash, which won her big smiles. I tried to remember more about the Silks, but couldn't. I'd never paid them much attention, and there was always so much of interest going on in the Trace clan. When Pearl turned back to me, I asked her, "What kind of work was Yancy Villers in?"

She shook her head. "I don't recall, dear. He may not have had to work all that hard. He married money."

"What about the grandmother? Who was *her* husband?"

Pearl thought. "I wasn't acquainted with her first husband—Theo's grandfather. I was busy raising my own family in those days and not much concerned with goings-on beyond my four walls. I know Ida was married briefly to Gordon Strub of the beer-brewing Strubs. But, again, I suppose there was that same clash of interests and wills. He was based in Milwaukee, and Ida's interests were here. Her daughter, Lara, was her only child, and Theodora was also an only child. The Port Jeff connection was compelling. So I suppose it just didn't work out. Neither one wanted to make a permanent move." Pearl looked at her desk, where a boy was waiting patiently. "Excuse me, Emma. Someone needs my help."

I flipped open my laptop and googled "Yancy Villers." No hits. The idea that Theo's father had married into money and moved away intrigued me. If Hazzard was blackmailing Theo, it was reasonable to assume that a money scandal might be at the root. It was also fair to guess that Villers had been keeping a low profile and living off his riches. Although maybe not showing up in Google was the result of his being unsociable. On a whim I googled myself. There were five hits—three linking to my position with Able, one to the Helping Hands, and one to an article in *The Record* about a cat rescue effort three years ago.

I googled "Villers" without the "Yancy" this time and came up with a Rod Villers in Cleveland, a Wilma Villers in Joplin, Missouri, and a photo of the "Villers Killer Cue" hanging up in a pool hall in Selden, four miles away. I decided to check that one out and noted the address and phone number in my book. I wrote down the other connections, just in case.

Then I did similar searches for Ida Silk Strub. Links popped up for the Port Jeff Ladies Bridge, the Beaver County Genealogy Project, and a book about furniture from the Civil War era.

I tapped my pencil on the edge of the table until Pearl gave me a look. Things had dead-ended for the moment. I shut my laptop and threw everything into my tote bag. LaRue was working, but I could grab her for a quick question.

When she saw me come in, she raised her eyebrows and set two sodas on a table.

"I gotta pick up an order, so make it quick."

"Think back, LaRue. Do you remember the arts and crafts club in high school?"

" 'Course. It kept me sane, as a lesbian in a world full of straight kids. I wasn't into boys, but I sure was into art."

"Theo was in that club." I explained about the yearbooks and how Theo wasn't in any club photos in her junior year. "Even her individual portrait was a retake."

"She must of been out sick."

"On every club's picture day?"

"Hang on." LaRue trotted off, burst through the swinging door, and burst out again with a tray full of burgers. When she had served her table, she was back, wiping her hands on her apron.

"She was in England."

"England? What are you talking about?"

"I just remembered. That fall, when I started ninth grade, Theo went to England to stay with her cousins." LaRue folded her arms. "The Silks of England. You never heard of the Silks of England?"

"No."

"Well, neither did I. But that's where she went. To her well-to-do cousins on the other side of the Atlantic, so she could learn how to sip tea with her pinky in the air."

"How do you know that?"

"Because when she came back to school after Christmas, she told us all about it. It wasn't like she just took off for England, Em. Grandma Silk fixed it with the principal."

"How long was she there?"

"The whole fall. That's why she wasn't in any pictures."

Back in the car I did a quick search on my computer for florists' conventions and found an obsolete registration form for last week's meeting in Providence, Rhode Island. I punched the phone number of the sponsoring organization into my throw-away phone.

A woman answered.

"Good morning, this is Val Sweet from the Long Island Floral Educators Association," I told her.

"How can I help you, Ms. Sweet?"

"One of our members, Theodora Silk, submitted a credit request form to us in regard to last week's event in Rhode Island. We give our members in-service credit for teaching or presenting their skills at conferences and so forth, and I need to verify that Ms. Silk actually presented at your event. Would you check that for me?"

The woman hesitated. "Have you asked her if she did?"

"Let me put it another way. She *did* tell me she presented, but our accounting division requires documentation, and it wasn't in her package. Sometimes our people don't submit the necessary paperwork, and that keeps me in a job, I guess." I laughed.

"Why don't you ask her to call us herself? We'd be glad to provide her with what she needs."

"I wish I could. Ms. Silk is out of town, and she specifically asked me to expedite this request while she's away. I was hoping you could help."

"Well," the woman said.

"Who am I speaking with, please?"

"This is Helen Fistwater. I'm in charge of conferences and special events."

"Ms. Fistwater, I do appreciate your help."

The woman was silent again. "I'll take a look," she said, finally.

She put me on hold listening to classical guitar. It took a very long time before she came back.

"Yes," Helen Fistwater said. "Theodora Silk presented on Friday at ten o'clock."

"And you know for a fact that the workshop took place?"

"I just said that, didn't I? What organization did you say you were with?"

"Long Island Floral Educators. I'm sorry, but our account—"

"You already told me that. And I'm verifying that Ms. Silk actually presented her workshop on Friday before a group of twenty-five people." There was a pause. "No, I'm sorry. She did present, but her workshop was moved to nine o'clock at the last minute."

"Do you know why?"

"I can't imagine why you would ask that."

"I have a lot of boxes to fill in here, so I'll just put 'rescheduled.' Not a problem."

"We switched her with another presenter to allow more time for curing."

The bouquet of roses was waiting outside my door when I got home. I was still lost in thought and almost kicked the vase over.

"Happy birthday, Emma Rose," the card said. "Hope to continue our conversation from last night . . . tonight. Tony."

I shook my head, smiling, and dialed his number.

"They're lovely, Tony. Thank you. But I can't see you tonight, remember?"

"Dinner with the family. I know. Can I at least take you out for a drink before? Or stop by later?"

"I can't promise, Tony. I have a million things to do, not the least of which is catch up on work."

I could hear the wheels turning. "Why don't we see how the day goes, and if you finish up early, give me a call. How does that sound?"

"Like a long shot." I hesitated. "How about this weekend? Give me a chance to clear my plate."

"Won't work. It's my grandmother's one hundredth birthday and the annual family get-together in Martha's Vineyard. Fifteen Italians sleeping in one house, can you imagine? I'm on the road early Friday morning."

"When do you get back?"

"Sunday night. Even that's a push. If I had my choice I'd come back Monday, but with a new business to tend to, no can do. By the way," he went on, "last night was amazing. *You*'re amazing."

I felt a pang. I missed him already.

CHAPTER THIRTY-FOUR

My family had commandeered a long table at La Casa, my favorite Italian restaurant, to celebrate my winning the bet. When I walked in, they broke into a round of applause and choruses of "Way to go, Emma!" and "Good job!" as I made my way past curious diners to our table.

Dad grinned widely and kissed me twice. "From your mother and me. Congratulations, sweetheart. Happy birthday."

"Thanks, Dad."

I did my ceremonial walk around the table, kissing everyone and shaking hands. I had to admit it felt bitchin'. Exceptional. It always feels good to win a bet against these guys. Uncle Sherm was there, and Uncle Pike with his crutches leaning against his chair, and Pike's current girlfriend, Anita, and Sandy and his wife, Elaine, and cousin Jerry and his wife, Carol, from upstate, and three of Pike's kids who live in the area with their significant others.

And Ned. I hit him last. It was my victory moment. I rested my hands on the back of the empty seat next to him and lorded it over him, a smirk on my face. I can be a real jerk when I feel like it.

Ned leaned away and looked up at me, the ever-present toothpick wiggling between his lips.

"So," he said.

"So," I said brightly.

"Good on you, Emma."

"You betcha."

"Real good." He indicated the chair.

Food had already started appearing—baked clams, calamari, eggplant, mussels, shrimp. Nothing I particularly liked. I knew Dad had ordered a variety of entrees and that I'd get my spaghetti and meatballs. Everyone dug in to the antipasto. I dug into my roll.

Having dinner with my family is a little like playing Double Dutch jump rope. The rope's already going and somebody's always jumping, and you just have to be brave and vault yourself in. With all the adrenaline going through me, I talked to everyone. Sandy asked how my head was and talked about his bumper crop of pumpkins. Uncle Pike and Dad argued about the Super Bowl, four weeks into the season. Jerry effused about foliage upstate while Carol dissected the latest season of *American Idol*. Ned poured me a glass of red wine and grunted a word here and there. Sherm shoveled in the food, not taking part in conversation.

When I got down to the last few bites of spaghetti and meatballs, I saw my chance.

"I want to know what the story is between you and Zahn," I said to Ned.

He gave me a quick look, his mouth full of sausage and peppers.

"Why?"

"Because he hates my guts. I want to know why."

"No, he doesn't. He just wants you to stay out of his business."

"He *got* me involved in his business yesterday. It didn't go so well." I sprinkled parmesan cheese on my last forkful of spaghetti. "Mainly, he doesn't want to hear from me."

"So why are you calling him?"

"Because I find out things. I'm in touch with what's going

on. I don't know. It's my civic duty. What happened between you two? How do you know him?"

He twiddled his fork in his pasta, then laid it across his plate. "It's a long story, Em."

"I have time."

"Goes back to my wild days."

I let out a short laugh. The busboy leaned over us to collect our dishes. Ned kept wiping the same corner of his mouth with his napkin. Finally he tossed the napkin on his plate and let the busboy take it away. He didn't look at me.

"Best left buried," he said.

"Everyone has regrets," I countered.

"Regrets." Ned bit down on the word. He unwrapped a new toothpick and put it between his teeth. Then he spent a few seconds studying the mural of the Italian countryside painted on the wall.

"We played on the same softball team," he finally said.

"You and Zahn?"

He nodded. "I was twenty-five. Not even—twenty-four. It was before the cat toys. I was working at the country club, collecting tips and meeting a lot of unhappy wives ten years older than I."

"Was that when you lived in Huntington?"

He gave me a rueful smile. "The basement apartment with the green drapes. Remember?"

"Mm-hmm."

A scoop of vanilla ice cream appeared before me, and I licked some off my spoon. Ned stared at his ice cream. I didn't say anything. It's no good asking him question after question if he's not ready. After the coffee was poured he continued.

"Before Pete joined the team, I was the best ball player on the Mo's Deli Grinders. We were in the playoffs four years in a row, babe—we won the league championship twice. Both of those wins were over the Ace Plumbing T-Bolts. Pete's team."

"What position did you play?"

"Centerfield. Not to brag, but I was the best centerfielder the Grinders ever had. *And* their cleanup hitter." Ned stirred some ice cream into his coffee. "The T-Bolts started having problems around that time, after the second championship. They lost their sponsor, and three of their guys dropped out for one reason or another. Pete was their best player, and he wanted to keep playing. So he was looking for a new team."

"And he played what position?"

"Shortstop."

"Ah." I could see where this was going.

"Pete knew some of my friends in the fire department, and they invited him to be on the team. We didn't have a shortstop after Roy left, so the timing was perfect. He started practicing with the Grinders that spring.

"Around the same time he was getting ready for the police exam. Pete wanted a job with the Suffolk County Police Department more than anything in the world. He'd had to delay it for some reason, but he was determined to get it done now. He was driven—obsessed." Ned waved his arm. "He could have gotten a job as a city cop. A lot of the guys in Suffolk, they come in through New York City, but Pete didn't want to do that. He wanted to put in his twenty here. I don't even think he was looking that far ahead. He just wanted to be a cop. You know what kind of work he was doing back then? Delivering propane."

I pushed my empty bowl away. "How did you guys get along?"

"On the team? Fine. Look, he was a great player. He was tall, he had a strong arm, he moved like greased lightning. And he could throw from the hole like nobody else. He was good at bat, too. The T-Bolts were our biggest rival, mostly because of him." Ned stopped talking, drifted off somewhere, then pulled himself back. "Pete was a helluva ball player, and he never let us forget it. He had all this pride and purpose and ego wrapped up in playing ball and wanting to be a cop. There were times I couldn't stand being around the guy, to tell you the truth. But when you're on a team, you play like a team. We had our best season the year he joined us."

The waiter refilled our coffee cups and Ned waited for him to walk away.

"By August we dominated the league. Completely dominated it. We knew we were going to make the playoffs, maybe get another trophy to put in Mo's window.

"Meanwhile, Pete had just aced the written exam for the department. He was flying high. He'd passed all the other screenings and evaluations, and the only thing left was the physical. He'd scheduled that for right after the playoffs.

"It was the second-to-last game of the regular season— Grinders versus the Kitty Boutique Hounds. Kind of a crappy team, but nice guys. We were ahead six to two in the bottom of the eighth. The Hounds had one man on base, and Ron Ventimiglia was at bat. He was their best hitter, which isn't saying much. Cal Ingraham pitched a curveball, and Ron blooped it into the outfield, right in my direction." Ned took a sip of his coffee and pushed the cup away. "The Hounds started yelling, 'Trouble!' but I had the ball. *I had the ball.* So I ran in. I didn't even see Zahn backing up. I plowed into him full force and we both went down." He took out the toothpick and flipped it into his ice cream dish. "Ball got away. I was okay, a little shook up. The Hounds scored two runs. Not enough to win, though."

"What about Zahn?" I asked.

Ned's voice was quiet. "Pete sprained his right ankle pretty bad. He was on crutches for the next six weeks. Of course, he missed the playoffs. Worse, he missed his physical with the police department. He was disqualified for that year."

The table had gotten quiet. Everyone was listening to Ned.

"So, he missed his chance," I said.

"Yeah. He missed it. He had to do it all over again the next year—all the tests. And then he was recruited. But he had to spend a whole extra year driving the propane truck." Ned shot me a hard look. "He blamed me for that, Em. Always has. He says he called the ball. I didn't hear him call anything. It wasn't my fault."

CHAPTER THIRTY-FIVE

A few minutes after nine I pulled into Honey's Billiards and parked under the halogen light. The squat green building had a shuttered, shifty look, but a few cars were clustered there, and I heard music coming from inside.

I grabbed my steno pad and made sure the badge hanging from my lanyard was partly concealed by my scarf. It was an old press pass that had once belonged to my friend, Noah Banks, who'd married me in the block corner in kindergarten. As long as no one looked too closely, it would work fine.

A few young guys were smoking outside Honey's front door. I passed them without comment. It was much larger and brighter inside than I'd expected. Two of the eight pool tables were in use, and a few people sat at the bar, most of them young and male. A blonde leaned her elbow on the shoulder of one of the men. The bartender, a man in his sixties with tattoos down both arms, cleared away empty glasses. A Garth Brooks song played in the jukebox.

On the paneled walls were racks full of cues and a few NO SMOKING signs that had probably been up for thirty years. Behind the bar, between a moose head and a Miller Lite mirror, I saw what had brought me to Honey's: a cue bracketed to a horizontal pine panel with a small handwritten sign beneath it. The ink had faded so much, I could barely read the sign until my hands were on the bar.

The bartender came and stood between me and the Villers

Killer Cue. He wore a gold earring and a World Series of Poker baseball cap.

"Evenin'." He slapped a coaster on the bar. "Somethin' to wet your whistle?"

"What've you got on tap?"

"Miller, Miller Lite, Bud, Bud Light, and Blue Point Toasted Lager."

"I'll have the Blue Point."

I watched him bend over to get a glass. He had a long gray braid that went most of the way down his back.

"I don't spot you as a pool player," he said, setting the beer in front of me.

"I play well enough," I countered.

"Those kids over there." He nodded at one of the tables. "They're here five, six nights a week. They're goin' to the state tourneys next month."

"Really. That's impressive." I took a gulp of the Blue Point.

"Sure. We got all kinds of champs comin' in here. And some not-so-champs." He gave me a sideways look. "But you're not here to play. Not meeting a friend, neither."

I extended my hand. "Right on both counts. I'm a journalist. Nola Banks."

"Well, howdy-do, Nola." He smiled, showing discolored teeth. His hand was rough and calloused. "Don Williams. Don't get too many journalists in here. What are you workin' on—pool story?"

"Yup." I clicked open my pen. "I'm writing about Long Island's legends of pool. History, you know."

"I don't know about legends. We got some capable players, though."

"Donnio!" One of the guys down the bar lifted an empty glass.

"Hang tight," Don said, and moved away.

I squinted at the sign below the cue. I could make out "High Run" and "Villers" and what looked like a first name beginning with "Y."

Don came back. He jerked his chin at my pad. "You got Fatty 'the Terminator' Arno in there? Smits Hooey? Bobby 'the Shark' Columbo?"

"Uh, not yet. I'm just getting started, Don. Reason I'm at Honey's is because of—*him.*"

He looked where I was pointing and turned back in surprise. "Villers?"

"Yeah. Heard he was a pool *monster* in these parts."

Don scratched his chin. "Don't know about that. He was good enough, though. Had one crazy run."

"Did you know him?"

"Probably the only guy here who did." His face darkened. "What's with Villers? You're the second in two days that's come askin' about him."

I sloshed beer over my chin and wiped it up with a napkin. "Geez, a writer can't get a break. What paper was he with?"

Don shrugged. "Other guy wasn't with the paper. He was a bum. Strung out on somethin'. Looked like a snake."

"You're right, Don, that was no reporter. What did he want to know?"

"Just asked if Villers'd been around lately." He leaned over the bar. "Yancy Villers hasn't shown his face here in eighteen years."

"No?"

"Not since that night." He jerked his chin toward the killer cue.

"Did the guy ask you anything else?"

"Nope. Said 'I'm gonna find that somvabitch' and stomped out. I figure Yance owed him money or was supposed to repay a favor or somethin'."

"Tell me about that night eighteen years ago."

Don folded his arms and leaned back against the wall. He seemed to be sizing me up. After a moment he gave a quick nod and started talking.

"Yance'd come in about every week or so, whenever he could get away without the wife takin' offense, I guess. Don't know too much about that part. He'd come in and get a game goin' with whoever was around. Sometimes that was me. If there wasn't nothin' happenin' at the bar, I'd shoot a rack.

"Saturday, the first of November, was a nasty night, blowin' and rainin'. Not much table action. There was a couple guys playin' eight-ball over there"—he pointed—"and Yance comes in drippin' and asks if I'm up for a game.

"I say 'sure.' So we set up, and I say, 'Yance, where's your cue?' And he says, 'I don't have it.' 'Well, where is it?' And he laughs sort of funny and says, 'It's buried in the backyard.' So I say. 'Well, what're you goin' to use, a turkey baster?'

"So he reaches 'round and takes one of the house cues off the wall, that have been around for a hundred years and I wouldn't recommend to anyone, and we start to play. Straight pool, fifty points. I break, I leave him a safety. Then he plays a safety. Then I fuck up, I leave him a hanger and he uses that to make his break shot. He pockets the next shot, and the next, and he keeps on pocketing them, one after the other. Before you know it he runs the rack. The other guys stop their game and come over to watch. Refill?"

"I'm good."

"So he sets up a new rack, makes his break shot, and pockets a few more. Now people at the bar come over, and some of the regulars show up, and they're watching, too. Yance is on a roll. He's playin' like a madman. Not drinkin', not talkin' to anyone, just a skinny old ball of sweat. Fourteen more in the pocket. Pretty soon we got a crowd six deep around the table. I've never seen Yance play like this before. Never seen *anyone* play like this.

"Meanwhile people are thirsty. I go over and I'm servin' drinks, and all I can hear is the knock as he hits each ball and the thunk as it goes in the pocket. I can't keep up with the drink orders, so I get out a big tub of beer, put it on the bar, and go to the honor system. I go back to the table.

"But I never get to shoot again. Yance keeps going until he gets up to sixty-two. *Sixty-two*! Then he misses. The crowd is wild, pattin' him on the back, offerin' him beers."

"He must have been stoked," I said.

"You would think," Don said. "He was smilin' and all. He was happy, but not really struttin'. The guys grabbed the cue, called it magic, wanted to hang it up like a lucky dollar in a diner. We made this"—he jerked his head toward the plaque—"a couple days later. We had a party for him the next Saturday and everyone came."

"How did that go?"

"Place was packed. More'n a hundred people. Except for Yance—he never showed up."

I wiped the condensation off my glass. "Why not?"

"Beats me. The dude gets an amazing high run. We make him this plaque, we're goin' to toast him and everything." His face clouded over. "You'd think he'd be appreciative. But nah. He never showed his face in here again."

Don shook his head and went over to refresh someone's drink. I put my elbows on the bar and rested my chin in my hands. When he came back, I asked casually, "Where do you think Villers went?"

Don shrugged. "You got a crystal ball?"

"I heard he has relatives in the Midwest. Maybe he moved to be near his family."

"Might have, I s'pose."

"Did he ever mention any family, besides the one here?"

"Nope. I don't know where Yancy Villers went." Don's voice was flat. "And to tell you the truth, Nola, I don't really give a shit."

I paid for my beer and left a twenty-dollar tip. "Thanks very much, Don."

He didn't touch the twenty. Just stared at it where it lay on the counter. On my way out the door, he called after me.

"What do I tell that snake if he comes in again?"

"Don't worry," I said over my shoulder. "He won't be back."

Chapter Thirty-Six

Thursday

The story about Sam broke the next morning.

PH.D.=PHONY DOC?

The Internet article said that Stony Brook professor Sam Benjamin, recently questioned by police regarding his role in a blackmail scheme, had falsified his credentials when he applied for a position in the English department, according to a faculty member who requested anonymity.

He had listed among his prior teaching positions a two-year stint at Harvard University in which he worked with other researchers on the literary origins of Shakespeare's early works when, in fact, he was never on Harvard's payroll and had not taught a single class there. No disciplinary action had been taken so far by the university.

LaRue stood over me with the coffeepot. "This gets better by the day."

"Un-fucking-believable."

"More coffee?"

"Hit me."

I went outside with my coffee cup and punched in Zahn's number.

"Major crimes."

"Give me Detective Zahn."

"He's not in. Can I—"

"This is Emma Trace. I need to talk to him now."

Silence, then pop music.

"Zahn," said Zahn.

"You are *so* on the wrong track," I blurted out. "Sam may not be perfect, but to suggest he's a *murderer,* to convict the man by public opinion? Do you know what life is like in academia these days? Do you have any idea what it takes to get funding?"

"What are you talking about, Trace?"

I started pacing. "I'm talking about the story on everyone's lips this morning. Sam lying on his resume."

"Hang on."

Paper rustled.

"Some jealous rival in the English department starts a rumor," I went on, "and all of a sudden you've got a scapegoat."

Zahn laughed.

"What's so funny?"

"This is the press talking, Trace. Not the police. Complain to them."

"You're the ones who pulled him in after Bisbee got himself killed. You're the ones who questioned him about the blackmail connection."

"You and a lot of other people are making that connection yourselves."

"You don't know Sam like I do. He wouldn't hurt a fly."

"Where's the sudden loyalty coming from? The other day you were calling him her boyfriend."

"That was Bellarosa."

"Right. Well, now that you've gotten this off your chest, Emma, do you mind if I get ready for work?"

I stopped pacing. "Detective, I think you should check out Theo. Theodora Silk."

"We've been through this, Trace. I'm not discussing the case with you. And I'm certainly not taking direction from you."

"I think she was a target of Hazzard's." I plowed on, praying he wouldn't hang up. "Her father, Yancy Villers, disappeared eighteen years ago, possibly with family money. Bisbee went looking for him before he was killed."

"Where'd you hear that?"

"The bartender at the pool hall."

"The bartender—Trace, what did I tell you about staying out of it?"

"Villers might be in Ohio or Missouri. I have some phone numbers. Wilma Villers in Joplin, age fifty-four, her husband, Tom—"

Zahn interjected, "Where are you getting all this?"

"The Internet." I took a breath. "I'm pretty sure Hazzard's murder weapon is in a garbage bag at Distant Shores."

"What a relief." Zahn's voice dripped with sarcasm. "I'll get on it right away."

"You have to listen to me, Detective. I tried to tell you at The Bench, but you stopped me."

He said nothing. I took a sip of my coffee and found it cold. Suddenly I realized that I was cold, too. A chill wind had whipped up off the harbor. The ferry blasted its horn and began to slide out of its berth. I remembered the missing photos at the museum.

"And another thing—"

"Enough," Zahn snapped. "No more things. You're pissing me off, Trace. Believe me, you don't want to piss me off."

I stood there breathing hard.

"You must think this is the only case I'm working on. I've got seven active cases right now. Contrary to popular belief, the police do not work twenty-four hours a day. I don't know where the hell you get off calling me at six-thirty in the morning, but

I've had enough of your impertinence." I heard his newspaper slap the table. "All your shenanigans—you could be tipping off the wrong people."

"But I'm—"

"You're endangering my investigation, Trace. I'll say it again—*my* investigation. Do not interfere. When I want your help, I'll ask for it."

Dead air told me he was gone.

"You won't get any medals for arresting the wrong man," I said. I flipped my phone shut and went back into the diner.

LaRue was standing near my booth, talking to Wendy, the other waitress.

"Just put some food out," Wendy said. "He'll come."

"Someone has to be there to grab him, Wen."

"The cat?" I asked.

"Poor thing is starving," Wendy said. "And there's something wrong with his foot."

"I'll bring over my cat carrier." I tossed a couple of bills on the table. "Try leaving a blanket and some food inside."

My mind was troubled on the short ride home. Maybe I shouldn't have called Zahn. But someone had tried to set me up, and it sure wasn't Sam. I had to do *something*.

I pulled into my parking space and sat in the car, gazing at the old house where I lived. It looked charming and vulnerable. I'd lied to Ned about having a good lock. In reality it was pretty crappy. I backed out and drove to the hardware store.

Chapter Thirty-Seven

For the next hour I entertained Bergamot with the power drill, chisel, and screwdriver, while the Rolling Stones played on the boom box. I gave a little cheer when I tried the new lock and the bolt slid smoothly in and out. Then I swept up the sawdust and tossed my tools back in the toolbox. I felt like a pro. After that I did a little editing, jazzing up the menu for a local seafood restaurant.

I was the first one in the library when it opened and spent the next several hours reading back issues of the local paper on microfilm, beginning six months before Yancy Villers had left town. Coincidentally—or not—his high run at Honey's had taken place during the same period that Theodora was sipping tea in England.

I read freely, looking for anything that might catch my eye. Unusual or disturbing events. Patterns, or breaks in patterns. And anything to do with a Villers or a Silk.

There were stories of feuding neighbors and dog bites, bank robberies and motorcycle thefts. As treasurer of the local Ladies Bridge Club, Ida Strub Silk had published occasional gentle reminders to negligent members to pay their dues. Egon Hoyt had received the Community Leader of the Month award for his Flowers for Angels program, which had raised fifteen thousand dollars for a local hospice.

A story in early December caught my eye. A newborn baby girl had been abandoned in a shoebox in a Port Jeff office building with her umbilical cord tied off with dental floss. The infant had been taken to the Sixth Precinct, where authorities pronounced her in good health, other than being completely soiled.

I skipped ahead to the issue about my high school graduation, which included a half-page photo of the entire graduating class—all ninety-two of us. I pulled out my pocket magnifier and scanned the faces until I found Theodora's glum puss in the back row. Could nothing cheer that girl up? I was right in the middle, grinning widely. Below the photo was a list of the graduates and their plans after graduation. I was shuffling off to Buffalo, and Theo was going to Cornell.

Only she didn't go to Cornell. She stayed home and got a job at Hoyt's.

Frowning, I put the microfilm back in its container and shut off the machine. Then I found a table nearby and opened my laptop. I was still seething about Zahn. I couldn't wait for this business to be over and for Zahn to disappear from my life. I logged into Suffolk e-Resources and set up a news search for "Peter Zahn."

I was surprised to see a long list of entries going all the way back to the 1970s, when he was only a child. As I perused the headlines, I noticed that a number of them were obituaries. Curious, I clicked one of the links.

NYPD COP KILLED BY FRIENDLY FIRE

An off-duty New York City police officer was shot and killed by a fellow officer last night while chasing an armed suspect through the 149th Street Grand Concourse subway station in the Bronx.

Officer Peter Zahn, thirty-eight, of the Domestic Violence Unit, was in street clothes and on his way home to his family on Fordham Road when a passenger on the Lexington Avenue

Express train began shouting taunts and waving a gun in a car crowded with commuters. Upon reaching the 149th Street station moments later, Zahn followed the passenger, Wayne Williams of 145th Street, off the train and attempted to arrest him. Williams shot Zahn in the right shoulder and began to run. Zahn drew his gun and gave chase, but did not immediately shoot because of the rush-hour crowds in the vicinity, instead shouting for Williams to stop.

Meanwhile, Transit Police Officer Vern Lewis, who had heard the gunshot from the street, rushed down the stairs as passengers fled the station screaming that there was a crazy person on the platform with a gun. Spotting Zahn, who he mistook for the shooter, Lewis opened fire and killed Zahn with a single bullet to the back. The suspect got away. With the help of witnesses Williams was later arrested at a bar on Prospect Avenue and will be indicted on charges of attempted murder. Lewis is not expected to be charged or disciplined in the shooting.

Zahn is survived by his wife, Helen, of fifteen years and a twelve-year-old son, also named Peter.

Stunned, I went back to the link list and read several more articles about the shooting and then one about the funeral.

THOUSANDS ATTEND FUNERAL OF SLAIN POLICE OFFICER

Thousands of police officers in dress uniform lined up five-deep for blocks around a Bronx church today to pay their respects to slain NYPD Officer Peter Zahn, who was killed last week in what is being described as a friendly fire incident.

The shooting has been classified as a line of duty death, entitling Zahn to an Inspector's funeral, the highest honor the department can give a fallen comrade. Zahn, who spent his entire career working in the Domestic Violence Unit and was devoted to the department, will be promoted posthumously to detective first grade.

As the flower-covered hearse passed by this afternoon, each attending officer raised a gloved hand in salute. Arriving at St. Raymond's Church, the hearse was surrounded by eight police officers who carried the casket up the steps while the NYPD Emerald Society Pipes and Drums wearing traditional Celtic dress played "An Inspector's Funeral."

Zahn was remembered during the service as an earnest and caring officer, one who was able to handle with authority and calmness the most difficult and volatile situations, which he frequently encountered in his sixteen-year career. During the eulogy there wasn't a dry eye in the tightly packed church.

The police commissioner spoke of Zahn's bravery on and off duty and described what happened as a tragic chain of events. "He was a man who made a difference, a man with a great heart, and a true hero," the commissioner said, as Zahn's widow wept openly in a pew. Addressing Zahn's young son, also named Peter, who valiantly held back his tears, the commissioner added, "Your father was a shining star not only to the department, but to all the people of the city of New York. His heroism stands as an example to each one of us to reach higher and to give more."

The mayor expressed the condolences of millions of New Yorkers in his moving eulogy. "With our hands and our hearts, we join *New York's Finest* in grieving this heroic man who gave his life protecting our city," the mayor said as waves of grief swept through the sea of blue. "He will not be forgotten."

Prayers were said for Zahn and also for Officer Vern Lewis, the police officer who mistakenly gunned him down.

After the service, Zahn's casket was draped with an American flag, and the eight pallbearers carried it back outside to the hearse while the Emerald Society Pipes and Drums played taps. Officer Zahn was buried in St. Raymond's Cemetery in the Bronx.

His death is under investigation.

Below the story was a photo of the graveside ceremony showing Zahn, Junior, his mother, and a sea of cops watching the casket as it was lowered into the ground. Zahn's mother wept on the shoulder of an unidentified man whose eyes were on the boy. The boy himself was staring, not at the casket, but at some point far beyond it, over the photographer's shoulder. Wind blew his fair hair across his face. His blazer was buttoned, his mouth set in a tight line. In his right hand he held his father's cap. I stared at that cap for a long time.

CHAPTER THIRTY-EIGHT

After lunch I called Charlie Steigbeagle. When I told him why, he grew angry.

"Those photos are irreplaceable. Why would someone want two old photos of a house?"

My question exactly. "What did they show?"

"The front of the house and the inside, bedrooms and attic."

"And you're sure they were on the wall before the break-in?"

"Of course, I'm sure," he snapped. "I've been in charge of the museum for twenty-five years."

I had about the same luck with Wilma Villers in Joplin.

"You people asked me that already. I'm not answerin' any more questions."

She thought I was the police. I didn't correct her. "It's very important for us to track down Mr. Villers. We need his help with a case."

"Like I told you people this morning, I don't know where he is. He hasn't been heard from in more'n twenty years."

"Might he be in touch with other members of the family?"

She laughed coarsely. "He threw 'em all away, the bum. Even my son—his nephew. Like an old shoe, he threw 'em away."

Or buried them in the backyard, I thought. Like the cue.

I filled my watering can, thinking about Theo. If her father had been such a bum, why was she protecting his secret? To spare the family embarrassment? It had to have been something shameful that would tarnish the family name. Was it awful enough to cause Theo to commit murder?

Suppose it was, and she did? If I were Theo and I'd killed to cover up a secret, where would I hide the evidence? A DVD, for instance, or a little blackmail book?

If it were me, I'd get rid of everything *tout de suite*. Especially the DVD, easy enough to toss. The blackmail book would be a little harder. But suppose I hadn't had a chance yet. If I were Theo, I wouldn't leave any evidence lying around the house for the police to find. I'd pick someone I trusted to safeguard my secret. Someone who would never betray me.

I watered my spider plant and waited for it to stop dripping. Someone like my grandmother.

I put down the watering can. Yes. Like the woman who'd raised Theo after her mother died, who'd proudly attended her high school graduation. The woman who would do anything to protect her granddaughter: Ida Silk Strub.

Immediately I got that little shiver that told me neural synapses were sparking. Connections were being made. I went into the bedroom and rummaged through my underwear drawer. My mom had given me a nightgown two years ago that I'd never worn. It was too short and ruffly, and it still had the store tags on it. If it must be sacrificed in the quest for truth, so be it. I pulled the nightgown from the back of the drawer, wrapped it in pink tissue, and stuffed it in a gift bag.

I found a blank DVD in my desk drawer and popped that in with the nightgown. The blond wig from the Bellarosa escapade might also come in handy. I dug it out of a drawer and tossed it in my purse. I grabbed my laptop last.

The Sunny Side Up had closed for the day. LaRue was filling ketchup bottles. I rapped on the window and she let me in.

"Don't *you* look like the cat that swallowed the canary."

I smiled and handed her the cat carrier. "I need your help, LaRue."

"Oh?"

She led the way to my usual booth. I yanked a napkin from the dispenser and shoved it toward her.

"Show me how the nursing home is laid out."

"Nanny's nursing home?" Her eyes bugged. "Why? You bustin' in?"

"Sorta."

LaRue pulled a pack of tropical gum out of her apron and popped two sticks in her mouth.

"What's at the nursing home?"

"That's what I'm going to find out. Tell me who and what I have to get by to get to somebody's room."

With a sly look, LaRue took a pen from her pocket and drew some boxes on the napkin.

"It's two stories. There's two wings on each floor and a nursing station in each wing. So first you have to get past the nursing police." She drew some squares in the hallways. "These are lounges where they have vending machines and stuff."

"Restrooms?"

"Here's the ladies'. I know about this one because this is Nanny's wing. There's others."

"Tell me about hallway traffic. Lot of residents walking around?"

"Not that many of them are walking, Swee'pea. The ones that walk go pretty slow. But you got people going back and forth. Cleaners and nurses. Aides."

LaRue popped a bubble. She jiggled her foot, watching me.

"How long do you need?"

"Five minutes."

"If you head over now, you got a nice window around four o'clock."

"How's that?"

"They all go downstairs to watch *Judge Judy*."

239

Perfecto. We both smiled.

"Just look like you know where you're going, and you'll be fine. Notice I'm not asking you whose room you're bustin' into."

"I noticed."

LaRue glanced at the cat carrier. "You think Bergamot would like a little friend?"

"He hates cats."

"I can't keep him, Em. He and Petey'll drive each other bonkers."

"Did you ask Wendy?"

"She's allergic."

"All right, if you catch him, call me. I'll bring him to the vet."

LaRue walked through the swinging door with the cat carrier, her ponytail bouncing as she walked. It sure was nice to look back there and not see Hazzard giving me the evil eye through the pass-through window. I could still feel her eyes on me, watching from the grave. What had made her hate me so much? I'd done nothing to her—*nothing.*

Then I had a new thought. What if Hazzard had not been staring at me that day, but at something *past* me, out the window, and I just happened to be in the way? A cold finger of fear went across the back of my neck. I turned my head slowly and followed the line of view from the pass-through to its ultimate destination.

Across the street, in the front window of Hoyt's Greenhouse among the paper autumn leaves and pumpkin cutouts, Theodora's pale face stared back at me.

My mouth went dry. For some seconds my eyes locked into Theo's and hers into mine.

She knew.

She knew that I knew she was the killer. And now she knew that I knew she knew.

CHAPTER THIRTY-NINE

It was three forty-five when I parked outside the Florida room of Distant Shores. For five minutes I sat there with the doors locked, half expecting Theodora to show up and try to add another murder to her roster. Finally I put on my wig, grabbed my gift bag, and went in.

The woman at the welcome desk had her nose in a book. I walked purposefully past her and past a group of people in wheelchairs waving big rubber balls over their heads to the tune of the Carpenters' "Close to You." In the "Charles" wing I wove through a procession of wheelchairs, each manned by an aide or a nurse. No one gave me a second look.

All of the doors were wide open, which was good, but there were no name tags, which was bad.

A whirring sound made me turn. A little man in a motorized wheelchair was buzzing down the hall without a nurse. He careened from side to side, narrowly missing the walls, while two pinwheels attached to his seatback spun madly. A few feet from me he accelerated slightly, did a three-sixty, and stopped on a dime.

"Nice moves," I said.

The little man smiled, his round face a map of wrinkles. He reminded me of Tyco Bass in Eleanor Cameron's book, *The Wonderful Flight to the Mushroom Planet.* He wore a bright red jogging suit and a cap that said *Don't forget my SENIOR DISCOUNT!*

"The nurses always holler at me, so I work on my spins when they're not around."

"Good idea. Say, do you know where I can find my great-aunt Ida's room?"

He shook his head. "We've got two Shirleys, a Frieda, and an Edna in this wing. No Ida."

"Okay, thanks."

"Allow me to accompany you to the other side." Tyco motored alongside me. "We'll find Great-Aunt Ida together."

"Oh, that's not necessary." His smile faded, and I felt I'd been rude. "I appreciate your help, though," I added.

The smile returned. "Follow me."

We approached a housekeeper on the other side.

"My darling Maria," Tyco said, "we are looking for this charming young woman's great-aunt Ida. Do you know where we might find her?"

"Ida Strub?" She pointed to the ceiling. "Upstairs, number seven."

"There you go," said Tyco.

I thanked them and scooted off to the stairwell before Tyco could say anything else. He and the cleaner would remember me and who I was looking for if asked, but I hoped it didn't come to that.

Another wheelchair parade was going by upstairs, so I hid in the stairwell until the coast was clear. The desk nurse was on the phone. Good. As I passed a cleaning cart I grabbed two Latex gloves from a cardboard dispenser and stuffed them in my pocket.

Ida's room was decorated like a Victorian rose garden, all teapots and doilies and tiny spoons in frames. A trellis on one wall displayed a dozen greeting cards, mostly of angels and praying hands. A small throw rug shaped like a rose lay in front of an antique dresser covered with framed family photos. I put down my gift bag and pulled on the Latex gloves. Most of the photos were very old. But a newer one in a mosaic frame caught my attention.

It was a five by seven of Theodora standing next to a small airplane, a headset draped around her neck. One hand was on her hip, the other resting on the cowling in a proprietary way, and she wore what almost passed for a smile. Theo was a pilot? Who knew?

I snapped a couple of pictures with my cell phone camera. The frame was surprisingly heavy. I turned it over, slid the metal fasteners aside, and lifted off the back.

Beneath the cardboard was a slim brown leather notebook.

I felt the adrenaline spurt through me as I opened to the first page. Tiny black letters filled the lines. The writing was in a sort of shorthand or code. I took a picture, then went through the whole book, photographing each page. I put the book back in the frame and replaced it on the dresser.

Four-twelve. The *Judge Judy* show aired in two thirty-minute segments back to back. I hoped Ida was in the habit of watching both segments.

Only one other photo frame was large enough to hold a DVD. I opened the back, found zip.

I circled the room counterclockwise, checking under doilies and behind plaques. I fanned through books and reached behind furniture. The closet was neatly packed with shoeboxes and plastic storage bins that offered myriad hiding places. Did Ida herself know where the DVD was?

I heard footsteps coming down the hall and ducked into the closet until they passed.

The shoeboxes contained dressy high-heeled and open-toed pumps stuffed with tissue paper. Shoes from the past. When I finished with the shoeboxes I rummaged through the storage bins. They held mostly sweaters and shawls.

I climbed up on a chair and felt around on the top shelf.

Maybe she'd thrown it away. Why keep an incriminating DVD, anyway?

Then I noticed a small CD player on the bedside table. Next to it was a basket holding six or seven CDs of big band music. I opened a few cases, and there on top of "Benny Goodman Live" I found a DVD labeled "CNN News-Archives."

Bingo. I hoped.

I pocketed the disk. It would take me less than five minutes to go down to my car, burn it to my hard drive, and return it to its case.

My phone said four twenty-eight. I peeled off my gloves, made sure the hall was empty, and headed for the stairs.

Tyco Bass pulled into the fast lane beside me. "Did you find Great-Aunt Ida?"

"I did, thank you."

"You look like a girl who enjoys Italian love songs. There's a concert tonight in the lounge. Beautiful songs. The singer will make you cry. Perhaps you would like to join me?"

I was surprised. "As your date?"

He waved his hands gently, as though he were stroking the air. "*Sì, bella.* We listen to some music, enjoy a little espresso, amaretti, biscotti—"

I smiled. "It sounds lovely, but I can't. Thank you for inviting me, though."

He gave me his crinkly smile. He really was rather adorable.

"If you change your mind, tell them at the desk. Tell them to tell Frank."

I was disappointed his name wasn't Tyco.

Frank took my hand and kissed it. *"Fino a quando ci incontreremo di nuovo, bella."* Until we meet again. He gave me a little salute and buzzed away, pinwheels spinning.

I was almost out the door when the woman at the welcome

desk called my name.

"I have a message for you. LaRue called. She wants you to meet her at Harborfront Park at five-thirty. Down by the rails."

I was puzzled. "She called here?"

"She said she couldn't reach you on your cell. You *are* Emma?"

"Yes."

"Good. I said I'd try and catch you on your way out."

I guessed LaRue hadn't wanted my cell phone to ring while I was in Ida's room. Smart move.

I got in my car and burned the DVD to my computer. Then I slipped past the welcome desk, and power-walked through the lobby and up the stairs. Behind me I could hear Judge Judy reaming somebody out in the lounge. I strode right into Ida Strub's room without looking.

She was there.

Ida was hunched in her wheelchair next to the greeting card trellis, working her jaws. She was draped in a black shawl, her knotted fingers lying in her lap like a pile of dry bones. Her skin was so wrinkled and pinched, it looked like a vacuum cleaner had been turned on inside her and sucked all the skin inward.

I braked to a halt. "I'm so sorry."

Her eyes rose slowly up my body and ran out of steam at about chest level. She didn't say anything, just kept up the jaw action. Her eyes were a watery, weak blue. After a few moments her eyes sank back down.

I put the DVD back in the Benny Goodman case and left the room.

CHAPTER FORTY

Built on the site of the former Bayles shipbuilding yard, Harborfront Park has a real then-and-now feel to it. The park includes an old chandlery, a playground, and an ice skating rink. A winding path takes you past grassy dunes and a striking sculpture of four seamen carrying the hull of a ship over their heads. Back in the days, schooners and whaling ships were built on land and launched into the harbor on the "well-worn ways"—rails that looked like train tracks. Some of those rails were unearthed like fossils when the park was built.

I stood on the rails now and waited for LaRue. A chill was in the air, a prelude to winter, and I zipped up my fleece. I'd left my car in the public lot on the other side of the ferry dock and walked over with nothing but my car keys. I was eager to get home to decipher the blackmail book and didn't want LaRue to lure me over to the Steam Room for fish and chips and beer. The sun was already below the horizon, the sky to the west golden with purple clouds.

I was still thinking about the revelation that Theo was a pilot. She'd kept that fact—like everything about her personal life—close to the vest. It made me very, very curious about her, to say the least. I wondered if either Ned or Sherm ever saw her around Brookhaven Airport. Of course, she might be based at MacArthur or Bayport or another airport. I made a mental note to ask Ned about her.

Being a pilot kind of put a kink in her alibi. Even if ten people vouched for Theo's presence in Rhode Island Friday morning, I knew she could have made it to Long Island in under an hour by plane. Ned and Sherm are always flying to Westerly for fuel, and that's how long it takes. She could have flown here, knocked off Hazzard, and been back at the hotel in time for breakfast.

A man passed by with two corgis. I gasped as something sharp dug into my back, below my left shoulder blade.

"Hand it over," Theodora Silk said in my ear. "Now." I felt her hot breath on my neck.

I stiffened. "Hand what over?"

"Don't play stupid, Emma. You're going to be dead in a minute. That's stupid."

"Not happening. LaRue's on her way."

Theo laughed harshly. "LaRue's not coming, you fool."

I had fallen into her trap.

"Put away the knife, Theo. I don't have your book."

"No?" The knife twisted against my back. "I think you do. And if I have to cut you up in little squares to find it, I will."

"You've already killed two people. Killing me will just get you a longer prison sentence. The police know where the book is and are on their way to get it. They may already have it."

"That's bullshit."

"Want to bet? They're way ahead of you, Theo. They've already done a voice analysis on the phone call."

Theo hesitated. She wasn't ready to kill me. First she wanted to know how much I and others knew. "What phone call?"

"The one you made from Anthony's. They have the blue bowl, too. With your fingerprints all over it."

"Impossible."

"Yeah, well, maybe they had to glue a few pieces together. The marvels of forensics."

While she chewed on that, I reached slowly into my left jacket pocket and pulled out one of the Latex gloves from the nursing home. I moved my right hand in front of my body where she couldn't see it and grabbed the other end of the glove.

"I was in Rhode Island on Friday, remember?" Theo said. "I did a presentation that morning. As you *well* know."

So that's where I'd slipped up. Helen Fistwater had called her.

"Doesn't matter. You could have gotten back here pretty damn quick in your airplane."

Theo jabbed the point of the knife through the fleece to my tender skin and dragged it toward my ribs. White pain and fear shot through me.

"All the evidence points to *you*, Emma," Theo snarled. "If you don't give me the book, the police will find it on you afterwards. I'll fix it so they do."

As she adjusted her grip on the knife, I spun around holding the glove taut and snapped it in her eye. Startled, she raised her hand to her face. I swung my leg up and kicked her hand, knocking the weapon onto the rocks in the harbor.

I turned and ran toward the lights of the ferry. My shirt stuck to my back where she had cut me. Glancing back I saw Theodora ten yards behind me, running awkwardly in her long skirt and loafers, the knife back in her hand. I angled out of the park and through the Danford's Hotel parking lot, keeping the marina to my right. Ahead of me cars were driving onto the ferry. To my left, steps led up to a line of shops that paralleled the marina.

I pounded up the steps, gulping air. Diving behind a dolphin statue I listened for the echo of her footsteps. Not a sound. I crept past the closed boutiques until I came to a second set of steps. Grabbing an umbrella from a stand, I leaned out and looked in both directions.

Theo was to my left, flattened against the wall with her face turned away, the knife clenched in her fist. I threw the umbrella down the steps. As she rushed toward the clatter I ran in the opposite direction and escaped down the last set of steps.

A metal fence separated Danford's parking lot from the ferry's. I hauled myself over it, ripping my jeans and nearly impaling myself on a pointed finial. The last few cars were driving aboard. I pulled up my hood and blended in with the walk-ons on the ramp.

At the top I broke away from the group and hid behind an SUV to watch for Theodora. The main deck on the third level was well-lit and populated, the best place to hide in plain sight, but if Theo found me there I'd have a heck of a time losing her when we debarked. I'd be a sitting duck. Staying below also gave me a good vantage point near the ramp. If she boarded the ferry, I could make a quick exit before we left port.

If she didn't board I had another set of problems. I didn't particularly want to be sailing for the next two and three-quarter hours while Theo broke into my car and stole my computer and all my notes. Surely she'd seen where I parked.

I scanned the interior of the two-level parking area. The upper deck, running along both sides of the vessel, was completely full. The lower deck was nearly full.

The crew began roping off the entrance ramp. I studied the maze of parked cars—had I missed her? Around me cars beeped as their owners clicked remote locking devices and headed for the stairs.

Three short whistle blasts and a long one, and the great vessel creaked in its berth. We began to move.

I stepped in front of a crew member. "Is there another way onto the ferry?"

"This is it."

I surveyed the main cavity again, then froze. Theo was inching along between two rows of cars on the opposite side, heading in my direction. Every few steps she bent down to look under the cars.

I crept along the outer wall in the other direction, toward the rear stairs. When I looked again, Theo was moving toward the rear, too, one row closer to me. In the dim overhead light the knife glinted in her hand. From here it looked like a small hooked-blade knife, the kind florists use to cut stems.

I felt around in the narrow space for something to use as a weapon. There were metal protuberances from the ship's body, and S-hooks and coils of rope, but everything was attached to the ship except for some lightweight chocks. I grabbed one.

Banging into a car's side mirror I made an involuntary sound. Theo looked up in my direction. The pilings moved slowly past open windows behind her.

I lunged for the stairwell door and ran up a flight, exited on the second level, and raced between the cars to the front stairs. Pulling open the heavy door I was blocked by a slow-moving couple with a cat carrier climbing up to the main deck. The door at the top opened and Theodora looked down at me. We eyed each other with the couple between us. Then I turned and dashed down the two flights.

Angling sharply toward the middle of the ferry where the big trucks were parked I leaped behind a yellow school bus. Through the driver's window I saw the door open and Theodora step out. I moved alongside the wheel to keep my legs hidden.

The great engine of the ferry hummed.

I could make it to the front stairs. I could. I looked under the school bus.

No loafers.

As I stood up Theo came around the back of the bus and lunged at me with the knife. I jumped aside, threw the chock at her face, and clambered over car bumpers to the next row. Through the window the twin smokestacks rolled by. Theo tore after me, swinging again and again with the knife and once catching the tail end of my jacket. I ripped free, rounded the outermost row of cars to the window, and hoisted myself up onto the ledge. The lights of the harbor looked far away.

Theo stood before me. Beneath her droopy bangs, her eyes bored into mine.

"Good luck covering up this one, Theo."

She took a step closer.

I leaned out the window and looked down. It was a twenty-foot drop to the water. A wave of vertigo rolled over me. I grabbed onto a window hook for balance and turned back in time to see a crew member disappear through a door on the second level.

"Who are you setting up to take the fall this time?"

She sneered. "I'm not the only one who uses a florist's knife."

My heart gave a jolt. Tony. She was setting up *Tony*.

"That's right, your new boyfriend." She took another step and raised the knife. "He won't even know what hit him. Just like you."

I said a quick prayer and shoved myself backwards off the ledge and out into space. I fell through the open air and crashed butt first into the cold, cold water of Port Jefferson Harbor.

CHAPTER FORTY-ONE

It was dark when I crawled up onto the rocks left by glaciers millions of years ago and sat against a boulder, gasping and shivering. Every muscle in my body burned with pain. Luckily, my skin was too numb to feel the gash Theo had given me.

The swim was easier and quicker than I'd anticipated. But there was still no time to spare. I had less than two hours to do what I needed before Theo got back.

My sneakers squeaked as I made my way dripping to the parking lot. Only a few people were around and they didn't pay any attention to me. Unzipping the inner pocket of my fleece, I found my keys and opened the car. I grabbed my phone and the I LOVE LIBRARIES tote and jogged home.

Less than a half hour later I was showered, bandaged, and wearing dry clothing. I called a taxi to pick me up. While I waited, I packed some toiletries and fed the cat.

I gave the taxi driver an address and popped the spare DVD into my computer. As we drove I burned the mystery video to the disk, transferred my cell phone's photo memory to my computer via a tiny memory card, and checked my voicemail. There was a message from Mom asking how my head was and one from LaRue saying she'd caught the little gray cat. When we got to Centereach I paid the driver, gathered up my stuff, and walked the last two blocks to the car rental office.

It was almost eight when I drove away in my Kia Soul. By now the ferry, and presumably Theo, were back in Port Jeff.

Maybe she'd already found my car and thought the worst. Or best, from her point of view. I stopped at the 7-Eleven for a Snickers and called Tony.

"Hi," he said in surprise.

"Are you busy?"

"No. What's going on?"

I heard cheering in the background. Football music.

"Are you alone?"

"Except for my roommates. Come on over, I'm just watching the game."

"I didn't know you had roommates."

"Temporarily. Where are you?"

He gave me directions to an address in Manorville, twenty-five minutes east. As I drove, exhaustion hit me. I opened the windows fully to keep myself awake.

The address turned out to be one of the big Monopoly houses that dot the former potato farms off the Long Island Expressway. I parked in front and went around to the side door, as Tony had instructed. He took one look at me and gathered me in his arms.

"Baby, what happened?"

I shook my head, and he led me inside to a dark-paneled, dimly lit bedroom. Some boxes and ski equipment were stacked against the wall. The bedroom door opened into a den with a bar. I heard football sounds coming from a television.

"They're upstairs," Tony said, in answer to my unspoken question. "No one can hear us."

For the first time since arriving I looked in his eyes.

"I need a favor."

"Sure."

"What time are you leaving for Martha's Vineyard tomorrow?"

"Nine or ten. I'm not on a schedule."

"I want you to bring these to Detective Zahn at police headquarters before you go."

I pressed my cell phone and the disk I'd copied into his palm.

"Do you have a piece of paper?"

I scrabbled in my bag for my pen but couldn't find it. Tony handed me one, along with a Post-it pad. His eyes never left my face.

I wrote down the number of my throwaway phone and stuck it to the jewel case.

"Tell him to call me."

"All right."

He put the items down, pulled me close, and kissed me. My lips were chapped from the salt water. I winced as his hand brushed the wound. He looked at me questioningly, but I shook my head again.

"*Sweet Emma Rose*," Tony said softly. "That's from a Van Morrison song, right?"

"Yes. How did you know I was named for that song?"

"Because you're a gypsy, and your caravan is on its way. Your folks Van Morrison fans?"

"They have a huge poster from his 'Moondance' tour in the living room and everything he ever recorded."

"Do you know why there's a radio in the song 'Caravan'?"

"No, why?"

Tony pulled me down gently to the edge of the bed and stroked my hair. "Because Morrison once lived in a house with an underground passage. Supposedly one time he heard a radio playing, loud enough to be in the same room. But the sound was really coming from another house a mile away."

"It came through the underground passage?"

"Yes. That's what he thought."

"I never knew that." I stared through the doorway into the den. Loud cheering broke out. Touchdown for someone. I looked back at Tony. His eyes were fixed on mine. "I'm a little bit like that. Ideas come to me from far away. I don't know where they come from."

We held hands without talking.

"Stay," he said. "We'll go to Zahn together in the morning."

"I can't, Tony. There's very little time. Very little."

"Why? What's going to happen?"

I shook my head. If I told him, he'd want to come with me. "There's something I have to do, and no one else to do it."

"Tell the police. Let them take care of it."

"They won't listen. They might start to, once they get those." I nodded toward the items I'd given him.

Tony's face was sober.

"What about that lightning you talk about?"

"What?"

"You know, standing under the right tree. I thought you believed in luck."

I looked away. "I do. I just want to make sure it doesn't run out this time."

A couple of hours later I was back on the expressway, heading to LaRue's and Ronk's condo. LaRue had made up the sofa bed. She eyed me dubiously as I set down my tote bag and put my sneakers under a heating vent to dry.

"I covered Petey's cage so he won't bother you."

"Where's our new friend?"

"You won't believe this."

She led me into the kitchen. The little gray cat was sleeping in the avocado plant, its small body wrapped around the stem.

"He ate a can and a half of Fancy Feast."

"Wow."

I noticed the thick bandage around his right front paw.

"You took him to the vet?"

"I had to. The poor thing was suffering. His foot was abscessed, and it got infected. Dr. Delgado had to anesthetize him and clean out the wound. He also gave him a shot of antibiotic." She pointed to a pile of medical supplies on the kitchen table. "He's going to need some care for a while. He might try and chew off his bandages when he starts feeling better."

"What caused the abscess?"

"I thought you'd never ask."

LaRue handed me a snap-and-seal sandwich bag. In it was a tiny blue chip.

I looked at her in surprise. "The blue bowl."

"You got it, sister." She grinned.

"He must have stepped on it after Hazzard was murdered."

LaRue nodded. "And the police swept up any other pieces."

"And took them to compare with the rest of the murder weapon, which went somewhere else."

"Distant Shores."

We looked at each other.

LaRue said, "So, where's the murder weapon now?"

"A little piece of it is in the room of every resident who went to arts and crafts this week. Some of it probably went home with grandchildren."

"What do you mean?"

I got my laptop from the other room and set it up on the kitchen table. I brought up one of the pictures I'd taken in Ida Strub's room.

LaRue stared. "Theo flies a plane? I didn't know that. But I don't see—"

"Not the photo. The frame."

The mosaic frame was filled with chips of every color, including mixing-bowl blue.

"Holy cannoli!"

"I missed it myself at first." Wearily I closed my laptop.

Her expression changed to concern. "Hey, you want a sandwich or something? When did you last eat?"

"I'm not hungry."

She opened the fridge. "I'll heat you up some of Mama's Italian wedding soup."

When the pot was on the stove, she came over and touched my shoulder.

"Show me."

I lifted up the back of my shirt. LaRue peeled back the gauze and stood there in silence. After a while she taped the gauze back down.

"Good Goddess. You're a mess."

"You think I need stitches?"

"I'm not a doctor. But it doesn't look too bad. Did you put anything on it?"

"Bacitracin. I used up the tube."

"I never thought I'd say this, Em."

"Say what?"

She stood over me in her pink fuzzy slippers with her hands on her hips. "You're the bravest person I know."

CHAPTER FORTY-TWO

Friday

I sat on the sofa bed under a batik throw and a tasseled Tibetan lamp. The laptop was on my lap, and the cat was on my laptop.

It was almost four in the morning. I'd slept soundly, falling instantly into a coma-like slumber after polishing off the soup, but for the last hour I'd been staring into the dark. I'd finally given in to the siren call of the computer. The sense that I was this close to putting it all together was overpowering.

"You were somebody's pet once, weren't you?" I lifted the little fellow off my keyboard and set him down next to me. "Who did you belong to, Chip?" He blinked and curled up in the crook of my leg.

I'd taken nine photos of the blackmail book. The first showed two columns of numbers—dates and amounts of bank deposits, maybe?

The other eight were of two-page spreads. Each spread had a name at the top and contained a jumble of equations, question marks, letters, and words. I flipped through the photos.

Kingpin
Granite
Cookiepuss
Frenchie
Icemom

Prof
Gogogo
Mr. Clean

"Kingpin" had to be Sally Bellarosa. The scribbles below his name were probably the blackmail hook, number of payments, and other details Hazzard felt were significant. Was Hazzard holding more over him than their affair? Did I care?

The "Prof" page sent a chill through me. Sam. One of the lines had an "H" with a line through it. No Harvard, I guessed.

Which one was Theo? After eliminating Mr. Clean for obvious reasons, I copied the notes from the other five spreads into my notebook. Then I minimized the photo files and opened my media player.

"What are you doing?"

LaRue stared at me from the hallway, a towel draped over her arm.

"I couldn't sleep. Is it morning already?"

"Hi ho, hi ho," she singsonged.

"Come in and look at Chip."

"Wait, I have to put my contacts in."

She shuffled off to the bathroom. While I waited I booted up the CNN News file I'd transferred to my computer.

The recording began in the middle of a story about six people killed during a Kentucky shooting rampage. I watched the whole gory segment. Next up was a story about a bride who'd faked having terminal cancer so she could collect wedding money for her honeymoon.

LaRue reappeared in her waitress uniform. "Look at you two," she said, petting the little cat, who was draped over my shoulder, his head smooshed into my neck. "My two survivors."

"Did you ask Ronk if she knows anyone who wants him?"

"Yeah. You. He loves you, Em."

"I'm telling you, Rue, Bergamot eats cats."

LaRue uncovered Petey's cage and went to work, and I went back to the film. Following the fake cancer story were stories about trapped miners and an Islamic center near Ground Zero. I didn't see the connection between any of these and Theo—or her father. I fast forwarded through two more segments before I realized I was going about it the wrong way.

If I wanted to record a news story, how would I do it? I'd turn on my recorder and keep it on until they went through all the stories and looped back to mine. *Then* I'd stop recording.

Duh. I fast forwarded to the last story.

It was a special report about Olympic skating hopefuls practicing in Lake Placid, New York. A couple dozen teens to young adults were shown working on their ice dancing, freestyle techniques, spins, and jumps in the legendary school that has trained figure skating champions for nearly a century. The CNN reporter had interviewed two students and their coaches, plus the mother of one of the students. All of the students were hoping to compete in the Winter Olympics.

One of Hazzard's targets was named Icemom. I went back to the photo files and opened up Icemom's spread.

Icemom
Gma's earring, 3 prls & pink st.
b-F?? crapster gone—GM&GD. ck house.
pu=ez

The shorthand was tough to figure out. Grandma's earring? Who or what was the crapster? "Ck house"—check the house for what?

I transferred Chip to the couch and went into the kitchen to make myself a pot of coffee and some toast. The only bread I could find had fourteen grains. All I wanted was one grain— wheat. The white kind. I hunted through the cabinets and came up with a box of Weetabix. Not Cap'n Crunch, but it would have to do. I dumped honey and milk on it and brought it back to the living room.

Then I cracked open my black and white notebook and started reading from the top—the whole enchilada. I now had pretty much all the information Hazzard had possessed before she died. All I had to do was put it together.

I reread the Sally Bellarosa episodes—the Sudzo King and the flea market, the bowling alley and the Bay Shore attack. Biz the Lizard. The disappearing trash bags. The library card and the yearbooks. Yancy Villers and the pool hall. Sam and Harvard. The mountains of microfilm. The photos stolen from the museum. The little gray cat and the blue chip.

It was like throwing a thousand-piece jigsaw puzzle up in the air and hoping for a miracle.

I googled "Villers Lake Placid" and "Silk Lake Placid," but nothing useful came up. I paired the two surnames with "Olympics" and "ice skating," again with no luck.

What did Theodora have to do with ice skaters in Lake Placid? I returned to the video and pressed play.

"Was that a sigh, or a category three hurricane?" Ronk stood in the living room, putting on her watch.

"Hey." I hit stop.

"So, here's my thought, ET. If you're going to get yourself killed, would you please do it *after* the thirty-first? And not before? Because we're planning a kickass Halloween party, and we need your Frankenstein mask for the front door."

"Will do." I smiled at the screen.

"I mean, show a little consideration here."

"No prob."

"Between the bird and the cat and everything else going on, I don't have time for another funeral this week."

I gave her a half-lidded look.

"Ronk, relax."

"What are you trying to do, Em?" She waved her arm. "Are you *trying* to get yourself killed? LaRue comes in and tells me you have a gash in your back this long, and you're afraid to go home. Sunday you were in the hospital with a concussion."

"That's because—"

"I'll have you know neither of us slept a wink the whole night."

"Ronk." I held up a hand to stop her. "I know who did it."

"Don't tell me. Tell the police."

"I am. This morning. They'll have all the evidence they need in two hours."

Ronk shook her head. "You used to be this timid little lamb. Lately you've morphed into I don't know what."

"Just call me ET-Rex."

"Ha."

"Ronk, you have any decent cereal in this house?"

She came over to the couch. "Is that that Weetabix shit?"

"Mmm-hmm."

"Come with me."

I put the laptop and bowl aside and followed her down the hall into the fitness-slash-crafts room. Ronk opened a bowling bag on the floor next to her golf clubs and pulled out two boxes of cereal.

"Honey Nut Cheerios or Frosted Flakes?"

"Ah, that's more like it." I grabbed the Frosted Flakes.

"Don't forget to put the box back when you're done. Are you going to be here for lunch?"

"I'm not sure yet."

"If you don't like LaRue's selections, you'll find mac and cheese in the golf bag."

After Ronk left for work, I viewed the Lake Placid story again. The interviews—the A-roll footage—began with a sixteen-year-old girl from Kentucky named Lorna Glen who was thrilled to be in Lake Placid. She was wearing Spongebob Squarepants earrings and a pink hoodie. The B-roll footage cut away to scenes of the local area and of high school students getting on buses. There was also film of the girl working in the rink with her coach.

The coach, a Russian woman and Olympic bronze medalist, spoke of her passion for encouraging students to develop their strengths and not fear the talent out there. B-roll was stock video of Olympic skating.

This was followed by a similar pairing of student-coach interviews, this time spotlighting a young man named Ivan Gregorovich and his mentor, a former ice dancing champion from Vancouver. The camera cut away to show the student heading into the local Starbucks with friends. Ivan's mother expressed her pride in her son and the fact that no one else in the family was the least bit athletic.

I went back to the beginning and took a closer look at the students practicing in the background. There were ten or twelve on the ice at any given time. They glided by the camera too quickly for me to pick up many details.

I heard lapping and turned to see the little cat on the floor beside me, finishing up the milk in my cereal bowl.

"How's the paw, Chip?"

"Meow," Chip said.

I brought the madras throw into the kitchen and made a nest on the table. Then I set Chip on the throw and carefully removed his bandage. His poor paw was all red and ravaged. I cleaned the wound, added a squirt of medication, and dressed the paw with a clean bandage. He didn't move the whole time, just gazed gratefully into my eyes.

It always amazes me that we can look at something so carefully and still miss the forest for the trees. Here was this little fellow who'd been limping around, fairly advertising a major clue, and neither LaRue nor I had picked it up because we were focusing on the wrong thing. I wondered if, despite my efforts, I was still missing something important.

I decided to review my notes from the back issues of *The Record*. It was all routine police blotter stuff and community news except for the abandoned baby story in the December 7 issue. Quickly, I did the math. That child, if she was alive today, would be eighteen—about the same age as the skaters in the video.

In the weird way the mind sometimes works, mine suddenly leaped from the skaters to an idea so improbable, far-fetched, and out-and-out bizarre that it took all my will to keep from dismissing it instantly. What if Theo had given birth to that baby?

What if that baby had been Theodora's?

Hypothetically, now. (Deep breath.) What if—what if Theo had never gone to England at all in her junior year, but was actually at home, waiting out a pregnancy? At the time, her father still lived there, and her grandmother, too. They could have taken care of her, brought her school work, whatever she needed. I pictured them shielding her behind drapes, smuggling her out the back door for doctors' appointments, allowing her a few minutes of fresh air now and then when no one was watching.

She would have been only sixteen and probably confused, shocked, and scared.

Her grandmother could have concocted the England trip as a way to conceal the pregnancy. That's the kind of thing Silks did. Silks didn't have babies outside of marriage. Certainly not as teenagers.

Who had the father been? I couldn't recall Theo having any boyfriends in high school. Had she dated someone secretly? Or, worse than that, had she been raped? The shame of a pregnancy from rape would be almost unimaginable for someone in her family. Her grandmother would have gone to any length to hide it.

So, suppose she'd been hidden away all those months—summer, fall, all the way up to the December birth. Suppose the pregnancy caused a lot of tension in the Silk household, created a rift between father and grandmother. Maybe they'd argued about how to handle it. Maybe Yancy Villers had blamed Theo, or maybe the situation had made a poor relationship with his mother-in-law even worse. It might have been quite stressful and unpleasant in the household—bad enough to drive him away.

Maybe Theo's shame had been so great that she couldn't see herself going through the adoption process. She might have agreed to it at first and changed her mind. But Ida Strub was a forceful personality—she was the one driving the bus. Maybe Theo believed she had no recourse but to go along with her grandmother's plans. What if she had given birth alone and panicked? Could she have taken matters into her own hands and abandoned the baby?

Motive to kill. There it was.

Sunlight splashed over the carpet. With a shake I brought myself back to reality. It was after ten and I should have heard from Zahn by now. I checked my cell phone and saw that I'd missed two calls from Tony. I punched in his number.

"What did Zahn say?" I asked when he picked up.

"Where've you been?" Tony said. I heard wind in the background. He was driving.

"I'm sorry, I didn't hear the phone."

"Zahn wasn't in when I got there. He and his partner were out on a case."

"Did you give the things to someone else?"

"Should I have? I wasn't sure what you wanted me to do.

That's why I called. I waited fifteen minutes for you to call back, but I had a ferry to catch."

I bit my lip. "So you have the disk and cell phone with you."

"Yes. If you don't mind someone else possibly opening the package, I can overnight them to Zahn when I get to the Vineyard."

"Where are you now?"

"New London."

I looked out the window, thinking.

"Emma?"

"When do you think you'll get there?"

"Three, maybe four if there's a lot of traffic on I-95, which it looks like there might be."

"It might not make sense to overnight them. If they don't go out tonight, they won't get to him until Sunday at the earliest. And you'll be back on Monday."

"If I survive Sunday."

"What do you mean?"

"The Jets are playing the Patriots," Tony explained. "My whole family's from Boston. If the Jets win, I'll have to sleep in the woodshed with the bats."

CHAPTER FORTY-THREE

I pulled up the Suffolk County Police Department's website and found the link to file an anonymous tip. I then reported the locations of a couple of items that might be of interest to police in the Jennifer Hazzard case. The site used encryption software to ensure that the tip couldn't be traced back to me.

Then I called Zahn from my throwaway phone and left him a message with my new number. I took a fresh cup of coffee and my computer out to the balcony and sat with my feet on the railing. From LaRue's and Ronk's second floor condo I could see a sliver of sparkling water in the harbor. Red and yellow leaves from the maples and birches below blew onto the balcony and whirled cheerfully around my chair.

As I expected, the Lake Placid skating school did not make public its student rosters. I googled "ice skating discussion forums" and three groups turned up. One was inactive, and another was mostly gossip about skating stars. The third group, On the Ice, had a more professional feel. There were discussion areas related to coaches, equipment, parent support, and various aspects of training. I scanned the discussion threads until one caught my eye. All the posts in the thread had been left the day before within a seven-hour period. The subject line was "Lorna on TV!!!"

skategirl1007: Hey everyone, did you see Lorna on CNN? Woo-hoo, GO LORNA!

happysk8s: Noooo!!!!! When was it?

skategirl007: Today, Greer. It was on a few times. Split jump, she did it perfect!!

nyzambonidriver: Yeah! I was in there, too.

skategirl007: I saw you go by, Scott!

ladyskater11: Ugh I missed it! I had soc class. Was I in there, Dee?

skategirl007: Lorna you just passed your Senior MIF, right?

lpblades: Yeah, and now I never have to do that #*@^&#% serpentine step sequence again! YAAAAY!!

The conversation continued with other skaters chiming in. I went to my black and white notebook and wrote down all the participants' names, matching real names to online handles wherever I could, until I had a list of seventeen names.

Then I opened a new tab, hopped over to Facebook, and did a search for "Lake Placid Ice Skaters." An official page and several unofficial ones came up. On the official page I found a post halfway down congratulating Lorna, Ivan, and the other students appearing in the broadcast. Under that were several comments.

Dee Cantone: Congrats Lorna and Ivan! Skaters, you rock!

Helen Pizer: Congrats to all you young people for your hard work. May you go far and find much success and happiness. Warm hugs!

Greer Lynn Applebaum: Yeah! Go skaters!

After adding Dee's and Greer's last names to my list, I clicked on Dee's Facebook page and read today's comments.

Dee Cantone: Par-tay tonight at my place!!! Lake Placid skaters, who's in?

Kevin Felker: There!

Leslie McGovern: What are people bringing? I can do wings.

Joe Morrisey: Beer.

Scott Brandwein: There! Crab dip.

Faith Devereaux: I'm going home for Thanksgiving. Sorry I'll miss your party, Dee!

Greer Lynn Applebaum: Veggies and dip.

Kevin Felker: Thanksgiving is next month. You Canadians have it all wrong.

Karen Carr: I'm in! Cheese and crackers.

Dee Cantone: Happy Turkey Day, Faith! We'll miss you! Kevin can you bring ice?

I filled in some missing last names from Dee's list of 639 friends. Then I clicked on the Facebook pages of the female students to see when their birthdays were. I always wonder why people make this kind of information public. I found what I was looking for almost immediately.

Faith Devereaux
Birthday: December 3
Hometown: Montreal, QC

Faith was the one going home for Canadian Thanksgiving. I checked out the other female students' pages, but no one else's birthday fell anywhere near the target date.

I studied her photos. Faith was tall for a skater, and thin, with a pretty, but secretive, smile. She had studied at the Mariposa School of Skating in Barrie, Ontario, before going to Lake Placid. She liked Bichons, the color purple, friendship rings, and Oreos dipped in milk. Her favorite movie was *Amélie*. She was passionate about the environment and the Montreal Canadiens. She liked to write poetry and had included a sample.

> If only I could love you, dear,
> I'd keep you safe from harm.
> I'd carry you through all the world.
> I'd shield you from the storm.
> But you were only in my dream.
> A wisp of cloud—unreal.
> You cannot love me back, dear,
> You cannot even feel.
> And this is why my heart and
> I will never
> ever
> heal.

Faith's wall was full of friendly hellos from her Canadian friends.

Katie Cohen: Can't wait to see you, Faithie!

Faith Devereaux: Katie! Gram gets here on Sun. and the fam feast is on Monday, so I'm busy except for Saturday. Brutopia?? Or shopping first?? Mom's coming with me to the A in the morning, but I'll be done early. Is Mollie home?

Katie Cohen: Mollie's in Halifax. I'm working 12 to 7. I'll see if I can get off earlier. Maybe if I tell them you're home! Haha right! What time do you practice?

Danielle Rosen-Leveque: Hey Faith! Where are you having Thanks?

Faith Devereaux: Dani!!! Are you home? We're having it at my house. Katie—at 7. Come watch me!

Soon-yi Lee: I'm home, too! Brutopia, woot!

Katie Cohen: OMG no I'll still be asleep!! I didn't even know the Atrium was open that early!

The last comment was posted at ten-thirty this morning. There was no response from Faith, which made sense if she was on the road heading home.

I googled "Atrium Montreal" and learned that it was an ice skating rink downtown. Then I fast forwarded through the news video looking for Faith. I recognized her right away. She wore black leggings and a red sweatshirt that said *Go Habs Go!*, her brown ponytail switching this way and that as she glided backwards past the camera.

If Faith Devereaux was Theo's daughter and Hazzard had figured it out—well, I had to give the pissant credit. But I couldn't go to Zahn with a birth date and an old news story. I needed proof.

I pulled up MapQuest on the Internet. In despair I noted that Montreal was more than 400 miles away. And what was I going to do when I got there—knock on her door? And say what?

The agency that had handled the baby's adoption would have any existing birth records, but they wouldn't release them to me. I wondered if I could track down the woman who'd found the baby. She might remember something—a birthmark, for example—that would help with identification. Coming up with her name might be difficult, though. It had been kept out of the newspaper stories.

I wrote down *The Record* reporter's name and called the paper.

"Deceased," said the operator who answered the phone.

Montreal was an awfully long drive.

I knew that if I called Ned, he'd fly me up in the Bonanza—no questions asked. I'd be on Canadian soil in two hours and be back in time for bed.

The thought nauseated me.

I did a search for commercial flights to Montreal—airplanes with nice big wings that were less likely to fall out of the sky. There was a three o'clock departure from MacArthur Airport.

Once again I enlisted my trusty Google search engine to fetch help, and it brought up a video that promised to banish my fear of flying in ten easy steps. I clicked "play" and sat back.

A woman in a white lab coat spoke in mellifluous tones, a smile playing at the corners of her mouth. "Are you comfortably seated? Have you removed all distractions? Silenced your cell phone?"

"Yes."

"Good," she said, as though she could hear me through the computer. "Now, I'm going to ask you some questions. If you answer 'yes' to three or more, you are an *excellent* candidate for this course. And I *promise* you that what you will learn in the next thirty minutes will prove to you what a *pleasurable* and *safe* activity flying really is. One. Does the thought of going to the airport stress you out?"

"Yes."

"Do you have sudden or prolonged panic attacks when you think about boarding an airplane?"

"Yes."

"In flight, do you often have fantasies about the airplane falling out of the sky and crashing?"

"What do *you* think?"

"Are you afraid of being hijacked?"

I glared at her.

"Do you fear heights? Do you dread being in enclosed or crowded spaces? Do you like to be in control of situations? Do you experience heart palpitations when you hear the engine make strange—"

I clicked *stop* and waited for my heart to slow down. Then I picked up the phone and called Noah Banks, my kindergarten husband. I hadn't talked to him in quite a while, so we had a minute or two of chitchat before I got to the point of my call.

"Are you still freelancing?" I asked.

"Photography, or the band?"

"Photography. What band?"

"I started a band with three other guys. Didn't I tell you? We're doing mostly parties now, but we have a couple gigs coming up."

"That's great." I shifted to my other foot. "Listen, Noah, I need a favor. I have a long drive ahead of me and not much time."

"Okay."

"Now, don't ask me any questions, because I can't answer. I need to borrow some of your cameras and stuff."

Noah cleared his throat the way he always does when he disapproves. "Cameras? Why?"

"No questions, Noah. I just need some equipment to make me look like a photographer. I'm not actually going to use any of it. I want stuff hanging from my shoulders, like light meters and all that other *chazzerei* you guys carry around."

There was a pause. "That *chazzerei*, as you call it, cost me thousands of dollars. I'd like to know what you plan to do with it."

"I can't tell you."

"Or you'd have to kill me?"

"Noah, trust me on this. I don't want to put you in danger."

"Oh, for Pete's sake. Can I at least ask where you're *going* with my cameras?"

"Canada."

"Canada!"

"It's only for one day. You'll have everything back by tomorrow night. Or Sunday. I promise. Definitely by Sunday."

I could feel him weakening.

"So, can I come by?"

Noah sighed. "When does this road trip start?"

CHAPTER FORTY-FOUR

It started as soon as I hung up. I gave Chip a kiss, grabbed my tote bag and the MapQuest printout, and left a brief note for LaRue and Ronk. They'd worry anyway, but it was the least I could do.

Noah was at the front door of his house in Terryville, peering out with hands on hips as I pulled into the driveway in my Kia.

"What happened to the Honda?" he asked when he let me in.

That was the cover question—the real question was something else. I looked at him and quickly looked away. Noah has very, very sad eyes. Maybe the saddest eyes of anybody I know. Whenever we make eye contact, for some reason I feel extremely guilty, even if I haven't done anything wrong. He has never asked me the real question. But I know it's there.

"The Honda's fine. This is a rental."

He nodded, looking me over. "And your face? That looks like a bad cut."

"Noah, I'd love to sit and chat, but if you'll just point me to the camera equipment, I'll be on my way." Then I felt a little ungracious. "I really appreciate your help."

"Well, I'm doubting my sanity, actually. If you were anybody else . . ." he said, his voice trailing off. I padded after him down the hallway to his office, past framed photos of winter beaches and night football games, sunflowers and sailboats. He had put down new carpeting and spruced up the place. It smelled new. It looked nice.

"Business going well?" I asked.

"Not bad," Noah said without elaborating.

The futon in his office was covered with equipment.

"Since you only want to pass for a photographer and not function as one, I'm giving you my old flashes and a case full of cords I don't use. Are you going to be indoors?"

"Yes."

He picked up a camera. "Take this one. It's got an eighty-five millimeter telephoto lens and a fast aperture so it works better in low light, for that touch of realism. There's an off-camera flash cord attached to the strap of the bag. On the other side is a pouch with your batteries, lens cloth, black tape, colored gels, and memory cards. Usually I put my extra lenses in there, too, but you're not getting those. You can use the spare room for your pistol and night-vision goggles." Noah gently wiped the lens of the camera and placed it back in its case.

"Can I have that one, too?" I asked, pointing.

"The Canon?"

"Yeah. I need more than one camera, Noah. I have to look like the real thing."

He picked it up as though it were a baby. "This cost me a few C-notes."

I smiled sweetly.

With a sideways look he placed the camera in the "yes" pile. "How are you getting to Canada?"

"I told you, I'm driving."

"Which—"

"No more questions, Noah. I'm serious."

"I was going to ask you which route you're taking. Getting through customs going up is not a problem. Coming back, if they decide to look through your car, you'll have to explain all this equipment. If you don't know what you're talking about, they'll know it."

"What do you recommend?"

"Come back through Vermont, it's less of a hassle. Don't take the Thruway." Noah frowned and picked up two lenses. "Should I throw in another lens? Nah." He put them back down.

"What's the name of your band?" I asked him as we placed everything in my trunk.

He looked almost embarrassed. "Caravan."

CHAPTER FORTY-FIVE

Getting around New York City is always terrible unless you go on Sunday at three a.m., which this wasn't. The Whitestone Bridge and the Hutch were moving at a crawl, and the Cross County wasn't much better. Once I got onto the Thruway it opened up.

With a jar of marshmallow fluff in the cup holder to stick a finger in once in a while and a working radio in the Kia, I was set. I fiddled with the radio dial until I found a station playing "Guitar Boogie."

I was still bummed out by what I'd learned about Zahn at the library. It kind of brought into question the whole tree-in-the-lightning-storm idea. If anyone had picked the wrong tree, it was Zahn's father. His death had turned Zahn's whole life inside out in the blink of an eye. But instead of retreating and blaming circumstances, Zahn had stood on this big, stinking pile of bad luck and made his way to the top. He'd risen through the ranks of the police department and become a detective.

It rankled to admit it, but he inspired me.

I stopped at the Plattekill service area to use the restroom and glanced in the mirror while washing my hands. My eyes returned a steady gaze. They looked like eyes that didn't give a rat's ass about luck or fate or lightning. Which was a good thing, because inside I was wishing I could hide under the covers until it was all over.

As I headed north, the Catskill Mountains rose on either side and fell away, followed by the Adirondacks. Several times I saw bands of Canada geese flying south through the bright sky.

The sun had gone behind the hills and the clouds had turned pinky-orange when I pulled into a gas station. Zahn called as I reached the pump.

"What's with the new phone number, Trace?"

"Oh, that. Makes me feel safer. Since that anonymous call, you know."

I got out of the car. A tractor trailer went by, blasting his horn.

"Where are you?" Zahn asked.

"Upstate."

"Where upstate?"

"Glens Falls. I'm at a gas station. Are you going to interrogate me every time I get in the car, Detective?"

"I'm not interrogating you, Trace. How'd the birthday dinner go?"

I took off the gas cap and inserted the nozzle. "How did you know I won the bet?"

"Wild guess."

"It was fun. I didn't know you and Ned played on the same softball team."

There was a pause. "Ned told you about the softball?"

"Yeah. He said you were great."

Another tractor trailer went by and drowned out Zahn's response.

"What did you say?"

"I said, he's giving you a crock."

"A crock that you were great, or that he meant it?"

Zahn laughed. "That he meant it."

I laughed, too. It was a good moment. Things relaxed between us. I wondered if Zahn had picked up my anonymous tip. Mentioning it on the phone would be akin to admitting I'd trespassed. In a way I was glad Tony hadn't gotten to him with the evidence.

"Before I forget, thanks for watching my back at the storage place." I pulled the nozzle out.

"Don't mention it, Trace."

"Goodnight, Detective."

As I put the gas cap back on I heard the sound of wings beating. I felt a breeze on my face and touched my cheek. Then I saw him—a bald eagle—fly past me at eye level. His white crown feathers gleamed and his wings spanned at least five feet. The eagle looked me directly in the eye as he flew past. At the end of the gas station he swooped upward, circling once above me. Then he glided to a nearby tree and landed on a branch.

Slowly I returned the hose to the pump. Cars whooshed by on the Interstate. In the Quik Mart, a man sat back reading the paper. I was the only one who'd witnessed it. I'd never seen a real eagle in the wild before, only the two that lived in the cage at the Holtsville Ecology Center. They'd been injured and couldn't be set free. But this one was free, and he was here—now—with me.

The eagle stared at me from the branch for a long minute. I stared back. Then he took off, circled again above me, and disappeared to the north.

A powerful feeling filled my chest. I felt brave and solid, as solid as the mountains. I didn't know if the feeling would last, but I didn't care. I was psyched.

The sky turned from deep blue to violet as I continued up I-87, singing along with George Harrison on "Handle with Care." Soon it was too dark to see the mountains or where the mountains ended. After a while I came to farm country with lights twinkling from farmhouses on either side. Lake Champlain was off to my right somewhere, and beyond that was Vermont.

A little after six, I stopped at a diner in Peru, New York. The temperature had dropped, and I wished I'd worn another layer. When I paid for my hamburger, I noticed some blue "Peru Indians" sweatshirts hanging behind the cash register and bought one.

I told customs I was visiting my cousins in Montreal for Thanksgiving and continued up Autoroute 15, listening to French folk songs and watching "Sortie" signs go by. Finally I saw the exit for Pont Champlain and navigated my way downtown.

I debated stopping to listen to some music, but all I really wanted was a hot shower and a good night's sleep. I pulled into the parking garage of a hotel on Sherbrooke and five minutes later was slipping my keycard into the slot of room 1616, with a "city view." The desk clerk had also offered me a room on the third floor, which is as far from the ground as I normally like to be, but something had made me pick the higher one.

The drapes were closed. After dumping my stuff on the bed I went to the window and, squeezing my eyes shut, pulled the cord. Metal scraped as the drapes parted, and I took a deep breath and opened my eyes. The earth fell away—rooftops, chimneys, lights, all below me. Quickly I shut my eyes, touching the wall for balance. Then I remembered the eagle, and the brave feeling came back. I opened my eyes.

Below me a thousand million lights twinkled like stars. I had never seen anything so beautiful in my life. I shivered, imagining what it would be like to be an eagle, circling high above the city.

I stood at the window for a long time, looking. Circling.

Evidence Locker
Box 15
Personal diary, page 166

Dear Diary,

It is safe. I know it is safe because the paper said someone took it. I was afraid it would be grotesque, but I was wrong. It was pretty, with tiny little fingers and eyelashes. I gave it one of Grandma's pearl earrings for luck.

Grandma did everything with me. That's all I'll say about it, Diary, except it's done and over with. And no one will ever know in fifty lifetimes. No one goes in that room, anyway.

CHAPTER FORTY-SIX

Saturday

When I got to the Atrium at seven, Faith Devereaux and her mother were already there. The indoor ice skating rink was in an enormous sky-lit room surrounded by a food court. I bought a cup of coffee, took a seat at the opposite end of the rink from the Devereauxes, and watched Faith put on her skates.

There were two other skaters on the ice, a man and woman practicing a dance routine. The first public skating session wasn't until ten. It was a good time to work before the crowds showed up.

Faith did some stretches against the barrier, de-ponytailed and re-ponytailed her hair, and stepped confidently onto the ice. She began her warmups, skating around the huge oval with long strides, doing forward crossovers as she passed me, then half-turning and skating backwards the rest of the way. Faith was wearing the same red Habs sweatshirt she'd worn on TV along with gray leggings and red striped legwarmers scrunched around her ankles. Her face showed animated concentration.

I turned my attention to her mother. She was sitting on the bench with her legs crossed, hands cupped about her knees, her chin tilted up. She nodded slightly as her daughter glided past her. A tiny smile curled at the edges of her mouth.

I slipped my trusty press pass and the straps of Noah's cameras over my head, slung the rest of the equipment over my shoulders, and headed for the other side of the rink.

"Good morning," I said to Faith's mother.

She looked up expectantly. "Well, you start your work day early." She smiled, her eyes grazing my getup.

"You should see me at eight p.m. I'm whipped."

Her laugh was like a bell tinkling. She patted the bench beside her. "What can I do for you?"

"I'm Nola Banks with *Young Athlete,* and I'm working on a feature about rising ice skaters and their families. I've been doing on-the-spot interviews in skating rinks, and taking pictures, of course. I'm a photojournalist," I added idiotically.

"Print or online?"

That took me by surprise. "Um, online. I've already been—"

"Do you have a business card?"

"Sure." I made a show of going through various zippered pockets. "I just restocked my bag, because I ran out last week in the field. Hang on, I think they're in here."

"Would you like me to hold something for you?"

"Oh, no, thanks." I unzipped another compartment and felt inside. "While I'm looking, may I ask you a few questions and then speak to your daughter?"

"How did you know she was my daughter?" The woman looked at me curiously.

"I just assumed. Forgive me—"

"She *is* my daughter, actually." The woman smoothed back her hair. She had a large forehead and an intelligent face. "Faith is getting ready for the North Atlantic regional qualifying competition in Lake Placid. She's been practicing for months. It's a very important step for a skater. Next are the sectionals."

"Could I have your names, first, please?" I grabbed a pen and pad.

"My daughter's name is Faith Devereaux." She spelled it for me. "And I'm Marie Devereaux."

"And you live in Montreal?"

"Yes. Faith has been skating in Lake Placid for the past year. She's home this weekend for Thanksgiving." She watched me write. "She was so pleased to be able to work things out so that she could study there. We were all pleased."

"That's terrific. Can you give me her coach's name?"

Marie Devereaux spelled it for me. "You can call the school and I'm sure you'll be able to speak to him."

"Has your daughter always wanted to skate?" There was only one question I needed the answer to, but I wanted to take my time getting there.

Faith's mother nodded. "Since she was three. I was a skater, and my husband is, and he still coaches hockey. So, Faithie grew up on the ice. My little snow bunting. She has more talent than my husband and I combined."

She flashed a brilliant smile toward the rink. I turned in time to see Faith execute a double left axel.

"She doesn't like it when I call her Faithie," Marie Devereaux said. "Please don't use it in your article."

"I won't. I'm glad you mentioned you and your husband. The purpose of my article is to explore family athleticism. Do athletic children take after their parents? That was going to be the basis for my next question."

"Well, it's funny you ask, because—"

There was a loud scrape as Faith braked to a halt in front of us.

"Mom, it's still too tight. I told you it would be."

"Well, Faith, honey, come sit down and we'll fix it."

"The tape hurts my ankle every time I jump. I'm getting a blister. Can we *please* go down to Klingbeil's and get some boots that fit?"

"I think we can manage that, honey. Faith, this is Ms. Banks. She's writing an article about skaters for—what did you say the

285

publication was?"

"*Young Athlete.*"

"I never heard of that one," Faith said to me. Her cheeks were as red as her sweatshirt. I thought I saw a resemblance to Theodora around the mouth and chin.

"It's new." I waved my light meter in the air. "An offshoot of *Sports Insider.* Your mom tells me you're getting ready for a competition."

"If I get through the regionals, I go to the sectionals, and if I get through those—" She shrugged and smiled. "Let's just say, it would be a real good thing."

"It sure would." I picked up a camera, hoping it was the low-light one. "Do you mind if I take a few photos?"

"Okay," Faith said. "Do you want me to start skating?"

"Let me get a close-up first." I twiddled with a few dials and remembered to take the lens cap off.

"Don't you need a flash in here?" Marie Devereaux asked.

"I think there's enough ambient lighting." I aimed the camera at Faith and then lowered it. I'd noticed something that made the hair on the back of my neck stand up. Faith was wearing a pearl pendant that looked a lot like the one I'd seen on Theodora. In fact, *exactly* like it. It had the same three pearls around a pink stone that Theo was forever worrying with her fingers.

"That's pretty," I said to Faith. "I've never seen a charm like that before."

Faith touched the pendant. "Oh, this? I always wear it, for luck."

"Do you believe in luck?"

"Absolutely. I consider myself a very lucky person."

I raised the camera again and pushed the button a few times, hoping to get at least one in focus. As Faith skated away, her mother said, "She works herself so hard. Sometimes I wish she'd ease up a little." She sighed, but I saw the tiny smile again. Helicopter mom.

"You were about to say something earlier, Mrs. Devereaux, when I mentioned families." I twiddled more dials and clicked the camera button a few more times in Faith's direction.

"Yes. I was about to say that it's funny, ironic actually, that you're writing about children inheriting their parents' athletic ability. I don't know if you can use Faith in your article, after all."

I looked at her. "Why not?"

"Because Faith is adopted. There's no basis for assuming that Faith's talent comes from my husband and me. We did encourage her. And she certainly has a gift. But it's not in the genes—that is, unless her biological parents were athletic. We have no way of knowing that."

"Is she Canadian by birth?"

She looked at me strangely. "Why do you ask?"

I shrugged. "I don't know. I guess, if she were from the States, or anywhere far away, it would make the athletic connection seem even odder. Sorry, it was a silly question."

Marie Devereaux looked troubled. Her eyes moved to Faith, who was executing a spin in the middle of the rink. "She was born in the States, in fact. But her home has always been here, in Montreal. We still live in NDG, in the house where Faith grew up."

"Endeegee?"

"Notre-Dame-de-Grâce. It's a neighborhood in the west end."

"May I ask you one more question?"

"Of course, Nola."

"What did Faith mean when she said she was a very lucky person?"

Marie Devereaux blinked. "I don't understand."

"She's in a sport that takes courage and skill and discipline, yet she speaks about luck."

Marie turned her eyes, which had been fixed on her daughter, back to me. She still looked troubled, but on top of that I saw a flicker of suspicion.

"I guess you would have to ask *her* that."

I turned and shot a few more photos. It would have been more realistic to take some using a flash or one of the other doohickeys in my goody bag, but I didn't want to make a mistake at such close range. "Mrs. Devereaux, thank you for your time. If you'd like to jot down an email address, I'll let you know when this goes live."

She took the notepad and pen I handed her, but didn't write. "Were you able to locate those business cards?"

"You know, I must have left them in my car." I tucked my camera away and gathered up my stuff.

"I think I'd like your phone number and email address." Marie Devereaux handed the notepad back to me. "If you don't mind."

"Certainly not." I said, scribbling. I tore off the top sheet and handed it to her. Our eyes met.

"I forgot where you said you were based," she said. "Stateside?"

"I don't think I said, but yes. I'm from the States."

Marie Devereaux leaned forward.

"That doesn't say Nola."

"What doesn't?"

"Your press pass. It says Noah." She flipped the paper from my notepad back and forth between her fingers.

"Typo," I said. "They run these things off by the dozens."

I was halfway across the Pont Champlain before my heart slowed down.

CHAPTER FORTY-SEVEN

"I have an idea," I said.

LaRue sat across from me at her kitchen table. Steam rose from two cups of tea.

"Shoot."

"Look at this." I unfolded the piece of paper that had been taped to the dash of the Kia and pushed it over to her.

She frowned. "Is this the code you were talking about? Who's 'Icemom'?"

"That's Hazzard's code name for Theo."

LaRue absently tucked a stick of gum in her mouth and read the lines I'd copied from the blackmail book. I stroked Chip and looked out the window into the night. The harbor parking lot was out there somewhere. So, with any luck, was my Honda.

I'd driven all day—first east through Quebec to Magog, then south across the border and into Vermont, where I'd stopped for a supper of pot roast at the P&H Truck Stop in Wells River. At the counter I was surrounded on both sides by guys in camo ordering elk burgers and maple syrup pie.

One of them looked at me and said, "Hey, Carl, is it flat-lander season yet?" and they all laughed.

"Turkey hunters," the waitress said, tucking a hefty cinnamon raisin loaf into a bag for me. "They're just funnin' you."

"What does the code mean?" LaRue asked now.

"I haven't figured out all of it, but I think Hazzard found Faith with the help of an earring."

"An earring?"

"Faith was wearing a pendant exactly like Theodora's—three pearls and a pink stone. Theo must have divided up a pair of earrings and put one in the shoebox with the baby."

"How sad."

It was. For the first time I thought I understood why Theo had kept the DVD instead of pitching it.

"How did Jennifer know that?" LaRue asked.

"I don't know yet. And I don't know how she knew Faith was that baby. In the news video Faith skates by too quickly for the pendant to be recognized. Maybe Hazzard posted a photo of the earring on eBay or genealogy sites, hoping Theo's daughter was looking for the match."

"Okay, go on."

" 'Ck house' was probably a note to check the house. Theo's house. For what, I don't know."

"Wasn't the Lizard murdered at the E-Z Storage?"

"Yeah."

LaRue tapped the paper with her finger. " 'Pu=ez.' That's the meeting place, Em. Jennifer picks up the first payment from Theo at the E-Z Storage. The next time Jennifer calls her, Theo goes to the Sunny Side and kills her, but she doesn't know about the notebook. The Lizard finds the notebook and sets up a meeting with Theo at the E-Z. She stabs him and takes the book."

"Right! Two questions, though. How did the Lizard figure out the meeting place? He wasn't that smart. And why didn't Theo kill Hazzard in the first place?"

"The Lizard didn't figure anything out," LaRue said. "He just asked Theo where she wanted to meet. About your other question, maybe Theo thought it would end with the first payment. Or"—Her eyes flashed—"maybe Hazzard found out some other stuff about Theo that was even worse than abandoning a baby."

I added honey to my tea. "I have a hunch the answer's in Theo's house. That's where you come in, LaRue. I want you to create a diversion."

She brightened. "You mean, find a way to get her out of the house?"

"You got it, babe."

"Like pretend to be the water company and tell her we're evacuating the block for a water main break?"

"Uh—"

"Or how about, I'm a funeral home and I need her to whip up some flowers for a funeral this afternoon. It's a rush because the family's florist pooped out." LaRue arched her eyebrows.

"That could work."

"How much time do you need?"

"An hour."

LaRue sipped her tea and turned her attention back to the code. "This is gonna be fun."

"Yeah, well, I'm glad you're enjoying yourself." I stood up with Chip and carried my cup to the sink. When I got back, LaRue was tapping the paper again.

" 'GM&GD.' That could be 'grandmother' and 'granddaughter.' Ida and Theo."

I thought about it. "Maybe 'crapster' is the father. Yancy Villers."

"Here it is, Em, right here. 'F' for 'father.' "

"Crapster gone," I said slowly. "The father gone. Okay. And his going had something to do with the grandmother and grand-daughter. And the house."

"Did the crapster move out before the baby was born?"

"Around that time."

We sat there staring at the code. An ambulance went by, its

siren waxing and waning. Chip arched his back against my hand.

" 'F' could also mean father of the baby," I said.

We both had the same thought at the same time.

"Oh, gross," LaRue said. "You don't think Villers was the father of Theo's baby?"

"He *could* be. He could have raped his daughter and had a history of molesting her. That would explain her rage. It could also explain why Villers moved out."

LaRue had a look of horror on her face. "That's *so* disgusting, Em."

"Go research funeral homes," I said. "It will get your mind off it."

Chapter Forty-Eight

Sunday

When the sound of Theo's Outback faded I sat up in the Kia, called LaRue, and let the phone ring once. I crossed the street to the Silk house, a three-story nineteenth-century Colonial on a narrow parcel. Half a mile away, LaRue was hiding behind the Sunny Side's dumpster, keeping an eye on the Greenhouse. We'd arranged for her to ring me when Theo left to deliver the flowers. LaRue had picked a funeral home fifteen minutes away, so I had a thirty-minute cushion after the call came in.

Lifting the latch to the backyard gate, I slipped through. The small yard had been pretty at one time. Now vines were everywhere—climbing fences, suffocating tree trunks, meandering through tufts of grass. A stand of paper birches overhung a miniscule pond ringed with high grass and wildflowers. The whole yard needed cutting back, and I wondered why Theo, who loved flowers, hadn't bothered to do it.

I slogged over to the birches. Their smooth white bark was crisscrossed with frowns and smiles. On some of the trees, the markings even looked like letters—I saw an A and a T and an H high up on the trunk. Paper birches on which Time had written.

The bartender at Honey's had relayed a crack Yancy Villers had made about burying his cue in the backyard. Was that what Hazzard had wanted to check the house for? The yard was a mess. I'd need a lot more than an hour to find an old buried cue—*if* he'd even been serious, which I doubted.

The house itself held more promise. Seeing, touching, smelling, and experiencing Theodora's world from the inside would reveal more in ten minutes than an hour spent digging in the yard. I jiggled the knob on the back door. Locked. Not a problem. I slid my trusty shopper's club card into the crack and forced the tongue back. This time I remembered to close the door behind me.

The kitchen was old-fashioned and tidy, with flowered curtains and a hutch full of what my father would call *tchotchkes*. Dust collectors. A clock shaped like a cat with a pendulum tail ticked the seconds while its eyes rolled left and right. Dried flowers overflowed baskets on shelves, windowsills, and atop the fridge. I found a note on the kitchen table.

21N 1-19 122.9
HWV—1157Z 26013G21 10SM FEW 35, 50 15/03 A2989
FC1230Z 24012G19 SKC
MVY—

Another code? I copied the lines onto a napkin and stuffed it in my pocket.

The first floor consisted of a formal dining room, parlor, small office, and utility room. On the dining room sidebar were a few photos of Silk women through the ages, confirming my belief that the men had been dispensable.

If Villers had raped his daughter, resulting in her pregnancy, that explained his disappearance. Staying here would have meant jail, if his actions had been discovered.

I climbed the stairs. There were two rooms on the second floor, one on each side with a small bathroom between them. The room to the left was Theo's. I could tell by the neat row of shoes next to the bed. I flipped through her desk calendar. The only appointment listed for the coming week was a dental appointment on Monday. The pages before and after the current week had a few notations for birthdays and anniversaries, but nothing unusual.

The other room appeared to be a guest room, with a carefully made bed and an antique dresser filled with sheets and comforters.

My phone rang once. Thirty-minute warning.

A steep, narrow staircase took me up to the third floor, where a pungent, stuffy smell assaulted my nostrils. It smelled as though no one had been up here in years. Again, there were two rooms, one on either side of the stairs, with a windowed alcove between them. Both doors were shut.

The door on my left opened easily onto a ten-by-ten room with slanted ceilings. The front and back walls were only four feet high—kneewalls. There was one window in the outside wall. The room had been painted an ugly pink and was filled with boxes, old lamps, a torn upholstered chair, and bins full of hangers, frames, and household goods.

The door on the right was locked. Out came the shopper's club card. In the past nine days I'd certainly gotten my money's worth from that membership.

A sour smell hit me full force when the door swung open. The room was a mirror image of the other, painted the same ugly pink except for the rear kneewall, which had been papered in a hideous blue floral print. But, oddly, the room was almost completely empty. In one corner was a braided rug, a wooden rocking chair, and a small table with an oil lamp. That was it.

Now, why would somebody lock a room that had nothing in it but a chair, a table, and a lamp?

I looked around, breathing through my mouth to filter out as much of the smell as I could. There was a small door in the front kneewall with a hook-and-eye closure. I bent down and opened it. Inside I found a toolbox and several baby food jars filled with nails. The toolbox was labeled Y. VILLERS.

I pulled the heavy box into the room and flicked up the latches. It was well made with three tiered trays and a larger storage area underneath. In the trays were the usual tools: hammer, pliers, drill bits, picture wire. I picked up the hammer. It was heavy and of good quality.

My dad has a toolbox just like it, and he treats all his tools like old friends. I know that if he ever moves to Florida, as he's threatened to do, that toolbox will go with him. I wondered why Yancy Villers hadn't taken *his* toolbox when he moved. Why would he leave it behind?

In all my research I'd found no record of Villers's address. Of course, he might be anywhere in the country. Or anywhere in the world.

But what if he wasn't?

I frowned at the hammer, turning it over and over in my hand.

What if Yancy Villers had never left? What if he was still *right here*?

Clicking on my keychain minilight, I poked my head through the little door and looked around. Crumbled plaster was strewn on the wide pine planks from back when someone, probably Villers, had broken through the lath and plaster to make the closet. I didn't see anything else in there so I backed out.

The rear wall was the only one covered with wallpaper. Why? I ran my hand over the paper. It was old and dry and the seams were pulling apart. When I pressed the seams together I saw that the pattern had not been aligned well. There was also excess paper at the top and bottom. Someone had done the job in a hurry.

Starting in the left-hand corner, I began knocking on the wall at varying heights and noting the sound it produced—the dense thud of lath and plaster. Slowly I moved to my right, knocking, until I got to a spot three feet from the end where the sound became hollow. Sheetrock.

I got the hammer and, on my knees, I swung the claw end into the sheetrock and pulled, ripping out a chunk of wall. I swung and pulled again and again, until I'd made a hole big enough to poke my arm through. I groped around inside until my fingertips brushed against something that felt like a wooden dowel. But I couldn't quite reach it.

I reached in with the hammer and hooked the claw end over the dowel-like object. This time something above my hand thumped forward against the sheetrock. Three small bones slid through the hole in the wall along the top of my outstretched arm and clattered to the floor.

I dropped the hammer. With shaking hands I pulled out my cell phone and called Zahn.

"I'm in Theodora's house," I said when he answered. "You'd better come over right away."

"Damn it, Trace, I want you out of that house—now!"

"I'm going. But, Detective—"

"I said, *out*! Get down the block, out of sight, *immediately.*"

Three floors below the front door clicked open. My phone spun to the floor and slid across the room.

Footsteps crossed the kitchen floor and keys clattered on the table. A kitchen drawer slowly slid open and shut. Then there was silence.

I leapt to the window and pushed up mightily on the frame. It wouldn't budge. The window had been painted to the sill. I ran through the room and across the landing. Tripping over boxes I lunged for the window and yanked on the frame.

Also jammed.

Where was my Swiss army knife when I needed it?

Footsteps started up the first flight of stairs.

I tried the window at the top of the stairs. Stuck. I ran back into the room with the bones and locked the door.

The floor creaked as Theodora rounded the landing and started up the second flight.

Grunting, I did battle with the window again—and lost.

The footsteps reached the third floor landing. A key turned in the lock.

I crouched in the corner behind the rocking chair and turned it around so it faced me. The door sprung open and Theodora stood there, her eyes like ice, a meat cleaver in her fist. With all my strength I picked up the rocking chair and lunged forward, knocking the weapon to the floor. I pushed Theo against the wall and trapped her between the chair rockers.

"You and Ida killed him together—didn't you?"

Her eyes were wild. I tried to kick the meat cleaver out of range but couldn't reach it. With a banshee yell Theodora pushed the chair back and whirled away. I crashed forward into the wall, let go of the chair, and jumped back, but not in time to stop her from grabbing the meat cleaver. I vaulted myself onto her back, forcing the arm holding the weapon forward and biting into her shoulder.

With a strength I hadn't seen in her before, Theo turned and swiped at me with the meat cleaver. There was a hissing sound as the blade missed my cheek by a fraction of an inch. I kicked her in the pelvis with my foot, and she reeled backwards.

"Bitch!" she screamed, raising the weapon again. "You and your stupid boyfriend! This could have ended with you!"

"What are you talking about?"

" 'Don't you worry, sweetheart, everything's safe with me!' " Theo said in mimicking tones. "Well, let's see how safe you are *now,* Mr. Hot Shot! *You and your whole family!*" She swung the meat cleaver across my midriff, ripping my jacket. I jumped back and landed hard on my butt against the papered wall. I braced my hands on the floor, pushing away a small object that came in contact with my pinky. A bone.

She stood above me, the whites of her eyes big.

"Put it down, Theo," I said in measured tones. "The police are on their way."

She burst out laughing. It was a guttural laugh, sending chills up my spine.

"Where I'm going, they can't catch me."

"You're insane. You need help."

Theo leaned over and stared me in the eye. "Your moron boyfriend. Somebody should tell him not to leave private messages in public places."

She raised the meat cleaver over her head and brought it down hard toward my head. At the last second I turned my face to the left to avoid the blade. It whistled past my ear and dug into the sheetrock behind me, taking a hunk of my hair with it and pinning me to the wall.

Theo gave another bloodcurdling scream and yanked on the weapon's handle. With both feet I kicked her hard in the midsection. As she fell back, I grabbed the oil lamp from the little table and spiked it at her feet. The glass smashed into a gazillion pieces, oil splashing everywhere. Theo lunged for the meat cleaver again and slipped in the oil, landing hard on her side.

I pulled at the knife handle, but my hands slipped off. Inhaling deeply I tore myself away from the wall, my hair making a sickening crunch as it left my scalp by the roots. I stumbled around in the puddle of oil and found myself running, falling, getting up, and running again. I lunged down the stairs. Behind me Theodora scrambled to her feet. I rounded the corner and ran down the second flight, my hand slipping along the rail. A fuzzy sound filled my ears. My heart was a wild drumbeat, and the visual sense was leaving me. As I neared the bottom the world began closing in from the periphery. Soon I would be in a tunnel. Soon I would faint.

I reached for the front doorknob, surprised to see blood on my hand, surprised at how slippery the knob was, used both hands to turn it, and then I was outside—running, running, away from the house.

CHAPTER FORTY-NINE

I fell to my knees on the neighbor's lawn, behind a beech tree.

Theo emerged from the house and glared around her. The back of her dress was dark with oil. After a few seconds she went back in and ran out with car keys. Then she thrust herself into the Subaru and backed out of the driveway at top speed.

I closed my eyes for a few moments to stop the world from spinning. When I opened them, I was in shadow. Two police officers stood over me, silhouetted against the sun.

"Are you all right, ma'am?"

I blinked a few times.

"Call an ambulance, Joe."

"No." I shook my head. "I'm fine. Don't call."

One of them lifted me to my feet and the other put a blanket around my shoulders. We started walking, or at least they started walking and I moved my feet a little in the air. I looked up. Zahn was watching me from the driver's seat of a blue Pontiac Firebird, pain in his X-ray eyes.

"You just missed her," I told him.

"It's okay, we're on it." He gestured toward the passenger door. "Get in." Someone opened the door for me and then I was sitting.

Zahn spoke into the phone. "She's on her way to Brookhaven. I need extra coverage. I want people in the parking lot, at the terminal, at Dowling, around the perimeter. Anyplace she can gain entry to the airport, I want you there. She may be armed. Cuff her and wait till I get there." He gave whoever he was talking to the tail number of an airplane—Theo's plane—and her tie-down location. Then he listened as the other person spoke. "Do whatever you have to do. Just make sure she doesn't take off."

You and your whole family, Theo had said. I thought of Tony at his family's house in Martha's Vineyard, oblivious to the danger ahead. It made my heart hurt to think about. I wondered what Theo had meant about private messages in public places. Something had obviously awakened her suspicions and caused her to drop what she was doing at the Greenhouse and come home.

Over the radio I heard the dispatcher's tinny voice calling for a police alert between Port Jeff and Brookhaven Airport and describing Theo's car model, color, and license plate number. The police were ready. They were going to catch Theo before she got to Tony and his family.

Zahn handed me a water bottle.

"Do you want to go to the hospital?"

"I'll be fine."

"We spoke to Tony Randazzo. Says he's in possession of a disk and your cell phone. True?"

"Yes."

"Is that your blood or hers?"

"I cut my hand, I think. Broken glass."

Zahn reached into the back and handed me a container of baby wipes. I cleaned myself off and gulped down some water. A shadow fell across us as an officer leaned into the driver's window.

"Crime Scene's on the way. Want us to start without you, Detective?"

"I'm coming in." Zahn turned to me. "What room were you in?"

"Don't you want the blow-by-blow?"

"Already had *that* in surround sound," Zahn said, waving his cell phone.

"Oh. Third floor, room on the right."

"Was there anyone else besides Theodora?"

"Just her father." The officer outside the window straightened. I touched the side of my head where there was no hair. It hurt. It hurt like hell. "Yancy Villers. He's up there, too."

"Where?"

"Behind the kneewall."

Zahn turned to the officer as he got out of the car. "As soon as I give the okay, seal it off. And get dental down here."

"Detective," I said.

He turned around.

"She's going to try and kill Tony and—the others, isn't she? That's why the police are waiting for her at the airport, right? To stop her?"

"Theodora Silk is not going to kill anyone else. Her party's over. There's some ice in that cup, Trace, if you want to hold it to your head."

Then he was gone, striding up the front walkway with officers flanking him on either side, looking tall and regal and in charge.

There was a silver lining to every cloud. The silver lining to this one was that my phone had slid under the chair while Zahn and I were connected.

The crime scene van pulled up and disgorged a photographer and several techs. They filed up the front path to the house. I watched their comings and goings for a couple of minutes. Then I opened the center console of the Firebird and thumbed through Zahn's CD collection. Linda Ronstadt, Faith Hill, the Eagles, the Byrds, Alabama, Emmylou Harris, Tanya Tucker, Buffalo Springfield, Jimmy Buffett, Alison Kraus, Iris DeMent, and Shakira. *Shakira?*

Zahn got back in and I slapped the console closed. He tossed a snap-and-seal bag into the cup holder. The bag held the note from the kitchen table.

"I left my phone in there," I said.

"Sorry."

Zahn put the car in drive and pulled away from the curb. We were silent for a while, lost in our own thoughts.

"You weren't surprised when I told you Yancy Villers was up there," I said.

"I knew he was. That's why I came with a search warrant today—to find Villers."

"You mean, you didn't come to rescue *me?*"

"Well, that, too." The corner of Zahn's mouth turned up. "Thanks to you, we didn't have to tear the whole house apart with pickaxes."

"I started the job for you."

"And left some hair back there."

"Better than leaving my head for you to find."

This time he laughed out loud. "You do have a sense of humor, Trace."

"It works."

"Better than luck?"

"Luck's good, too, if you can get it."

Zahn turned south and headed toward the expressway. It was one of those windy Technicolor October days. Purple, gray, and white clouds scudded past one another in a patchwork sky.

"How long have you known it was Theodora?" I asked.

"Since the day Hazzard was murdered."

My eyebrows went up. "All this time you knew about Theo's father? What he did to her, and what—what she and her grandmother did to him?"

"Yep."

"You know, I thought you suspected me at first."

"You were never under suspicion, Trace. We were interested in you because we thought you might have seen something."

"But—my library card. And that letter I wrote—?"

"What letter?"

"You didn't find a letter?"

He looked at me.

"Never mind," I said. "It's not important."

"Oh, I remember," Zahn said.

We stopped at a red light.

When we were moving again he asked, "Why do you think Theo framed you?"

"I've been trying to figure that out myself. Maybe she knew Sam dumped me for Jenn. Everyone else in town seemed to know. I was a convenient scapegoat." I looked out the window. "Maybe *she* found that letter."

Zahn made a noncommittal sound.

"You know, I went up to Canada and found her daughter."

"I know."

"You do?"

"Sure."

"Why didn't you stop me?"

Zahn smiled again. "You were safer out of the way."

We started moving again. I had about a hundred questions I knew he'd never answer. I asked one I thought he would.

"Did Villers have a record?"

Zahn held up a finger to signal me to wait and turned up the radio volume. After listening briefly he picked up the transceiver.

"Turk, anything?"

"Negative," came the reply. "Any minute now, Pete."

Zahn lowered the transceiver to his lap. "He did have a record. When Villers lived here, he had a habit of inviting little girls down to his basement so he could 'photograph' them. He was arrested twice for child molestation. That was back in the days when the addresses of child molesters weren't made public, and people didn't know when one was living among them. School authorities suspected him of molesting his daughter, but, when asked, Theodora denied it, and so did her grandmother.

"Since he never held a regular job and was estranged from his family, Villers's disappearance didn't arouse any suspicion. Ida Silk said he'd moved away, and no one questioned it. When we looked at credit reports, driver's licenses, and so forth, we discovered he'd never left this address. It was just a matter of finding where they'd put him."

I tried to imagine Theo's desperation, at sixteen, when she found out she was pregnant. I pictured her cloistered away in the big house, every day getting closer to childbirth, talking to her grandmother deep into the night about what they should do. Ida probably came up with the idea to kill Villers. It must have taken both of them to stuff him into the wall. I guessed they hadn't done such a hot job of spackling and tried to cover their sins with wallpaper.

"Why are you telling me all this?"

"Because it's going to be in all the papers this afternoon, after we arrest her. You're not hearing anything the rest of the world won't know very soon. You can't tweet it without your cell. And you're not going to leak it any other way, because you're with me."

I looked out the windshield quietly. We were on the expressway now, heading east. There was something I still wanted to tell him.

"Remember when I called Bisbee to set up the meeting?"

Zahn nodded.

"I didn't realize it until today, but he gave away that he was expecting a call from Theodora."

"How do you figure that?"

"Because he answered the phone, 'I see what's going on.' But Bisbee wasn't saying, '*I see* what's going on,' he was saying, '*Icy,* what's going on?' "

"Ah." Zahn brightened.

The radio buzzed to life.

"No sign of the suspect yet, Detective," said a disembodied voice.

Zahn's face registered concern. "Where are you, Jenkins?"

"William Floyd Parkway, just north of destination."

"Dispatch, ask all cars to report in," Zahn said. "Someone must have spotted her by now."

The dispatcher made the call, and there was a flurry of "negatives" over the airwaves.

"Damn it." Zahn stepped on the gas. We accelerated and moved into the left lane for the last two exits.

I didn't know if I'd get another chance to ask my next question. "What did Theo mean about private messages in public places?"

Zahn set his mouth grimly. "Tony told me that when he couldn't reach you on Friday, he left a voicemail for you at Hoyt's saying he'd taken everything to the Vineyard. He wanted the receptionist to tell you if you stopped in or called. Theodora Silk picked up that message."

I said in alarm, "She must think he has the original evidence, then. But he doesn't. He only has—"

Zahn put up a hand to stop me.

I said, more to myself than to him, "She thought I gave it to Tony." My heart sank. Maybe I should have told Tony my suspicions. I'd been afraid that that knowledge would make him vulnerable. In reality I had put him in more danger by not telling him.

"That's what I'm worried about," Zahn said. He pulled off

the expressway onto the William Floyd. We sped the last three miles to the airport.

Bonomo and two officers in street clothes met us in the parking lot. Bonomo held a walkie-talkie.

"She's not here," he reported.

"What do you mean, she's not here?" Zahn barked. "This is where her plane is. She hasn't sprouted wings in the last half hour, has she?"

"Pete, there are a dozen of us surrounding the field, and another dozen patrol out looking for her. She'll turn up. She can't get far without the plane."

"What time is it?"

"Almost twelve."

"Give me that."

Zahn grabbed the walkie-talkie from Bonomo and pushed a button.

"Dowling, come in."

"Carter here, Detective. She's not here."

"Is there any other access to the field?"

Bonomo walked into the terminal.

"Barbed wire fences run the perimeter," Carter replied. "Lester and Sylvestri are in the woods, looking for the vehicle."

Zahn dropped the walkie-talkie to his side. He nodded toward the guard booth at the entry gate. "What about the guard?" he asked one of the officers. "You talk to him?"

"He didn't see her. He keeps a log of every vehicle that goes through the gate. Security's tight."

"And the terminal?"

"They didn't see her either."

"Detective!" An officer hurried toward us from the field. "Her airplane's gone."

"Gone! What do you mean, gone?"

The officer looked shamefaced. "Her tie-down is empty."

Zahn looked around at the group in disbelief. "Nobody bothered to check until now that her plane was on the field?"

Without waiting for an answer, he strode into the terminal. I followed him. Bonomo was talking to Leo, behind the desk.

"She didn't fly today," Leo was saying. "If she flew today, I'd be the first to know. The tail number of every plane that lands at or departs from this field gets written down right here." He held up a lined sheet. "And I monitor Unicom, I woulda heard her."

"What's Unicom?" Zahn asked.

"The pilots' advisory frequency. One-twenty-two-point-eight. We don't have a tower here, Detective. The pilots announce themselves on Unicom when they're in the pattern. The ones that have radios do, anyway. And I got these for anyone I can't make out on the radio." He pointed to a pair of binoculars hanging from a peg.

"Take a look at that list and tell me if she flew yesterday."

Leo flipped back a page and ran his finger along the names.

"Yep. Here she is. Departed yesterday afternoon at four-eighteen."

Zahn looked at Bonomo. "Son of a fucking gun, she moved her plane. She moved her plane to another airport. Get me Martha's Vineyard on the phone," he said to Leo.

"I called them already," Bonomo said guardedly. "Police are stationed at both Vineyard Haven and Katama airports. They'll arrest her when she lands."

"Well, that's one thing right." Zahn paced to the glass doors and looked out. Then he faced Bonomo, hands on his hips. "We have her and she knows it. She's looking at jail for the rest of her life with no parole. So she moves her plane so she can proceed with a plan that she has zero hope of carrying out. What am I missing here, Turk?"

"Do you have an office we can use?" Bonomo asked Leo.

Leo showed them into a room behind the counter. Through the window I watched their lips move as they discussed what to do. Zahn paced back and forth, doing most of the talking. Bonomo leaned calmly against the wall, his hands in his pockets, nodding at times.

"I'm going to find Ned," I said to no one in particular. I ran outside and waved at the guard.

"Did Ned Trace come through yet?"

He nodded. " 'Bout an hour ago."

I ran across the taxi area and along the row of parked airplanes, but halfway from the end I stopped short. I could see from here that Ned's hangar door was open and the Extra was gone. He was flying.

"Can I help you?" I turned to see a woman squatting on the wing of her airplane with a bungee cord in her hand, an open flight bag next to her. Her plane was an old low-wing with red and black stripes on its sides. She was in her fifties, and she looked very comfortable up there. She looked kind of cool.

"I'm looking for Ned Trace. Do you know him?"

"He just taxied out. I can try and catch him before he takes off." Concern creased her face. "Are you okay?"

I nodded. "Tell him Emma's here, and it's very important."

The woman spoke into a transceiver, her eyes not leaving my face. "Extra in the runup area, would you return to the hangar? Emma's here. She says it's urgent."

I heard Ned acknowledge the request, then I ran the rest of the way to his hangar. Ned taxied up and shut off the engine. He opened the canopy and stared at me.

"What happened to your hair?"

"Later. You know that murder I told you about?"

"Yeah." He hopped out.

"The police are ready to make an arrest." I gave him the

short version of the day's events, ending with Theo moving her plane.

"She knows the cops are onto her, and she doesn't care. She's flying to Martha's Vineyard right now to try and—kill Tony—and his family. Including his hundred-year-old grandmother."

"Tony's the guy you're seeing."

"Yes."

Ned frowned. "Why him?"

"I can't go into it now." I blinked back tears. "Theo's insane, Ned. She's lost it. And it frightens me. She's very clever and so far she's been able to evade the police."

"But you said they're ready to grab her when she lands."

I shook my head. "I have a bad feeling about this. It's turning my stomach into knots." I pulled the napkin out of my pocket and handed it to him. "I found this note in code at Theo's. Does it mean anything to you?"

Ned took a small magnifying glass out of a zippered pocket and polished it on his jacket.

"Don't tell me you lost your glasses again," I said.

"All right, I won't." He passed the magnifying glass over the napkin. "This isn't a code. It's a weather briefing. I can translate it for you."

"Hold on." We both looked up to see Zahn getting out of the Firebird, with Bonomo right behind him. Zahn carried the plastic evidence bag. "I want to hear this, too."

CHAPTER FIFTY

Zahn walked up to Ned, and they stood eye to eye. Or eye to shoulder, since Zahn was half a foot taller. After a moment Ned thrust out his hand.

"Pete."

"Ned." They shook as though their hands were hot potatoes.

"Been a while."

Zahn's face showed no expression. He cleared his throat. "This is Detective Harris Bonomo. Tell us about this briefing." He placed the bag with the original note on the wing of the Extra where we could all see it.

21N 1-19 122.9
HWV1157Z 26013G21 10SM FEW 35, 50 15/03 A2989
FC1230Z 24012G19 SKC
MVY—

Ned unwrapped a toothpick and angled it in his mouth. "The first line is airport information. 'Twenty-one-N' is the airport identifier for Mattituck. One and one-nine are the runways, and one-twenty-two-point-nine is the Common Traffic Advisory Frequency. That's the radio frequency pilots use when they're taking off or landing."

"Turk, call Mattituck with a descrip," Zahn said. He turned back to Ned.

Ned pointed to the next group of figures. "Below that we

have the identifier 'HWV,' Brookhaven Airport, followed by the weather conditions at the field at the time she called—wind, visibility, temperature, and so forth."

"If she was planning to fly out of Mattituck, why did she get Brookhaven's weather?" Zahn asked.

"Mattituck doesn't have its own weather equipment," Ned explained. "Pilots make do with the conditions at Brookhaven or Gabreski. The time was eleven-fifty-seven Zulu, or seven fifty-seven Daylight Savings Time. Wind out of the southwest at thirteen knots—"

"Is all this important?" Zahn interrupted.

"Wind might be. It was gusting to twenty-one. If the conditions were similar at Mattituck, I'd call that a challenging crosswind, given that you've got a fairly narrow runway. Visibility ten miles, few clouds at three thousand five hundred feet, few clouds at five thousand, temperature fifteen Celsius, dew point zero-three Celsius, altimeter two-nine-eight-nine. That last number refers to atmospheric pressure."

Bonomo returned to the group. Zahn looked at him.

"Her car's at Mattituck, but the plane's gone," Bonomo said. "According to the airport manager, she just took off."

Zahn checked the time on his cell phone. "Continue."

Ned frowned. "It looks like she intended to be wheels up by about eight thirty. See the third line? 'FC.' Looks like she picked up the forecast showing that eight-thirty winds were predicted to be out of the southwest at twelve gusting to nineteen. Sky clear."

"So, she meant to go earlier, but her plans changed." Zahn gave me a penetrating look.

Ned looked thoughtful. "I don't know that I'd want to launch a taildragger on a north-south runway in that kind of crosswind, but for a good pilot in a heavier airplane with tricycle gear, it would be fine. What does she fly?"

Zahn consulted a pad. "A Cessna Skylane."

"That would work." Ned rubbed his chin in silence.

"What?"

"Well, the surface conditions at the Vineyard are missing. Also the weather en route and the return flight forecast. All she has here is 'MVY'—Martha's Vineyard—with a dash after it."

"Maybe she was going to update it later," Zahn said.

Ned shook his head. "Any pilot worth her salt pays attention to the return forecast, if she wants to get home that night. She's flying VFR, of course."

"What does that mean?" Zahn growled.

"By visual flight rules, not instrument rules. When you fly IFR—by instruments—you have to file a flight plan with the FAA. That puts your flight on record. Meaning the police have access to it. When you fly VFR, a flight plan is not required. If she's heading out to commit murder, I seriously doubt she's filed a flight plan."

I was still pondering the briefing. "Maybe—" I stopped.

Zahn turned to me abruptly. "Maybe what?"

I felt the blood drain from my face. A cold sweat broke out on my forehead. I looked at Zahn, then Bonomo, then Ned.

"Spit it out, Trace," Zahn ordered.

"Maybe she's not planning to land at Vineyard Haven *or* Katama." My eyes locked with Ned's. My voice was so low I could hardly hear myself. "Maybe she's not planning to land at all, in the ordinary sense."

You could have heard a pin drop.

"The house," Ned said. "You think she's planning to crash into the house."

"Holy shit," Zahn said.

"That's it, don't you see?" I said to Zahn. "That's why she didn't care about the surface conditions or return forecast. She's not *going* to the airport. And she's not coming back. That's what she meant when she said that where she was going, we couldn't catch her."

Zahn pulled out his notebook. "The house is in Gay Head."

"She could easily locate it with Google Earth," Bonomo said.

"How many people are staying there?" Ned asked.

A thousand expressions flitted across Zahn's face in a millisecond. "Fifteen." He pushed buttons on his cell phone and held it to his ear.

"Can we get her on radar?" Bonomo asked.

"Not unless she has her transponder on, which I doubt," Ned said. "She's probably flying too low to be picked up, anyway."

Zahn snorted. "What good is *radar*? What *fuck*ing good is *that*?"

Bonomo spoke woodenly. "The Air National Guard is based at Gabreski. They can contact her by radio, try and talk her down. Intercept her, if necessary."

"Are you serious? They're going to send over a Delta Dagger to bring down a Skylane?"

Bonomo turned to Ned. "So, there's no way to determine exactly where she is?"

"Not unless you fly up there yourself, Detective, and look for her." Ned pointed to a spot on the map. "If she just left Mattituck in a Skylane, she's going to be out of New York airspace in twenty minutes. She'll be at Martha's Vineyard in forty. We have a very small window in which to act. So we can—"

"Ned, when I want your opinion, I'll ask for it," Zahn snapped. He paced to the hangar and back, speaking into his phone. "Vineyard Police, please. Suffolk County Homicide."

Bonomo said, "What about evacuating? There are fifteen people in that house, and neighbors—"

Zahn cut him off. "What do you think I'm doing? I know how many lives are at stake, Harris."

"Right." Bonomo lifted up both palms and stepped back.

Zahn finished talking, snapped the phone shut and turned to Ned. "What's the cruising speed of the Skylane?"

"Hundred fifty miles an hour." Ned folded his arms and leaned back against the plane. "Now, the Extra cruises at two hundred. If I take off now, I can catch up with her before she gets there."

"Ned!" I protested.

Zahn rolled right over me. "Catch up with her? *Then* what are you going to do, Davy Crockett? Tell her to pull over to the nearest cloud?"

"Divert her," Ned said calmly. "Make her land somewhere else."

"Out of the question. Not only is it dangerous, but it would be irresponsible of me as lead detective to allow you to do that."

"I can do it, Pete. I've got the means, and I've got the skills. I know that airspace like the back of my hand. It's our only chance, and you know it."

Zahn moved his face up close to Ned's. "Over my dead body, cowboy."

"You've got a better idea?"

Zahn clenched the plastic baggie in his fist. "I'll call the FAA. I know some people—"

"That bureaucracy?" Ned broke in. "By the time they do anything, there will be a big boom a hundred miles east and a heap of burning, twisted metal and flesh. And you'll be on the news tonight—and not in a good way."

I strangled a cry. Zahn strode back to his car and tossed the baggie through the window. He put his palms on the roof and leaned over, tapping his foot. I'd never paid attention to his shoes before, but he was wearing those fine Italian leather boots you see on movie stars. He rejoined us. "You think you can catch up with her?"

"We're cutting it close, but I can if I leave right now."

"Okay. For lack of a better idea, let's do it. I'll go along to handle communications."

"No, you won't." Ned grabbed a parachute pack out of a storage bin and put it on.

"Yes, I will." Zahn began to remove his overcoat.

"You're not flying with me, Pete. You're too charged up. I need a copilot who will follow direction and not be a distraction. Someone I can trust." Ned tossed me a parachute. "I'll take Emma."

"Like hell you will." Zahn stepped closer to Ned and looked down at him. "This is my case, and it's my call."

Ned shook his head. "This is my plane, and I'm pilot in command. And you're not flying." He looked Zahn in the eye and added, "It wasn't your call then, and it's not your call now."

Zahn blanched. Two pink spots appeared in his cheeks.

Ned looked at me. "What do you say, Em?"

I held out the chute. "I'm sorry, Ned. I can't."

Ned put his hands on my shoulders. "Yes, you can. Think about Tony. Think about his grandmother." He tossed his toothpick aside. "On second thought, forget about them—think about me."

"You!"

"I could use an extra pair of eyes in the cockpit."

"To read the instruments, no doubt."

Ned squinted at the windsock in the middle of the field. "Not just that, Em. You know this woman, her history. The two of you have a connection. This plan of hers—you might be able to talk her out of it."

"We're going to talk to her?"

"We can try."

I bit my lip and looked down at my sneakers. They'd been with me every step of the way for the past ten days. Buddha-bagging, laundry-nabbing, and bowling alley tours. A pool hall cue quest and a meet-up gone sour. Several break-ins and a swim in the Sound. Even a trip to Canada and back.

They hadn't counted on getting in an airplane, though.

No sirree, not by a long shot.

Nunh-uh.

Fuggedaboutit.

On the other hand, unless we stopped her, Theo might wipe out an entire family. *Tony's* family. I was being given that chance—the chance to be an eagle.

"I won't minimize the risks," Ned said. "Shit can happen. We might run low on fuel if we're up there too long. We might have to land before we catch her. We might have to perform some unusual maneuvers. And Theo's a loaded gun—there's no telling what she'll do, in her state of mind."

"I understand." We locked eyes. "Okay, I'll do it. I'll go with you, Ned."

"That's my girl." He helped me put my arms through the parachute straps.

"If you kill me," I added, "I will never forgive you."

He winked at me secretly. I climbed into the front seat and let him buckle me in. "Okay, then. Mandatory passenger briefing. Feet off the pedals. If the plane catches fire or loses a wing, the canopy will pop open. Pull the quick release on your harness and dive out. And don't forget to open your chute. And please don't throw up. I just cleaned the Plexiglas."

"I hate you."

"You'll get over it." He put the last buckle in its clasp, hopped in behind me, and pulled the canopy over us. Then he started the engine, and the three-blade propeller became a deafening blur.

Between the headphones I was in a little cocoon of relative quiet. I let the white noise of the prop lull me into a trance. If I was going to die, might as well zone out first. I glanced at the pavement two feet away. Soon it would be a lot more than two.

"Any loose change in your pockets?" His voice through the mike was calm.

"Loose—where's the rearview mirror in this thing?"

"No rearview mirror. Why?"

"I'm sticking out my tongue."

He laughed and released the brake, and off we rolled. I took a quick look back at Zahn. He was standing with his hands at his sides and watching me with that look I couldn't identify. He lifted one hand slightly as if he meant to wave, then put it in his pocket.

We zigzagged down the taxiway to where the runway started. Ned pivoted 180 degrees and began to click things on and off and vroom the engine. Zahn and Bonomo were two sticks in the distance.

A pre-puke rumbling began in my stomach as we pivoted again. My teeth started chattering like castanets.

Ned said, "Brookhaven traffic, Extra departing two-four, northbound."

"Oh shit, oh shit, oh shit, oh shit, oh shit—"

He gave it full throttle and we were rolling down the runway, faster and faster, past the big numbers, past the stripes. A deer grazing at the edge of the woods looked up as we went by. Then we were nose up, rocketing into the sky, and I was flattened against the seat back, looking at blue.

"Oh shit, oh shit, oh shit, oh—"

"Where you off to, Ned?" came a voice through the radio. "Block Island? Columbia?"

"Vineyard. What's up, Rick?"

"Hangar party at Ed's. You coming?"

"Can't make it, buddy."

"Okay. Good flight."

"See you."

319

Ned hung a sharp right to avoid hitting a flock of starlings.

I squeezed my eyes shut and leaned left. Ned hung a left, and my headset banged into the canopy. Then we jerked right again, then left. I reached out for something to grab—nothing but cold metal tubing. My fingernails dug deep into my palms. Seconds passed like years.

Ned said, "Hang on, Em. You're doing great. Tell me what the instrument on the right says."

"I can't."

"Why not?"

"My eyes are shut."

"Well, open them, you turkey."

I opened one eye, then the other. Sky in every direction. Clouds below us. *Below* us. I blinked back tears and focused on one of the three dials. "Four-thirty."

"It's not a clock, but thanks." Ned leveled the plane out. "Altitude four thousand five hundred. What about the one on the left."

"One seventy. Knots."

"Excellent."

"What's the one in the middle for?"

"That's the G-Meter."

He banked the plane to the left. Connecticut's shoreline appeared through the glass. Then he banked right, and I saw the fishtail of Long Island's east end. My stomach made a dive.

"We should catch up to her pretty close to the Vineyard," Ned said.

"How close?"

"Depends on how fast she's going. With any luck, before she begins her descent. What *is* that? Do you hear a clicking noise?"

"It's my teeth chattering."

Ned made a left and we aviated across the Sound, among the clouds. Sunlight splashed us at intervals. The airplane's clear canopy gave me a three-hundred-sixty-degree vista. When I looked down I saw the Bridgeport ferry chugging across the Sound like a child's toy. I suddenly realized I'd been holding my breath. I thought of the eagle, and exhaled.

How ironic. Only a little more than a week ago I'd been searching like a madwoman for the one thing that would keep me on the ground. And I'd found it. But the box with the radio was still sitting unopened on my kitchen table, and here I was—in the air.

"There's the Jamestown Bridge." Ned's voice brought me back to the moment.

"Where are we?"

"Near Newport. Rhode Island. Martha's Vineyard will be on our right. Keep your eyes peeled."

"Look, there's a plane."

"That's a Mooney. Look for a high-wing. The tail number won't be visible until we're right on top of her."

What if we don't—? I banished the rest of that thought. We *had* to find Theo in time.

The engine noise dropped a bit as the plane nosed down. The Jamestown Bridge was now far behind us.

"What are you doing?" I asked.

"I want to come in above her, but not by much."

"Is that Martha's Vineyard?"

We had been flying over water most of the way, just off the New England shore, but now we cut to the right, across a larger body of water. Ahead I could see some flat pancakes of land.

"That's Cuttyhunk. One of the small islands on the way to the Vineyard. What's our altitude?"

"Three thousand two hundred."

More nosing down. We leveled out under a broken layer of clouds. Just below the horizon I saw something moving—a white high-wing.

"There she is!" I pointed.

Ned banked to the right to follow my finger.

"Let's take a look."

He closed in quickly on the moving aircraft, slowing down just behind and above it, so he could sync the Extra with its moves.

"It's a Skylane, all right," Ned said. "Can you read the numbers?"

"No."

"She's at two thousand, give or take, heading of one-three-five. Yup, she's aiming for the west end of the island."

"How far is it?"

"Twenty-five miles. Why'd they have to get a place in Gay Head?"

"What's bad about Gay Head?"

"Cliffs. High population. Hold on, it's gonna get a little rough."

Ned swooped down and pulled up alongside the Cessna. He flipped us ninety degrees so that we were flying sideways—a wing up, a wing down. The top of our canopy faced the other plane.

"That her?"

I looked up through the glass. Thirty feet away, Theodora's cold, white face turned toward me. Shock registered. She turned away.

"That's her."

Deftly he straightened us out.

"November-four-one-five-zero-Juliet. Theodora! There's no one in the house. Turn around *now* and go back to Brookhaven." Ned fiddled with the radio, repeating the message on different frequencies.

"She's still descending!" My eyes went to the altimeter: one thousand eight hundred.

"Okay. Let's see how she likes smoke." Ned hit a switch and there was a loud roar. He made a sharp left and climbed away from the Cessna, then angled down and to the right, pulling ahead of her with white smoke billowing behind. I looked back. Theo flew straight through the smoke and out the other side. Ned turned steeply to the right and circled back, punching through the trail of smoke. The smell of oil penetrated the cabin.

Theo flew on, diving with a single psychopathic purpose toward certain death.

"Em, you're on frequency. Try and raise her."

"Go back, Theo!" I shouted. "Tony doesn't have the book! You're making a big mistake!"

No answer. We kept dropping.

Ned lined up next to Theo and added power. We began rolling around the Cessna as though we were rolling around a barrel. As we went over the top, I looked down through the top of the canopy and saw Theo's white face looking up at us. Her mouth was moving.

"Keep trying!" Ned shouted.

"Nobody has to die, Theo! Turn around and go home!"

Her voice came through the static.

"Burn in hell, Trace."

Ned rolled around her again, but Theo didn't flinch. We dropped another hundred feet.

"You have a choice," I continued. "You don't have to do this, Theo. You have the freedom—"

"Freedom! What freedom?"

"The freedom to choose life—for yourself. For Tony. For his grandmother! You don't have to crash."

"A joke! Silks don't have freedom!"

I looked down at the instrument panel. One thousand three hundred.

"*You're* free!" she screamed. "Yes, *you,* Emma. You can do anything! You don't have to protect your name!"

Cuttyhunk passed under us.

"It's too late for me now!" Theo shouted. "I have to pay the price to save the Silks! The Silks!"

"Ten miles!" Ned yelled over the noise.

"What are we going to do?" I yelled back.

Ned didn't answer right away. He switched off the smoke and veered away from the Cessna. Was he giving up?

The altimeter needle kept sliding. One thousand one hundred feet, one thousand feet.

"Ned! Stop her!"

Ned added full power and headed straight for the 182.

"No!" I shrieked, pulling my knees up.

At the last second, Ned pulled hard to the left. With a loud crack the Extra's right wingtip struck the left side of the Cessna's tail and ripped a horizontal panel off its hinges.

We turned steeply left and I saw cliffs below, houses. People running. Something falling.

Circled back and she was in front of us again. Wobbling. But—incredibly—she was still flying.

Eight hundred feet. Seven.

The right half of the Cessna's tail was still intact. At full throttle Ned charged again and pulled off to the right. I braced myself as we struck the tail with our left wing, shearing the matching piece and its hinges right off the plane. The amputated panel hurtled past us.

For an instant Theo's plane seemed to freeze in mid-air. I caught a glimpse of her horror-stricken face in the window. Then the Cessna tipped over and plummeted nose first into the ocean, just off the cliffs of Gay Head.

We circled in the Extra, our eyes on the spot where the Cessna had penetrated the ocean's surface, watching the ripples go out and out until there were none left. A few pieces of debris bobbed in the waves. Ned resumed level flight and angled left past the cliffs, tracking the south shoreline of the island.

He was the first to speak.

"You all right, Minute Mouse?"

"I think so. You?"

"Yes."

We were flying very low over the water and had slowed down considerably. A crowd of people on the cliff held up their cell phones.

"How far is the airport?" I asked.

"Hang on. I don't—we've lost power."

"What—?"

"We're out of—oh, shit." His voice sounded strangled. "We're landing, Em. When I give the signal, pull the quick release on your harness."

"Landing *here*?"

Without another word he jettisoned the canopy.

"Mayday, Mayday, Extra ditching—"

I heard a splash as the canopy made impact.

Ditching?

"—south of Chilmark. Mayday—"

Ned pulled my headphones off. Wind slapped my hair against my face. I thought of Dad, Mom. LaRue. Zahn. My cats.

Scaredy cat! Scaredy cat! We're going down, scaredy cat!

The airspeed and altimeter needles wound down. Time wound down and condensed into one infinite moment. Where was the signal? All was silence. Everything gathered into a tunnel before me. I pulled up my knees and waited as the stick came back.

Deep breath.

Who will take care of my cats?

Who will—?

Scaredy cat!

We slammed into the water. Flipped over.

Upside down, cold waves rocking me, I tugged at my harness.

Other hands pushed mine aside. I looked down—or up, I wasn't sure which—at Ned's figure floating before me, his hair waving like seaweed, as the air left my lungs.

CHAPTER FIFTY-ONE

Monday

Because of Twitter, the airplane chase went viral in ninety minutes. People standing on the cliffs at Gay Head sent their videos to YouTube and Facebook, and Ned was convicted by popular opinion of murder-by-airplane. Since he wasn't arrested on the spot, the police were criticized for being behind the stunt, and everyone from the boating population to the air safety people to the community watchdogs in Martha's Vineyard had something to say. Speculation and public outcry were rampant, and the police were forced to have a press conference.

LaRue and I watched the whole thing from my couch. Since Ned and I were in good shape after being rescued by the Nantucket Coast Guard, the hospital had released us with antibiotic ointment and a couple of Band-Aids.

Zahn and Bonomo stood behind the police chief, while Ned, his hair combed back, stood to their side. Cameras flashed nonstop. The chief did all the talking. He explained that the woman in the downed plane was a triple murderer who was wanted by police. She was believed to have killed a blackmailer and a second person who'd gotten involved with the blackmail scheme. Police had also uncovered evidence indicating that she and a relative may have done in her father twenty-three years ago.

The blackmailer, Jennifer Hazzard, had originally moved here from New Jersey, where she'd accumulated a veritable parade of blackmail subjects, from teachers to bartenders to city employees. In fact, she had largely supported herself on the revenue from these activities. And as she'd been about to be caught, she was motivated to move to Long Island, where she'd picked up right where she left off in Jersey—getting the dirt on local people and making them pay to keep her quiet.

The police chief described how Hazzard had worked briefly for the Silks as a housekeeper several years ago and found a diary written by Theodora Silk containing records of childhood abuse at the hands of her father. According to the diary, the father had repeatedly raped his daughter, resulting in her pregnancy at age sixteen. Because of the pride attached to her family's name, Theodora had been forced to leave school under false pretenses to hide the pregnancy. The father's remains had been found in the family home, leading police to believe that the daughter and another relative had conspired to kill him and hide the murder. Theodora had given birth to the baby alone and abandoned her in a public building. The child had been rescued and later adopted. Hazzard's acquisition of this information had led to the blackmail arrangement, which lasted until Theodora decided to take steps to stop it.

The police had uncovered the diary early in the investigation. They had also obtained evidence of Theodora's presence at the Hazzard crime scene through surveillance videos. Theodora had disabled newly installed cameras at the floral shop but had been spotted running from the murder scene by the camera at the liquor store two doors down. Through police perseverance, the weapon had been located and traced back to her.

Her alibi—that she'd been at a floral convention in Rhode Island at the time of the Hazzard murder—fell through when police learned that she was a licensed private pilot. By flying her airplane, she was able to return to Long Island Friday morning, commit the crime, and be back in Rhode Island in time to present a workshop at the convention. Her aircraft was on record as departing from Brookhaven Airport on Wednesday night, returning at four a.m., departing again at seven, and returning at two. Records showed it had landed and departed from Providence at times that coincided with this flight schedule. She had also made a fuel stop at Westerly, Rhode Island, after the murder.

The second person she was believed to have killed was Clifford Bisbee, who may have learned of the blackmail scheme through direct conversation with Hazzard or by witnessing payoffs. He was a neighbor of hers, out of work and on drugs, and looking for a source of income. Police had put together a picture that included Bisbee's obtaining a notebook in which Hazzard kept her blackmail accounts. It was not known how he got the notebook, but he'd attempted to use it to blackmail Theodora Silk and at least one other person. He'd been stabbed to death at the E-Z Self Storage four days after the first murder. The weapon had not been found at the time, but the wounds were consistent with those that might be made with a florist's knife. Forensics experts had matched the wounds to a knife in Theodora Silk's possession.

Police had evidence that Silk had believed this blackmail notebook and an incriminating DVD were in the possession of someone at Martha's Vineyard. She had decided to fly there—not to confront this person, but to kill him and at least fourteen other people who were in the house at the time enjoying a family reunion. She'd intended to crash her plane into the house. It was a suicide mission.

Suffolk County Police had made numerous calls to alert the family to the danger and had worked closely with police authorities at the Vineyard as well as with the Coast Guard. Police had been stationed at both airports in Martha's Vineyard. Everyone was well aware of the serious nature of the situation and in constant communication. After thoughtful consideration, as events unfolded, it had been decided not to broadcast to the community what was happening so as not to cause panic or risk intensifying what was an extremely volatile situation. It had to be handled very carefully. Police had ultimately decided to send a very fast aircraft with a highly skilled pilot to divert Theodora Silk and force her to land at Vineyard Haven Airport, where she would be arrested by police.

The airplane she was flying, a Cessna Skylane, could have killed any number of adults and children, both in the target residence and nearby residences, as well as on the street and in the playground, if she missed her target. The airplane dispatched in pursuit, an Extra 300L, was not only swift and agile, but was constructed of fiberglass-like material, so that if involved in an unanticipated collision or forced to land, it would not come apart. As everyone could see by the events that ensued as well as by the forced ditching in the bay, the airplane had *not* come apart, and the pilot and his copilot had survived unhurt.

In closing, the police chief expressed his and the department's gratitude that unknown numbers of lives had been saved in this mission and that it had been carried out with the utmost professionalism, courage, and fortitude. For this he thanked lead Detective Pete Zahn and his partner, Detective Harris Bonomo, as well as all the authorities who had worked with them to solve the case and bring it to a safe and timely conclusion. He then opened the floor to questions.

"Okay, here we go," LaRue said.

CBS News was up first.

"You said, 'unanticipated collision.' How do you characterize the repeated impacts between the Extra and the Skylane? Did the pilot of the Extra have your permission to bring down the other aircraft by whatever means possible?"

"The pilot's orders were to preserve the lives and safety of innocent people," the police chief answered. "He performed a heroic act in the execution of those orders."

"Did he not put himself and his copilot in danger performing those actions?" another reporter asked.

"Who was the copilot?" someone else put in.

"Ladies and gentlemen, one at a time," said the chief. "As you can see, the pilot, Ned Trace, is standing right here next to me. The airplane, as I mentioned, was built for aerobatics and made of highly impact-resistant material. The pilot and the other party were fully aware of the risks before the flight."

"What about the DVD and the notebook you spoke of?" FOX News asked. "How did they come to be in the hands of a person going to a family reunion in Martha's Vineyard who was not described as being involved in this case at all?"

A number of voices rose at once, and the police chief put out his hand.

"I will not get into the specifics of the case beyond what I've already told you. For reasons of privacy, the names of witnesses and others connected to the case will not be revealed."

"But shouldn't the police have contained all the evidence so that the situation didn't snowball to this degree?"

Zahn stepped up to the mike.

"The case was always under our control and the evidence contained. What was perceived by Theodora Silk to be damaging material was not original evidence. We had the originals at all times."

"Oh, snap," said LaRue.

Zahn continued. "The police rely upon agencies and individuals for help. We were grateful to obtain leads and assistance from a variety of sources. And we encourage the public to continue to be aware, to keep their eyes open, and to report circumstances that seem in any way unusual."

"Leads—he means you, Swee'pea."

"Some acknowledgment. I risk life and limb, and all he does is lump me in with the group." I took a handful of Wheat Thins and passed LaRue the box.

"Oh, look," LaRue said. "Ned's getting a certificate."

Sure enough, the police chief was shaking Ned's hand and giving him a framed certificate. The camera zoomed in on it. The chief stepped back and beamed at Zahn, motioning him over. Zahn stepped forward, and both he and Ned clenched their jaws and glared at each other. Then they smiled woodenly and shook hands. The camera flashes accelerated.

"Aw, isn't that sweet." LaRue filled her mouth with Wheat Thins.

Chip jumped up on the ottoman where Bergamot was sleeping and curled up next to him. Bergamot opened an eye but didn't move.

"What I don't get," I said, "is how Theodora and her grandmother killed Yancy Villers."

"I think they tricked him. They made him build them a closet in the upstairs room. So he busted through the wall and cut out some studs to make room for shelves. Then Theo snuck up behind him and bonked him over the head with a hammer and he fell in."

"With Granny's permission, of course."

"Granny was there distracting him so he didn't turn around."

"You know, they really should make this into a movie," I said.

"I'd go," said LaRue.

Zahn stopped by later with my cell phone.

"You look none the worse for wear," he said.

"Gee, thanks. I see you're still pumped from the press conference I wasn't invited to."

"Be glad you're out of the public eye, Trace. The public can be cruel."

"Actually, I just got calls from *Good Morning, America* and *The Today Show.*"

"No kidding."

"No kidding. And I've been mentioned in eleven thousand tweets. Some people think I acted very heroically."

"As the police do. As I do. Are you going on TV?"

"I haven't decided."

Zahn stood in front of me. "What's eating you, Trace?"

I looked up at him. The X-ray eyes were soft. "Why didn't I get a certificate, Detective? Why wasn't I up there with Ned and all of you? You didn't even acknowledge what I did to help your case. Which was a lot."

"Our job today was to clear up misconceptions." He made an offhand gesture. "Your being there would have raised more questions. We did you a favor by not inviting you."

"Right."

"Not to put too fine a point on it, Trace, but you almost blew the case a couple times."

My mouth dropped open. "Blew the case!"

"Running around after Bellarosa. Making deals with Bisbee."

"You wouldn't have *had* a case without them. If I hadn't led you to Sally, you never would have known Hazzard was blackmailing him. If I hadn't—"

"Trace, that man almost killed you."

"—talked to the Lizard, you'd never have known about the notebook. And how about the television at the Sunny Side? And the nursing home?"

"Before you go on, let me point out that anonymous tips work both ways. The good part for me is that I don't have to ask questions. I don't have to get anyone in trouble for, say, trespassing."

I shut my mouth.

"While you're at it, consider yourself lucky that the camera was off at Hoyt's. That was a misdemeanor. You got off easy, Trace."

"We're lucky we didn't get killed," I retorted. "Where was Theo while we were back there? Waiting for us to leave so she could smash the bowl and sweep up the pieces?"

Zahn gave me that funny look again.

"What? What are you looking at me like that for?"

Instead of answering, Zahn tossed a paper bag he'd been holding onto the couch.

"What's this?"

"Open it."

Inside the bag was a stuffed Snoopy wearing aviator goggles. Snoopy the Flying Ace. I picked up the Snoopy and looked at Zahn.

"Thank you," he said.

I got a lump in my throat. "I don't know what to say."

" 'You're welcome' works."

"You're welcome." I looked back at Snoopy. I'd been wrong about Zahn. It looked like I'd been wrong about a lot of things. "I had no idea about the diary."

Zahn turned to leave. "See you around, Trace."

"Wait. There's one thing I can't figure out."

"What's that?"

"What pointed Hazzard to Faith? Out of all the eighteen-year-old girls in the world?"

He folded his arms. "That was luck. Theo's the one who found her. Faith had posted in some online jewelry forum, hoping to find a match for the earring and so find her mother. Theo wrote the girl's name in her diary, and Hazzard figured out the rest on the Internet."

"And the stolen photos? Did Hazzard take them?"

Zahn nodded. "A week before she was killed. One of the photos showed the upstairs rooms before Villers had taken up occupancy and the wallpaper'd gone up. It was all part of her blackmail ammo. Steigbeagle didn't notice the photos were gone until after the break-in."

"Oh. And Detective?"

"Ye-es?"

"You like cats?"

"You got it all," I said to Tony. "The barrel rolls, the landing in the water, the helicopters. Everything."

I was talking to him on the phone while scrolling through the photos he'd emailed me. At the first sound of airplane engines low in the sky, everyone had run out of the sports bar in Gay Head to see what was going on. It was six minutes into the first quarter of the Jets-Patriots game, and Tony and his three cousins had just started in on the hot wings.

"My favorite is the one where you're being lifted up to the helicopter," he said.

"Yeah. Wait'll my mom sees that. So, you had no idea it was me in that plane?"

"Nope. Say, I'm at a total loss here, Emma. What can I possibly give the girl who saved the lives of my whole family?"

"You still owe me dinner at Tara's."

"Tara's? Let me take you someplace special. Elegant."

"I'm not a big fan of elegant, Tony. Tara's is perfect."

"Then Tara's it is. How about tonight? You feel up to it?"

"Sure. By the way, who won?"

Tony's voice was dark. "Lord Voldemort."

"I'm sorry."

"Yeah, me, too. Not going to happen again. In a couple months the Pats come to the Meadowlands, and we're going to kick Tom Brady's butt all the way to Secaucus."

CHAPTER FIFTY-TWO

Thursday

I waited in the hall outside the English department office for Sam to finish with his former student.

Down the hall, at Sam's real office, the Smart Squad was replacing the nameplate on the door. This was a major project requiring three people. They'd walked past me single file—one holding a level, one a toolbox, and one a ladder—wearing overalls like characters in a Richard Scarry book. The nameplate itself was six inches by one-and-a-half inches and needed two tiny screws. Our tax dollars at work.

The department door opened and a young woman hurried out. Sam waved me in. I followed him into the undergraduate director's office and sat down. Sam sat behind the desk.

"I thought we'd be more comfortable here. My office is in boxes."

"This is fine, Sam."

"Coffee?"

"I'm not staying. I just came by to wish you well."

He nodded curtly.

"What's next?" I asked. "Any plans?"

Sam clasped his hands before him on the desk. His eyes showed strain. Since our breakup I'd thought of myself as the one who'd lost everything. I'd been dumped, left by the roadside. But now I knew that wasn't true. In Sam's face I saw an entire, carefully built world going down the toilet. "Well, I didn't exactly anticipate making a change at this point. This was supposed to be it. But now—" He shrugged. "Immediate plans, I'm going to London to continue my Shakespeare research. Maybe stay a year. After that, we'll see."

"What about Ruby? And your house?"

"My brother will stay in the house and look after her. He just lost his job, too." He smiled sadly. "Look at *you*, now—I have to congratulate you, Emma. And your uncle. You and Sully are quite the heroes."

I squirmed at the reference to Captain Sullenberger's famous landing in the Hudson.

"Everywhere I look I see your story—in the paper, on television, on the Internet. You've got a fan page on Facebook with hundreds of followers. You even made it to Oprah. Wow."

"It's the near-death thing, Sam."

"And all for Tony Randazzo, restaurateur. Are you two serious?"

"We only just met."

He closed his eyes halfway. "Ironic, isn't it, Emma?"

"What is?"

"I always had the feeling you'd up and leave me one day. You'd get the bug like everyone else in your family, and that would be it."

My heart quickened. "You're the one who was sleeping with Hazzard."

"That was once. After that it became something else."

"How stupid do you think I am? The phone calls coming in at all hours, the mysterious appointments with 'students'? And what about the time I caught you and Hazzard having lunch at that French restaurant?"

"That was so she could pick up her check." Sam stood up and walked to the window. "I brought it all on myself by my poor judgment and feeling of invincibility. You know what I found out? None of us is invincible."

Coming here had been a bad idea. I had hoped we'd find closure, but it was not to be. Life never lives up to my fantasies. I looked at the back of Sam's head.

"Be well," I said. I did not ask him to stay in touch.

Driving my Honda down Dune Road in Westhampton Beach, I felt a stab of pity for Theo. She hadn't had a single break growing up. From the father who'd abused her to the mother who'd failed to intervene to the grandmother who'd taught her that murder was the answer, she'd had bad luck by the barrelful.

It hurt my heart to think about Theo's suffering. Briefly, I wondered if I, in her place, would have acted any differently.

But no. I couldn't see myself taking another life or abandoning a baby, even with all the bad luck in the world heaped on me.

At least Faith Devereaux had turned out all right. *She* was going to be fine. Better than fine—amazing.

I let go of the day and began to smile. The smile got bigger and bigger until my whole self was nothing but a living container of buoyant happiness. I parked at Ned's beach house and trotted up the steps.

"Pizza delivery," I called through the open door.

"Come on up."

Ned was in the living room on the second floor, stretched out on the modular leather sofa facing an immense picture window that overlooked the ocean. A colorful bouquet was on the coffee table.

"Flowers from Zahn?"

Ned grimaced. "From the girls at the FBO."

I pushed them aside and opened the pizza box. Pepperoni, mushrooms, and onion for him. Plain cheese for me.

"Nice do." Ned nodded toward my head.

"Not too short?"

"You look sophisticated."

"It's only until my hair grows out."

We munched in comfortable silence.

"When are you buying another plane?"

"This week. Why?"

I shrugged. I heard the buzz of an airplane in the distance, and I remembered Mike, the young instructor I'd met at Brookhaven Airport. I pictured myself sitting next to him in a tiny airplane with lots of clocks on the dashboard, heading out over the bay for a discovery flight. "It's too bad about the other one."

"It's okay. I'm looking at a newer model. Or I might get an Edge."

"Hmm." I looked at all the framed posters of advertisements for Ned's Runway Pies lining the walls and nodded. "Well, we were certainly lucky."

"You don't really believe that, do you, Minute Mouse?"

I looked at him. "No, I don't, actually. Not anymore."

He took a swig of soda and wiped his mouth with his sleeve. " 'Luck is the residue of design.' "

"Who said that?"

"Branch Rickey. Famous baseball guy."

The buzz of the airplane got closer. I looked out at the beach and the seagulls dipping and floating on the air. I turned back to Ned.

"Minute Mouse?"

He smiled. I smiled back. Then a small yellow airplane appeared in the corner of the window, flying from right to left, and we both turned to look.

ABOUT THE AUTHOR

Toby Speed lives on Long Island and is the mother of three fabulous daughters. *Death Over Easy* is her first mystery. Although most of her research took place on terra firma, she learned how to fly an airplane to write this book. Learn more at *tobyspeed.com.*